Y0-CBD-372

Feast or Felon?

Here is critical praise for James Lileks' *Falling up the Stairs*, the debut adventure of Jonathan Simpson, Middle America's food reviewer/sleuth . . .

"[An] alternately hilarious and harrowing spoof . . . James Lileks satirizes just about everything. . . . The action here is fast paced . . . countless and extremely funny one-liners . . . a laugh-out-loud narrative . . . concentrated with humorous retorts and word play. . . . It's all great fun. . . ."
—Stephen Schwandt, *Minneapolis Star-Tribune*

"Sexual adventure and food terrorism . . . sheer love of story floats the whole enterprise. . . . Lileks' voice is so likable, his hero so endearing, that you can forgive just about anything."
—Carolyn See, *Los Angeles Times*

"Major league funny stuff . . . Lileks' feel for his newspaper colleagues is unfailing and an endless source of great, nasty little one-liners. . . . A witty romp through a bizarre world of self-delusion and cynicism. You'll love the ride. . . ."
—John Louis Anderson, *St. Paul Pioneer Press*

Just what has James Lileks cooked up for Jonathan Simpson this time? If you liked the appetizer, you'll love the main course . . .

MR. OBVIOUS

Books by James Lileks

MYSTERY

Falling up the Stairs
Mr. Obvious*

HUMOR

Notes of a Nervous Man*
Fresh Lies*

*Published by POCKET BOOKS

For orders other than by individual consumers, Pocket Books grants a discount on the purchase of **10 or more** copies of single titles for special markets or premium use. For further details, please write to the Vice-President of Special Markets, Pocket Books, 1230 Avenue of the Americas, New York, NY 10020.

For information on how individual consumers can place orders, please write to Mail Order Department, Paramount Publishing, 200 Old Tappan Road, Old Tappan, NJ 07675.

Mr.
Obvious

JAMES LILEKS

POCKET BOOKS

New York   London   Toronto   Sydney   Tokyo   Singapore

The sale of this book without its cover is unauthorized. If you purchased this book without a cover, you should be aware that it was reported to the publisher as "unsold and destroyed." Neither the author nor the publisher has received payment for the sale of this "stripped book."

This book is a work of fiction. Names, characters, places and incidents are products of the author's imagination or are used fictitiously. Any resemblance to actual events or locales or persons, living or dead, is entirely coincidental.

An *Original* Publication of POCKET BOOKS

 POCKET BOOKS, a division of Simon & Schuster Inc.
1230 Avenue of the Americas, New York, NY 10020

Copyright © 1995 by James Lileks

All rights reserved, including the right to reproduce this book or portions thereof in any form whatsoever. For information address Pocket Books, 1230 Avenue of the Americas, New York, NY 10020

ISBN: 0-671-73705-8

First Pocket Books printing May 1995

10 9 8 7 6 5 4 3 2 1

POCKET and colophon are registered trademarks of Simon & Schuster Inc.

Cover art by Ben Perini

Printed in the U.S.A.

The following, while based on true events, is a work of fiction. Repeat: the following is fictional but based on true events.

—J.A.S.

Mr.
Obvious

Crash Dummies

I KNEW WE WERE UNFIT FOR ONE ANOTHER THE NIGHT WE were watching *Casablanca*. I remarked how it was good that the Germans didn't win the war, and she got mad at me for spoiling the ending.

The entire relationship had felt dull and impermanent, like something you put in a bus station locker. It should have been better. She was quite pretty, although in a way that only made sense on television, where she worked as a third-string newscaster. She had the brains of a sparrow, but she also had the practiced vivacity of someone who can speak whenever pointed to. Granted, she rarely spoke for longer than fifteen seconds at a time, and her conversation always seemed to end portentously, as though we were about to go to film. When no film ever came, she had a tendency to repeat what she'd just said with the cadences of someone wrapping it all up and then hand it off to me. And thus it was in bed, too. We had slept

1

together about fifty times, like Edison doggedly trying to invent the lightbulb. I think he got it right on the fifty-first try.

I wish I could remember more of her. The name is simple to call up: Tara. (Mother went into labor during a showing of *Gone with the Wind,* she said, or so the story went.) This gave her the pretext for innumerable bad southern belle imitations, and I once pointed out that she was named for a house, not its occupant, and it would be more accurate if she simply stood still, perhaps creaked every so often, or burned down. As for the particulars of her life— childhood tales, favorite foods, everything else she'd spilled on the first date—I can't remember.

Of course, there's a lot I don't remember. Getting shot in the head will do that to you. I lost about an ounce of brain when they tweezered out the bone fragments. What is peculiar is that I know what I don't remember: I don't know Firsts. First kiss. First drunken, slurry, terrified loss of virginity (I'm assuming). First cigarette. This was all sent up the hospital flue. I do recall, of all things, my circumcision. I get angry when I realize that they never even *considered* a local anesthesia. I don't think that qualifies as a First—more like an Only. Which sheds some light on the brain's filing system: big dumpsters with general concepts stenciled on the side. I am glad they didn't remove the bin marked Never Again. God knows what I would lack the sense to try.

I know I don't recall the first time she told me she was married. If she did.

First, Only, Never Again. Getting shot in the head fits into one of these. I suppose I shall have to wait the rest of my life to see which.

It happened the day that awful TV movie aired, the one in which I was played by an actor noted primarily for the incandescence of his teeth. Being the Local Man on whose life this movie was based, I was doing a small amount of publicity for it. I was scheduled to appear on the Josh Carlton show that afternoon to sing about the stupid thing.

I woke late, Tara having rolled out and snuck off hours before to report on a hobo convention or some such perennial botheration. I took coffee in the dining hall, shivering. August, and the house was cold. It was like this every morning and had been since I inherited this big stupid ugly pile of rock from a certain bilious relative who had looked around her family, decided who she disliked enough to impoverish with real estate taxes, and landed on me. I do not complain: Few people who make a hundred dollars a week as a food reviewer for a free weekly newspaper own a twenty-room mansion. I pay the taxes by renting the main hall out for weddings and receptions. The latter are more fun; I like coming downstairs from my room in a suit and mingling and dancing with the bride, pretending I'm one of the guests. Find the wedding pictures of a Minneapolis couple, and there's a good chance I'm in the background, drinking their liquor. Archeologists will judge me a very popular man or some sort of fertility shaman. I'd prefer the first.

What a house of this scale needed, of course, was servants, and I had two: Trygve and Grunewald, an elderly pair that had served the various idiots who'd occupied the house for several decades. They had left a couple weeks earlier for a year in Europe, paid for by Trygve's overstuffed bank account. (I got the house but he got all the money or what hadn't been dissipated by the last generation of wastrels.) I missed them; Grunewald knew every secret trick of the old place and would be downstairs beating the furnace with a wrench and swearing chunky German imprecations. But I had been busy generating kilowatts with Tara and hadn't yet missed them too much.

I had a roll and read the paper, then showered and left for the radio station. A Minnesota August, soupy and torporous, waited outside. In a couple of months, of course, the skies would whip up a wind and spit out small shards of snow like someone feeding panes of glass into a jet engine. Enjoy the fetid humidity while you can, I suppose. I got into my car, turned it around in the deserted garage, built to hold a half-dozen big, shiny plutocrat autos, and headed toward the radio station.

I got as far as the driveway. My next-door neighbor, a fierce sliver of desiccated Scotch womanhood who stamped around the neighborhood in a walker and hissed at the children, lay in wait on the sidewalk. Next to her stood a nervous man. She was the sort of hateful neighbor who regards your presence on earth as a violation of some old zoning ordinance the city council would enforce if it weren't packed with coloreds and atheists. She had filed exactly one hundred and twelve complaints against me with the neighborhood council, beginning with the reasonable objection to rezoning my house for receptions. That was followed by an increasingly surrealistic set of charges that suggested some sort of dementia or a neurological condition that expressed itself through uncontrollable spasms of legal actions. Lately she had been suing me in small-claims court. I rolled down my window and held out my hand. It was time for the ritual dispensing of the summons.

"When?" I asked.

"Next, ah, Friday," said the man. He handed me an envelope with a return address full of names and ampersands, embossed in gold—the sort of letter that meant money or punishment. He stepped back. Cue the harridan.

"And there'll be no squirmin' out o' this one," she hissed. "Ah got the drapes ta prove ma point." She glared wickedly at me, stamped her walker twice on the ground, and withdrew. The man nodded at me and followed her up the sidewalk.

We went through this once a month. Last time I was accused of interfering with her television reception by hanging huge sheets of tinfoil in my living room. Dismissed. The previous grievance had me digging tunnels beneath her house to release noxious vapors. Dismissed. I ripped open the envelope to see what I had done now. Ah: I was using my X-ray vision to set her drapes alight.

Josh Carlton. The Voice of Reason, Your Friend in the End, Your Boon After Noon, the Twin Cities's least-listened-to talk show host. I'd done his show the previous year, when I was on the shilling circuit for my true crime book. It was an account of my rather inadvertent involvement two years ago with some terrorists—food poisoners, actually. Marxist nutritionists. Long story, a cautionary tale for food reviewers whose newspapers have a leftist slant: If there are any vegetable-liberation activists out there, they'll hold you too close to their bosom.

And, in my case, jab a gun at your temple as well. They were attempting to change America's eating habits by violent means and spent half a year poisoning waffle mixes and grain shipments, pausing only to send terse manifestos to me in the hopes I would publicize and support their bratty rumpus. I didn't, which earned me a nasty episode at my house one night—hostages, police, gunfire, all the messy terrorist clichés. No one I was worried about got hurt, although the police shot one of the terrorists in the kitchen, right where we put old newspapers before taking them out to the trash. Can the Sunday paper

5

absorb four quarts of blood? Maybe in New York, but not, as I learned, in Minneapolis.

I wrote what I thought was an appropriately hard-boiled recitation of the events, and it was published in paperback as *Dead Bread,* with an embossed foil picture of a beautiful woman clenching her throat in agony. It was a slim book, with Many Shocking True Photos, such as Trygve pointing grimly to a bullet hole in the dishwasher. There were no photos of the dead terrorists; Grue had the joint mopped and waxed before the police photographers got there. *Dead Bread* was read mostly by people on the bus or by people coming home from jobs they did not enjoy. I sometimes felt bad for figuring out the identities of the terrorists when I did. If I hadn't solved the case for a few more weeks, I'd have written a longer book. The people on the buses would have gotten a better value.

In any case, it was sold to television and promptly made into a dreadful movie, entitled *Give Us This Day Our Deadly Bread,* due to be aired that night. I'd been sent an advance cassette. I was played by someone who had been in a successful situation comedy ten years before and whose most recent work, as I noted, consisted of hour-long infomercials for teeth-whitening salves. My then-girlfriend—since departed to cloud the minds of other hapless men—was played by a woman so gorgeous she probably had to be kept in a dark box lest she blind people but whose acting ability was an illusion created by styling irons and camera angles. They also made her a blonde, when she was really a redhead. It was as if someone had corrected the color of my life. I hated the whole thing.

I'd done some talk shows around town to promote the stupid thing. I did *Town Talk,* where I was joined by several other local crime authors, each of whom wrote fiction and consequently looked down on me as someone who had such an impoverished imagination he had to rely on a shootout in his living room for material. I did *Daybreak Twin Cities* with some people whose relatives had expired from eating tainted food. On the monitor, I saw one identified as Brother of Muffin Victim, while another was labeled Wife Died of Toast. I nearly burst my eardrums trying not to laugh at that, issuing high, pained squeaks whenever I looked at the monitor and hence was very unpopular by the end of the program.

Strangest of all was *Talk of the Town with P.D. Spaunaugle,* a cable-access program in which the host, a wiry fellow in a chef's hat and sunglasses, spent the half hour shouting out the most baroque libels I could imagine—that I was a fraud and a cheat, I didn't write the book, I had been arrested for sodomizing lost dogs, I fed the neighborhood children sugar-coated lead chips, I had a tattoo of Trotsky on my right buttock, and so on. No calm denial or wry look of amazement could turn him aside, and the matter came to blows. He shoved me into a camera. As I fell backward, my legs became tangled with his, and he fell face first into the lens, chipping a tooth. Close-up of tooth. Close-up of howling Spaunaugle. End of show.

Spaunaugle staggered off, cursing and kicking people. The show's producer apologetically helped me up. He explained that every show ended this way, it was all a joke, the Talk Show as Performance Art. They would, in postproduction, put in disclaimers. No one took it seriously. Because it was on cable access, no one even saw it.

I didn't. Although a friend told me that every one of Spaunaugle's remarks brought the words TEMPORARILY UNSUBSTANTIATED ASSERTION flashing on the screen, my replies earned the words PREDICTABLE DENIAL. To prove it was Art, my friend added, there was a credit at the end thanking a local corporate endowment for funding.

As I said earlier, I'd done Josh Carlton's radio show before, after I'd hosted the hail-of-lead party at the manor. Back then my stories were raw and jerky. Now, a year later, I had them as buffed and polished as pearls on a string. I didn't pretend to be spontaneous anymore. Instead, I concentrated on sounding bored and rehearsed—less entertaining, but far more honest.

I arrived at the station an hour early, and rather than sit inside the station and freeze—Minnesotans seem to think air conditioners have two settings, Off and Pluto—I decided to sit outside and coax a tan out of the sun. KTOK was located in a featureless cube on the top of a hill, on the edge of a cracked and weedy suburban highway. Across the road was a bare savanna, its sole crop the massive KTOK tower; the metallic trunk of an extraordinarily single-minded tree. Guy wires anchored it to the earth, keeping it straight and true. The red warning light atop the tower blinked on and off, keeping the time for some stately gavotte the rest of us couldn't hear.

While I loafed outside, host Josh Carlton drove up in a sputtering Buick. He parked and walked over, looking hard at the ground. He gave me a brief look as he climbed the steps, then stopped, peered over his sunglasses, and smiled.

"The three o'clock victim," he said. He sat down on the steps, sighed. "How are you, Jonathan? Still reviewing meals the rest of the world can't afford, I suppose."

"Not true," I said. "Last week's piece was on hot dogs." My editor had given it the headline Frankly Speaking, as I somehow knew he would. "That's as proletarian as it gets."

"I guess." He stared off at the tower. "Well. You're not going to write a piece about my show or anything, are you?"

I said I hadn't planned on it. He sighed. "I could use the publicity. On the other hand, it'd be like sending a strip-o-gram to announce a fuckin' funeral," He frowned. "The book comes in today. Ratings, to you civilians. Already got my ass hiked up, waiting for the kick. I'll probably pull a low three." The local papers ran the ratings in agate type every quarter, and I had watched Carlton's ratings descend for the last year, a point at a time, like an old man working his way downstairs. Carlton's tone of voice suggested that that the bottom step was swabbed with grease and that he'd feel these ratings in his tailbone.

"Maybe they won't be so bad."

"They'll suck." He took out a cigarette, produced a Zippo, and looked at it with a queer expression, as if seeing his reflection in the chrome. I saw the word *Nationwide* engraved on the lighter. "You know," he said, snapping open the lighter, "you *ought* to write a book about me."

"Sure." Humor him. "I do have one more book to go on the contract. Another true crime book." I sighed. "There's so damn few serial killers around here, I don't know what I'll do." I took the Zippo from his hand and lit a cigarette. "Kill a guest or something, and we'll talk."

"Write one about talk radio." He was staring at the hills, deep in some private funk. "What it does to you. It's like prostitution, blowing the mike to make it happy. Be nice, be nice, be nice. Drives you nuts."

"It's a job."

"So says Mr. I-Eat-Out-Every-Day-for-a-Living. Let me tell you about jobs. I dreamed last night I was a crash dummy. And for some reason I thought it was a fuckin' promotion. I had this whole crash dummy family—crash dummy wife, little crash dummy kid in the back. I kept getting mad because he wouldn't stop flying from the backseat through the window—you know, 'Junior, will you please put on your seat belt? No, Daddy doesn't have to put his on, Daddy is testing the airbag.' And my crash dummy wife, no face, right, but she's got this wig all crooked on her plastic head. After every head-on collision, she'd say 'Do you know where we're going? Let me look at that map.' Into the wall, *wang!* Into the wall, *wang!* Alllll night long." He shivered. "I woke up on my stomach with my forehead pressed up against the headboard."

"Shouldn't we be going in? I imagine you'll want to get ready."

"Ready for what? I read the papers already. Taxes are down and the crime rate dropped last month. No poking John Q's two favorite bruises today. Can't even count on thieves and politicians. I'm dreading the open line hour." Another long pull on his cigarette. "Hello, who's this sorry fool?"

A car had pulled into the KTOK lot. A small woman in a black dress got out and stamped up the walk with such fury I feared she would stop, grab her legs, and rip herself in half like Rumpelstiltskin. She threw us a look that was meant to send us both to hell and roll boulders over the hole. She stabbed the building's front door buzzer and demanded admittance.

"The new sales rep for my show," Carlton remarked after she'd gone inside. "It can be a frustrating experience." He got up and squinted at the hills. "Let's go commit some radio."

Carlton invited me into the booth, where it was cool and quiet. He turned down the lights, so all you could see was the console, glowing like a dashboard. Two round oblong mikes hung from poles like perfect fruit with a skin of foam. A plate-glass window separated us from the control room, where there two were young men: One seated at the controls wore a T-shirt that said NO FAT CHICKS; the other was a grinning flathead who appeared to made entirely of barrels of varying sizes. He had the anti-fat-chicks man in a headlock and was pretending to beat his co-worker's skull with his free fist.

"My crack production team," said Carlton. He hit a button and leaned toward the microphone. "Get in here, Dagler. We need to confer."

Dagler appeared a minute later, gave me a nod so brief it could be mistake for an involuntary tremor, and smiled broadly at Carlton.

"What's your favorite punctuation mark?" Dagler said.

"What? A colon."

"Well, I could have guessed. And you?" Dagler looked at me.

"Upside-down question mark."

"Ah, for the Spanish market, sure." Dagler threw a magazine at Carlton. "Look at that. FCC approved the petition of that station to include an exclamation point in its call letters. Can you believe it? I say we go for a period. Nice and blunt. Can't you hear it? *KTO Period.* It has authority."

Carlton scanned the article. "Yeah. I read that. Still can't figure out how they do the ID."

"They say *WDC Exclamation Point* when they do the legal ID, then WD*C!,* like they're all excited, the rest of the time."

Carlton passed the article to me. I read: "The FCC has decided that in standard nonlegal usage, inflection can be considered an acceptable means of identifying the station."

"Trust me," said Dagler. "KQ will beef up the heavy metal on their playlist and petition for an umlaut."

"While we are awarded null signs by general fucking acclaim."

"Hey, cheer up. It's a two-count'em!-two-guest day. That animal-rights guy I told you about? He's here. His other appointment canceled on him, so we'll do him in the three o'clock, then do Simpson. Hi, Simpson." He turned and pumped my hand, giving an innocent and squinty grin. "So let me brief you. He's—"

"I know, I know. He's an earnest little specimen who's pissed off because cows are too stupid to run away or fight back, and so they end up as shoes or supper. I have to treat him nice, don't I?"

"Very, very nice. You got the memo. 'We're the talk station, not the shout station.' Words for us to live by if we want to keep ourselves in leather and steaks, buddy."

"What did that memo *mean?* Who ever shouts on this station? You got fucking Dobbs in the morning, couldn't raise his voice without a block and tackle. I'm so hemmed in by the format and the stack of be-nice memos I get every damn day I don't dare get excited."

"But you want to start yelling," said Dagler. "It's in your voice. You're not a happy man. We've had this conversation. It's why I like you. In another market, we will scream and rant, but for now . . ."

"I don't believe in another market." Carlton glowered at the floor. "There is no afterlife. Only this stupid Scandinavian be-nice happyface world. For this I left New York."

"For this you left Iowa. You left New York for Iowa, remember? And I'm the guy who knows that when you say New York, you mean Syracuse and the three

A.M. traffic desk job. Don't complain. And don't pick a fight with this guy, okay?"

"Well, stop booking controversial guests then." He turned to me. "Is that pathetic? I'm asking him to stop getting interesting shows on the air and get me more guys like you and this animal lover. That's what it's like. Last week I had this woman who wrote a book about the myths of penis size. Nice, straightforward book. Pretty good show, lots of calls. Then the program director acts like I've brought on a lobbyist for the American Sodomy Institute and starts telling me that my audience is all old and impotent and Lutheran. Or if not Lutheran, then so devoutly Catholic they're probably listening while Jesuits whip them with wet leather strips, and I can't say penis on the air, ever. Want to see the memo?" He leaned back to a stack of papers.

"Josh, you just don't have the juice," said Dagler. "Not right now. Not today."

Today was said a little too gently. I sensed imminent talk about the ratings. Josh suddenly looked like he was going to a funeral held by a religion that doesn't believe in the afterlife.

"I put the book in your box," said Dagler. "You didn't look at it, did you?"

"No. Let it degrade. Let me smell it in a few months' time." He rubbed his eyes. "All right, tell me."

"One."

"One?" Josh Carlton shot back in his seat like someone fielding a cannon ball. "One what? One point nine?"

"Uno. No dos. It's seasonal. Everybody's down in this book. Hey, hey! Don't get purple on me!"

"For Jesus' sake! A *two share!* A two share means we have nothing but people who have died and left the radio on! A one share means their batteries finally

13

went dead! I could lean out the window and shout and get a goddamned one share!"

"You're taking this personally. Don't. This station sucks. Life's a bitch," said Dagler. "Then you're live."

The show did not go well. I listened from another room, drinking watery coffee and wincing as Carlton tried to keep depression and fury from flooding his brain and drowning the guest. Josh sounded like a man who realizes he no longer wants to make love to his wife. She gave him a one share.

He was talking with a sallow gent named Sid, executive director of People in Partnership with Animals—a name that suggested barnyard fowl in business suits scowling over prospectuses and vetoing deals. PIPA was attempting to pass a National Animal Moratorium Day, during which no one would eat meat or wear leather or drop harsh corrosive chemicals into the innocent eyes of gentle bunnies. Josh asked Sid what he would do if he was charged by a wild, foaming warthog on Moratorium Day.

"Well, run," said Sid.

"Say you trip. Bust a leg. It happens. The warthog is still coming. Crazed and hungry. You have a gun, but it's Moratorium Day. What do you do?"

"Look, it's a ridiculous situation. But even so, I could never, never harm an animal, not as much as a guppy. That's what we're about."

"I am all for animals being undisturbed," Josh said. "Except when I'm hungry. Then I want them dead and seasoned and undisturbed."

"Oh, but why is it all right to kill something just because you're hungry? That's hardly fair, is it? I mean with all the grain and lettuce and beans in the world, why do we have to kill?"

"Because it's nature's way. Nature is just one feral-snarling cockfight," Josh said. "Look at a shrimp.

Dead, I can enjoy its flesh. Mm-mm. Alive, it will be enjoyed by some other big fish. What's the difference? Are we evil because we've somehow softened the savagery with the invention of cocktail sauce?"

"Well, no. That shrimp was alive once. I respect life. You seem to—"

"And if the shrimp was poorly refrigerated and I get live salmonella bacteria scurrying through my veins and die, is that exactly respecting my life?"

"Well, you asked for it, didn't you?"

"Say I suddenly double over in pain from salmonella. Would you take me to the hospital?"

"Of course."

"But that means helping to kill the poor, defenseless salmonella germ."

"Oh, don't be silly."

"Not at all. If all life is sacred, then killing anything is wrong. Do you know that there are insects that live on those stalks of wheat you so wantonly cut down for your food? That you kill millions of dust mites each time you shower? There's a genocide in every day, friend . . . I think we have to check weather now."

There was a weather break, which consisted of: hot now, hot tonight, hot tomorrow. Generally, hot. I looked into the studio through the window. Josh and his guest endured the break in hard, frigid silence.

"Dust mites are different," said Mr. PIPA when the weather was over.

"We're back on KTOK," said Josh. "Talking dust mite rights with People in Pederasty with Animists or something. Well, Gus, look. I'm not going to stand here and feel guilty for being at the top of the food chain. If the animal kingdom had an opposable thumb and access to firearms, we would all live in fear of being dragged back to some squirrel's lair for supper. I don't particularly take pleasure in this. I'm just happy to be on the side with the firepower.

Doesn't mean I won't help, say, a dog in trouble. But it means that if I see a man passed out in the street, a dog passed out next to him, and a bus rushing out of control toward them, I will not have to perform some elaborate moral calculus before I decide the human is more worthy of being saved."

"Really? I'd save the dog. Wouldn't think twice."

"The dog? Ha-ha! Really."

"It depends, I suppose. If the man is in a three-piece suit, that says to me greed. It just does. I know I judge people by their clothes and I know that's wrong, but that's how I am. Whereas the dog is not greedy and hasn't hurt anyone."

"You have a point. I'd argue that it's wrong if I argued with anyone. But now, we have a call. Let's go to line 1 for our first caller. Tim, you're on."

"Hey, Josh! It's Tim! Remember?"

"We get a lot of Tims. Jog my memory."

"Aw, I'd rather give you a fun fact. Collect 'em all! So then: Did you know that when a man is shot, the impact actually lifts him off his feet?" Breathy voice, thrilled with itself. "Did you? Didja know that?"

"Ahhh, I'm not certain what this has to do with animal—"

"You don't believe me? Well, you know what they say. Learn by doing." *Click.*

"That was Tim, calling in from Venus. Good connection. Any listeners out there not currently engulfed in a fever delirium are invited to call us here, 555-8255. We're talking with Gus Sidwell—I'm sorry, Sid Guswell. Or Well Sidgus. Sounds like a Scottish dish, eh? Sidgus. Let's get back to saving dogs and people now. Suppose the man is dressed in common laborer's clothes, so we know he's not greedy, and the dog is rabid, foaming at the mouth and has passed out from exhaustion from biting an entire sixth-grade class during recess. Still going to save the dog?"

"Depends. I'd have to know more about the dog. Is it the last of its species?"

"If I could ask, what does that have anything to do with it?"

"It's very important to preserve genetic diversity."

"Which should go for the man as well, eh? I imagine he has genes that are responsible for more interesting things than 'correctly identify cat urine.'"

"I'm just saying I'd have to know more."

"Okay, it's Albert Einstein passed out in the street, and some mongrel dog is passed out next to him, and the bus is coming."

"Why do you persist? There's no way I can tell by looking that it's a mongrel. How do I know it's not the last of its breed?"

"And you'd let the greatest physicist of the twentieth century get turned to jam by a bus to save some dog specially bred by Chinese emperors to have a high butt and a low bark?"

"I can't make those value judgments."

"You have to. Here comes the bus."

"Since we're discussing principles, and since I am always true to my principles, I'd save the dog. I'm sorry, but that's just the way I am."

"Okay. Okay. There's a woman in the road, really cute, gorgeous, great build, and next to her is some mange-ridden rabid mutt you've just watched kill a basketful of innocent kittens, tip over an aquarium and kill all the fish, eat the family parakeet, and snap up a dozen hamsters like popcorn. Who do you save: beautiful woman or psychopathic animal-slaughtering dog?"

"Well, first, it's a rather heterosexist assumption you're making."

"What in God's name do you mean?"

"That I'd want to save the woman because she's attractive and I want to sleep with her."

"So it's an attractive guy then. Same scenario."

"And it's still inappropriate. You don't save someone just because they're attractive."

"So it's a gay man with elephantitis in the road with the rabid dog!" Josh shouted. *"Who do you want to save?"*

"It's still not fair. Maybe the dog could be used for research that would cure rabies, I don't know."

"Aha! So you support animal testing!"

"No, no, absolutely not! But if they just took some of its blood—"

"No time to draw blood. The bus is coming. Save the cute guy or the rabid dog."

"I can't say which I'd save."

"If that's the case, you are either a liar or an idiot, and if I ever come across you passed out in the street, I am going to find a dog, club it unconscious, throw it next to you, and pray that someone who believes exactly as you do comes across the scene."

This was the first part of the show. Forty minutes of the same followed, with Josh swinging between rude snarls and simpering noncommittal demurrals. At the bottom of the hour a man in a suit—the program director, no doubt—entered the studio; I heard Josh shout "Fuck you" a minute later. The program director left red faced and steaming.

After this merriment, it was my turn.

When I got in the booth and settled into my chair, Carlton didn't acknowledge me. He fell silent for a few minutes, only to get up and leave without a word when the network news came on. I was wondering if I'd have to start the show myself when he reappeared with a mug of coffee. His hands were shaking. Coffee leapt from the cup. He drank half of it, pulled a bottle of Clan Anderson from his jacket, and glugged two fingers into the cup. He waved the bottle at me.

"Note the cheap brand," he said, and he took a sip

and muttered something. "Put that in your piece. Not only does Mr. One Share drink on the job, he drinks the cheap stuff. Listen, radio is a hard business. No security. Only a fool drinks good liquor on the job. Ahhhhhh." He grinned. "I'm in the mood to be fired, and it feels uncommonly good." There was something sharp and unpleasant in his eyes. I looked down at the note pad where he scrawled questions and notes. There was a big blue one in the middle, surrounded with a thicket of smaller ones.

"Stand by," said the voice under the table, like some troll with an FCC license. "Thirty seconds out of traffic, then the shout, then twenty seconds bumper music, post at seventeen seconds. What did the PD have to say? Didn't he like that hour?"

"Post at seventeen," Josh muttered. Another draught of hot coffee. A minute later there was the chorus of breathy white folk crying "Jawwwwwsh, Carlton!" then music kicked in, something with a rubbery bass and a brittle drum. Carlton stepped in a moment before the melody arrived, parried it away, and introduced himself. Dagler pulled the music down, and there we were.

"Josh Carlton back with you on this fine fresh Monday afternoon. The time is somewhere after four, and as for the weather, well, I'm in a small windowless room. Why you'd depend on me for weather I can't imagine. You want to know the weather? Go look out your goddamn window." Dagler's eyes went wide, and he hit a small red switch, presumably the panic button. Drums kicked in and the white folk sang "KTOK! KTOK! We're here, we're always here, KTOK!"

"Sorry about that," said Carlton. "Lost my entire training for a second. Years of not cussing, right out the window. If I had a window, that is; I'm sitting in a windowless room, and I can't see shit."

"KTOK! KTOK! We're here, we're always here, KTOK!"

There were now fists pounding on the studio door, vainly trying the locked knob. "Anyway. Hope you caught the last hour, a fascinating conversation with a total idiot with a clean colon and an empty head, a common combination nowadays. Hey, here's our general manager, Peter Garth, waving at us from the control room!" There was a man standing behind Dagler shouting silently at Carlton. "Penis, penis, penis, penis, penis," said Carlton. "Penis. Now that the daily business is out of the way, let's get down to our guest. With me today is another shameless self-promoter, Jonathan Simpson. A name as limp as the man himself. I believe you're here to rehash some ancient history for us?"

"Ah, I gather, yes. It's about the movie—"

"Oh, yes. Your movie. Your *TV* movie. More about the Alimentary Instruction League, right? Now we all know you've pretty much made a career out of your involvement with those terrorists—"

"Well, wait a minute." P.D. Spaunaugle-style ambushes from Josh Carlton—who'd have thought? But I shouldn't have complained: a TV movie had been made of my life, and I was now public property. "I'm not making a career of this," I said. "It's just the natural progression, isn't it? Something happened to me, I wrote about it, and a studio bought the story. If a gaping chasm should suddenly open beneath your chair and you were dropped into a ninety-foot pit, and one of those horrible person-in-a-pit rescue vigils followed, I think you'd go the same route."

He smiled sadly. The smile of someone who believes he would never be so lucky. *Fall in a pit, get trapped, be pulled out shivering and half mad, and then sell the rights? Naw, stuff like that doesn't happen to folks like me.* He took another drink of Clan Anderson, then announced a break for weather.

Carlton rubbed his eyes and, without looking at me, said, "Sorry. A bad day. Nothing personal."

"Something probably not evident to the listeners."

"No one's listening," he said, doodling another set of ones. "No one's listening."

"Traffic for thirty," said Dagler, sitting behind a glass wall that separated the booth from the intercom, "then back to you. For the moment. I hope you know what a poor impression you're making with your employers." Carlton nodded.

After traffic—the usual horror story of vehicle fires, jackknifed semis, and drivers slamming on the brakes for no good reason—we came back. Carlton gave me the sad smile again and reintroduced me.

"When I said you've made a career out of this, I mean that you've done well. You have a nice job and a nice house, if the TV show is true, and you get to see your life on TV. I should get in such trouble." The strange, sad smile again. "Tell us: What's the movie like?"

"It's awful."

"Oh, I'm sure it's not—"

But I interrupted him and spent the next ten minutes keelhauling the movie. Carlton sat back, watching me, doodling. He leaned over only to announce a commercial break. We sat in silence listening to a commercial for *Deadly Bread.* Tomorrow night, on KBAE, which, I recalled, was the parent company of this radio station. Tara's employer, too.

The show ended with Carlton telling everyone he'd see them down at the Groutfest at the Civic Center, provided hell froze sheer and solid, and he signed off for the hour.

"I'll walk you out. I owe you that much."

Some repayment. We exited the building in silence. Other KTOK employees looked away as we passed. Carlton stopped outside the door and shook a cigarette from his pack with trembling fingers. He looked out over the brown field across the road that held the station's transmitting tower: a three-hundred-foot spire projecting his inadequacy over the state. I took out a cigarette and waited. Carlton wanted to talk about something, I could tell.

He looked out to the tower in the fields, shielding his eyes, cigarette standing up in his fingers like an empty flagpole, trembling.

"You need a light?" He shook his head, lit his cigarette, and snapped the Zippo shut.

I heard a *crack:* sharp and distant, like a cable snapping. Something shattered above me, and I shot a look upward. The neon *T* in KTOK had exploded, showering a mist of glass and chemicals down upon me. Severed wires hissed and popped. I put up my hand to shield my face, feeling the moment expand like an accordion, gathering wind to blow one long discordant chord. I tried to turn away, but I'd sunk to my ankles in terror. That sound, that clean final break, that was a gun, that—There it was again, then a grunt. Something slammed into my head and shoved me on my back. I heard Carlton's lighter clatter to the ground, then I was face up on the pavement, fire pouring from my head. Carlton gasped and shouted something at me. I saw the words float down like white scraps of ash, melt on my face, and flow out the place in my head where everything else was going—numbers, words, faces, days, all pouring out.

Then a black ring circled the world, and the ring fell in on itself. Something flew past and took me with it. *Do you know where we're going?* I thought.

Let me look at that map.

Lazarus's Travels

1

ANGELS SINGING. DOING A POOR JOB OF IT, TOO.

They were singing on the other side of a wall. They stopped. Feet shuffled in my direction. Light fell on my face. A voice, the head angel perhaps, said "Hmm . . . no use singing for him," and the angels moved along and started singing again, their voices growing faint.

I tried to tell the angels I was very much interested in their songs. *Anything! Kumbaya even! Just come back!* Not as much as a croak emerged. The pilot light of my vocal cords had been extinguished. I couldn't even move my head to look toward the wall. My neck felt like the cap on an old bottle of syrup. Sitting up was out of the question. Some vast and silent wind kept me flat on my back. My inability to move I ascribed to the state of being dead.

If this was heaven, though, it lacked. I had at least expected to have to haul my soul through customs, pay the duties. Maybe this was where they made the flesh cool its heels while they took the soul into the room with the bright lights and rubber hoses. While I laid here, my soul was confessing to shoplifting a *Playboy* in seventh grade, and we were both going off to the sulfurous Jacuzzi below. If I was already in hell, I thought, noting the contours of the room I appeared to be in, it bore a remarkable resemblance to a motel room.

Although in hell, nothing would be sanitized for your protection. And in hell, the angels would sing nothing *but* Kumbaya.

It took a few minutes of thoughts like those to wave the fog from my brain. Eventually my rational faculties bustled in and started ordering my thoughts around. First conclusion: I was in a hospital. Second: Since there were no sniffling relations at the foot of the bed wailing novenas and slaughtering lambs for my recovery, I must have been here for a while. To my left was a series of machines, with lines and blips measuring out my finite allotment of heartbeats. To my right, an IV unit dangled from a pole, dripping something cold into the shoots that ran into my arms. Beyond that, a keystone of light from the hallway spilled onto the floor. My eyes adjusted, and I saw the room in detail: a TV set bolted to the wall, a table with no flowers or cards, windows with the curtains open to the flat night sky.

Why am I in a hospital?

Snow was falling outside the window.

The sight of snow put a match to my voice, and I howled and howled until two nurses hustled in and turned on a light over my bed. *Ouch! Jesus!* I tried to shout. It was like highway warning flares had been shoved down my optic nerves. The nurses soothed me with meaningless sounds. They smiled at each other, and one left to fetch a doctor or an insurance claims adjuster, whichever was more important. The other one hushed me and smoothed my hair, beaming down at me.

"Snowing," I tried to say. I sounded like branches scratching on a screen window. I pointed at the window with one of the dead tubes of meat that had previously been my fingers.

"I know, I know," she said. "You're back in time for Christmas."

"Which. Year."

"The same year where you got hurt. Just be calm. It's all going to be fine."

"Have I. Been in. A coma?"

"Yes."

I lay silent for a while. And this was the year I was going to get my cards out early.

The doctor came to see me the next morning. I had been given a cursory examination the night before by a yawning young intern in a Santa Claus suit. He had been touring the pediatrics wards, handing out toys to the shut-in children. So blind with exhaustion, he handed both nurses and me a set of wind-up teeth before he realized he was here on business. He said I was fine and yawned his way back to handing out chattering choppers—probably not the best thing to give a kid facing surgery, when you think about it.

After he left, the nurses on the floor came to meet me, one by one. My lack of sociability was put down to my disorientation when it was, in fact, the realization that these women had been giving me intimate sponge baths without my knowing it. The nurses made sure I was comfortable, then faded off to other duties, checking in periodically to make sure I had not dozed off again, this time for keeps.

I laid there in the dim light, eyes wide as headlights, my brain pawing through a hall of mirrors. Why was I here? What had happened? And, most important:

"Can I smoke in here? And how about some coffee?"

It was the next morning, and the doctor, a coffee-skinned man reeking of tobacco, his nameplate reading R. Phranjari, shook his head.

"You want a cigarette?" he said. His accent was Indian, and it made the English language sound as though it were leaping for a stick. "I should have thought that would be out of your system." He opened a folder, looked at some papers and frowned.

"I always have one when I wake up."

He shrugged and looked at some more papers and scowled. "This would be a good time not to be smoking," he said. "Your wound and resultant hibernation brought down your blood pressure, which, we noted from your records, was very high."

"I'd have preferred medication that wasn't ballistically administered."

He went on examining my chart, glowering at the monitors.

"Excuse me," I said. "Sorry to bother you. But how long—"

"Three months, four days. Minor." He gave my monitors a small sneer. "There is a man down the hall who has been in a coma for six years."

"I have a short attention span."

Phranjari nodded briskly. He withdrew a small mallet from his pocket and whipped the sheets off my body. "Knees first. If this is painful, that is a good sign."

"Wait a minute, all right? Could you tell me exactly why I am here? What happened? Did I cut myself shaving, slip in the shower—"

"You were shot in the head," he said. He struck my

26

kneecap with his mallet. My leg jumped as though it had decided to audition for the Rockettes. I gave a cry of pain. Phranjari smiled, sheathed his mallet, and slammed the folder shut. "You were shot exactly here." He rapped a knuckle on a spot above my right temple. "Luck was with you, unlikely as that is seeming to you now. There was neither heavy blood loss nor damage of cortex. The level of responsiveness of your autonomic functions indicated quick recovery, certainly nothing to indicate three months of comalike behavior. At the time a fast recovery was being envisioned." He scowled. He'd probably lost money in the coma pool.

"There are tests to be done," he continued, "and there will be a psychiatrist along later for the parts of the brain I can do nothing about. Also much physical therapy. You are a wasted man, but a coma will do that."

"I was shot in the *head?*"

He nodded. "It will please you to no possible end that the man who did it languishes in jail as we speak. It was in the news very much. You missed a time of great drama."

"So-so-so——"

"No need to be thanking. It is my job." Apparently he had led the police hunt as well.

"Why am I alive? Why am I talking? Shouldn't I be staring at the ceiling and drooling?"

"I will explain at a point in later time. Suffice to say there was little neurological damage. We did take out a smallish portion of your brain, but as you can see you are doing well without it. You were not shot directly in the head, which helped. The bullet entered the arm of your friend who was also there being shot. It struck a bone, exited his arm, and traveled into your brain, by which time, of course, it had slowed down. You owe your life to his radial bone."

"I'll send it a card." I started to say something else, but Dr. Phranjari held up a hand.

"I have to go. There are many injured brains to see. I will be back. Dr. Oong will be along shortly. Good day." And I was left alone again.

Bastard. Dump that in my lap and stroll away. I did not like having part of my brain gone and being told I was doing fine without it.

"Who knows what was in that part?" I yelled at the door. "I had phone numbers in there! Combinations to locks! Concepts of right and wrong!"

No one burst in the door to soothe my nerves, kiss my stitches, tell me it was all right.

Okay. Shot in the head. Think about this.

I was awake and yapping away, so I was obviously not going to spend the rest of my life as an incontinent zucchini, dusted off every afternoon by bored orderlies who gave me insulting pet names. Hands and feet responded to commands, so I'd be up and walking, probably in front of a car, soon enough. Best of all, my memory was still intact. I knew who I was, what I did, where I lived. At this point everything else was frosting.

Or did I remember everything correctly? After all, there was no assurance any memory I had was real. If you're illiterate, you don't know if the card catalog is in the proper order. Maybe my memories had all leaked together, and I confused my last girlfriend with my second-grade teacher and heretofore would only be attracted to old women who smelled of glue. Perhaps the several hundred thousand television programs I've watched had been refiled as Real Memories, and I was condemned to a life of sitting around the bar insisting I helped Gregory Peck and Zorba the Greek destroy the Guns of Navarone, while my friends exchanged tired, sad looks.

I felt panic bolting up my throat. Even if I thought I was all right, that too could be a trick of my jumbled brain. That was the essence of madness: not knowing how mad you were.

I closed my eyes.

The day of the shooting was indistinct, like grainy film, the voices out of sync with the sound. I saw a man with headphones, a bottle of scotch in each hand. I saw a sad man driving a bus over Albert Einstein. No, no. That wasn't right. Think. Oh, sure. Mr. Save-Everything-from-Plankton-on-Up. The radio show. Right?

I remembered leaving a room, standing on the steps of a building. Someone standing over me shouting . . . swearing, it seemed. After that, nothing.

It came back—wheezing and limping, but it returned. I spent a few hours reconnoitering through my memory, grazing back through my life until I hit the thick hedge of infancy. Everything seemed to be still there, and a few memories profited from being taken down and dusted, particularly a few humid numbers from adolescence. My brain worked then. This was looking good. I'd be out of the hospital in no time.

Out, less a few ounces of brain matter, probably unemployed. I recalled having a few days sick leave stored up, but this was pushing it.

Just two minor questions.

Who? And for Christ's sake, why?

When I awoke on the second day, I called for the nurse and requested a phone. "There were some people I was supposed to meet for supper," I said. "I imagine they're starting to get concerned."

I didn't know who to call. Grunewald and Trygve, I had realized, would be in Europe for months. I called home just to make sure, and the phone rang forever. I laid there listening to the ring, imagining every empty room of the house. Jesus, what had happened to the people who'd rented the place for a wedding and found it locked?

Then I called my employer, the *Metropole,* and told the receptionist my name. She said there were some messages for me to pick up. She could read them if I liked; there were only three. I told her to put me through to my editor, Fikes, and waited, listening to the Muzak. It was a popular song I'd never heard. Realizing I had been asleep long enough for a song to make it to Muzak made me feel clammy again, as did the thought of talking to Fikes. He didn't much like me.

He had apparently had time to change his mind.

"Simpson! God! Jesus! Mary! Joseph the carpenter! You're awake! Can you hold?" *Click.* Muzak. I had the brief feeling I had awoken in an alternate world, one where the phlegmatic Fikes, he who could not speak a sentence without a murmur of pain and disgust as though his tongue had gout, was actually possessed of a lively personality, one that liked me. Then he returned, his old self again. *"Mrrgh.* Sorry. Had to kill the Simpson Coma Watch for this edition. In fact for you I'll hold the edition. Are you up to talking? I'd prefer an exclusive. Remember, you're still on salary."

"So I still have a job."

"Mrrrm. You did the right thing in coming out before the insurance bailed out. That was a decision I was not looking forward to making. But you're still one of us. So what do you say? Interview? Fifteen minutes, *mrggghm?"*

"I haven't the faintest idea what I'd say. I just woke up. I'm not even sure what happened."

"Even better. Let me be the first. Somebody took a shot at Josh Carlton, Christ if I know why. The bullet took a bounce worthy of Lee Harvey Oswald and hit you in the head. They've a suspect in jail, gentleman by the name of Peter Byrne, and I understand they've a rather tight case on him, too. Which is the problem, according to the reporter who has been working on this. He will explain the rest."

"Why is the tight case a problem?"

"Ahh . . . I'll let him explain. Very complicated. I'm not sure I like where he is taking the paper on this, but I won't say any more. Just tell me when the convocation can begin."

I said he could come by in the afternoon and then said I wanted to go to sleep.

"*Mrrrgh*. One more thing. Are you up to composing a piece on hospital food? Sort of a mock highbrow take on postcontemporary gruel."

I'd think about it. *Click*.

Thirty-six hours out of a coma and I was already on deadline.

2

TARA ARRIVED WITHIN THE HOUR. SHE BLEW INTO THE room with the air of a mannequin that had been granted one day of life and by God was going to make the most of it. She stopped and regarded me for a second with total horror: *Icky! Icky!* But then she squared her beautiful shoulders and shook her beautiful hair and took my hand. The camera wasn't running yet; I appreciated the effort.

I cannot of course remember the first time I saw Tara, which must have been through the cool glass of the TV set. I remember the first time I saw in her in the flesh, though. She was across the room, drink in one hand, cigarette in the other, yelling at a man with such gusto that his face was about to ripple with *g*-force. I liked the look of her. She had long, black wavy hair and a body that looked like the sign for infinity set on its end. I edged my way across the room until I was behind her, watching her hair bounce as she went at the man like a backhoe on a stump. He was tall, thin, with small eyes glaring out from a face nearly entirely overgrown with red foliage. Her victim's eyes darted left and right for rescue, as though some social version of paramedics would burst in, check his vitals, declare him hopelessly defeated, and immediately administer five minutes with a fawning sycophant.

"Jerk it, yank it, stick it in an electric socket for all I care," she shouted. "I just don't want it near me again!"

"Thank you," he said. He turned, a limp chamois, and was pulled as though by rollers into the crowd of the party. She then turned around and threw her drink in my face. Or so it appeared. Actually, someone had been attempting a Lindy hop on the dance floor and had thrown their partner into the crowd. She'd sailed backward flailing for purchase until she hit Tara. Tara's martini went into my face and soaked my shirt. Her face banged into mine and her cigarette went right up my sleeve, where I did not find it for another minute.

After that I smelled like gin, but as I found out when I kissed her later, so did she. Hardly a basis for a relationship, of course, but at the time it explained the kiss.

We left together that evening and did not part until the gunshot forced the issue. Our six months together was not all that bad. At first I felt unworthy and expected her to leave me on the grounds that she was a figment of my libidinous imagination. But then she grew tiresome. She demanded of me a level of ambition equal to her own. I couldn't do it; no one could. Tara would have berated FDR for not seeking a fifth term. She was a one-person paving crew, and you either jogged alongside the machinery or laid down and became part of the road. When I failed to accede to her appetite for a large, remunerative career, I became a nonentity. Toward the end of the relationship she looked at me as though she could detect the faint outlines of the furniture behind me.

If we'd been allowed to let the thing die its natural death, it would have ended according to the familiar pathetic script. I'd have gone over to collect the various bits of jetsam that had drifted into her apartment, at the same time returning sundries, cosmetics, odd bits of undergarments, and unused contraceptives. It would be horrible. Intending to drive the last few nails in the coffin, we would end up arguing about the right kind of nails. In the end I would stand alone on her porch with a box of my belongings, looking forward to a life of frozen pizzas, dead plants, and convenience-store beer.

Thank God someone shot me and saved me from all that.

"Jeeez, Jonathan, you look, like, *horrible.*"

"I've been on the Coma Diet." I smiled.

She hesitated at the doorway. "Gunshot wounds are not contagious, Tara," I said.

She nodded, set her lips, and came over to my bedside. She patted my shoulder like it was made of pie crust and sat down on the bed. A few seconds later a cameraman entered, a rheumy-eyed soul who looked like an elf thrown out of the toy makers' guild for moral torpidity. He started looking around the room for a good angle, throwing me looks that put me on a level with stuffed animals and wax fruit. He turned on the lights over my bed, held a light meter to them, and scowled.

"Light's bad in here," he said.

"I know," I said. "My life passed before me and I could hardly make it out."

"I gotta go get light," he said, and he waddled from the room.

Tara let out a long sigh, then put her arms around me and gave me a hug. It was as intimate as someone reaching around a dummy to fasten the buttons on its shirt.

"I've thought about you everyday," she said.

"I wish I could say the same, Tar."

"You look cute with long hair."

"I get completely shaved tomorrow for some tests. I'll look like a recruiting poster for the Hitler Youth."

"Are *they* back?" she said with irritation. "Okay. Does anything hurt? Everything work, y'know, upstairs?" She tapped her head.

"It works well enough for me to wonder what I am doing here. Who the hell would shoot me?"

"You're a public figure," she said. "It happens."

"In movies it happens. I'm a food critic. My occupational hazards are brucellosis squitters and salmonella. Getting shot was not in the job description."

"Well, it's not like they were aiming for you anyway, so don't get too full of yourself. This is a freak thing."

"Articulate as ever, Tara. Cause of injury: freak thing."

She scowled.

"What about Josh Carlton?" I said. "No one's filled in any details at all. For all I know he's in the ground."

"Worse. He's working nights." Tara was pawing through her purse for her notebook. "The station demoted him to the midnight-to-three shift, put this raving maniac in his place. Josh just got hit in the arm, you know. Poor man. Couldn't even manage to pull a career opportunity out of that." She shook her head.

Shoot her in the right arm, and she'd turn it into a anchor job.

"The nurse said that someone named Tara Greasy was coming up to see me. I thought it cruel and inaccurate, unless you were suddenly neglecting your appearance."

"*Gruesse.* She must have taken it off my driver's license. Didn't recognize me from TV, I guess. My married name is Tara Gruesse."

"You got—you did? You married a guy named Greasy?"

"It's just pronounced Greasy. And don't *be* that way."

"*Married.* Jesus. Where did you meet the swain Greasy?"

"A long time ago. At the hearing. Federal courts. I—"

"Reporter, huh. *Times? Press-Dispatch?* I *knew* I'd lose you to one of those alcoholic—"

"He's the cops reporter for the *Times,* and he is not alcoholic. He is *brilliant.* Don't be this way, Jonathan."

"Brilliant and alcoholic are not mutually exclusive. And since when do you get married in three months? It took me four months to get you to commit to a lunch date on a weekday."

"I've known him a while."

"Fill me in. Were you married to him while we went out?"

"Of course I was. What, you think I meet a guy and marry him in three months?"

"Sorry. Low of me to think otherwise."

She looked at me with an expression I couldn't read, a nursery rhyme in Sanskrit. I couldn't tell if she *had* told me, and the memory was a fleck on Phranjari's gloves washed down the drain, or if she hadn't ever told me and was using my interlude of drastic slumber to cover for herself. I didn't care if she'd lied, but I was piqued to find out why she might.

All sorts of interesting things occur to you when you sleep with people you really don't care for.

She was still looking inscrutable, so I put on my sad-eyed, wasted coma patient look, and she pursed her lips and looked away. "You'll meet him. You'll like him."

"I'll meet him? Why in God's name should I want to meet him?"

"He knows all about us, and I think he's curious to see who you are. It's all in the past, anyway, over and done. Although I guess for you it's like yesterday?" She bit her lower lip.

"Don't worry," I said, smiling. *"Mazel tov,* you wonderful, crazy kids you."

"Oh, I knew you'd be cool about it." Hug and a peck; immense relief, I could tell. She checked her watch. "Anyway, we'll discuss this later. When Frank comes back with lighting, I'll have to do a straight interview. I have to get it in by two, so it'll be fast, and *no* questions from you. Leave it to me. What I've done on this story is the best I've ever done, and you waking up—well, that's just the perfect kicker."

"What if I relapse?"

"A postscript. Final tragic note, that's about all." She shook a hank of hair out of her face. "Well, you asked."

3

TARA'S INTERVIEW WAS SHORT AND BRUSQUE, WITH THE standard ration of sympathy she doled out to all those whose adversity is bad enough to land them a spot as lead human interest on the prenetwork news show. At one point the cameraman commanded me to smile. When I'd given a grin of insufficient luminescence, he told me to imagine a date with the lovely lady interviewing me. We both turned to the camera with bright, insane smiles of horror.

That was the photo they freeze-framed on the evening news. Either someone at editing desk had it in for Tara or the publisher had ordered another we're-here-for-you promotional binge that required the reporters to be photographed digging victims from collapsed buildings and delivering the babies of unwed mothers.

The next day the *Metropole* reporter showed up. Around noon, just as I was looking at a plate of lurid gruel and wondering if the energy required to eat it would leave me too exhausted to throw it up, the door blew open and in came Hitch Marty, so named not for an Festusesque crimp in his walk, for a stint in the service, or for a resemblance to a fat film director, but for his constant nervous tick—hitching himself up as though some great invisible hand was forever yanking at his underwear. Every thirty seconds or so his shoulders would bunch up, his eyebrows would arch, and he would stand on tiptoe. Hitch struck you as someone so intensely horny that he probably gave himself concussions when he masturbated. But he had recently taken up with a stunning woman who outclassed him by several degrees, so that didn't explain his peculiarity.

"So," he said. *Hitch!* "You got shot. Single gunman, they say. Hah!" Hitch was an intense Kennedy buff. "Like a duck they lured you into that spot! Triangulated fire! Bang! I suppose the Magic Bullet Manufacturing Company made the one that went into your head!"

"I don't want my shooting to spawn a cottage industry for conspiracy buffs," I said.

"Just kidding. I figure one shooter, but two people present." He opened a notebook. "You like *Star Trek?* It's been a great season so far. Three months you've been down, right? I envy you, all that new *Star Trek* just waiting. Plus *Playboys.* Okay." *Hitch.* "It's like this. Two guys witness the shooting—a station employee driving up for his nighttime shift and the operator of a gas station on the other side of the highway. Both saw you do the big dive. The station owner hears the second shot—"

"There was another? One wasn't good enough?"

"The first one hit the T in the station's neon sign, blew it out. Bang! The second hit Carlton in the arm, smack! The bullet exits and smacks you in the head. *Whap!*"

"Please."

"Anyway, the owner heard where the shot came from, saw you down, calls for help. Shortly afterward he sees an old red Cadillac, a real gas-suckin' boat, flying outta this road behind his gas station. The road went along the field where the KTOK transmitters sit. I been out there, it's a service road, little traffic. The police got good tread castings. Anyway, police and ambulance get there pretty quickly, and the officers get the description of the car from the gas station guy. One unit goes in pursuit, can't find the car. Go figure:

Big red Cadillacs, they don't blend right in. The other units investigate the area around the towers. They find two spent rifle cartridges, footprints in the mud, tire tracks, candy bar wrappers, cigarette butts. Based on this, they had a suspect in custody in two days."

"Someone with a bad cough and cavities drive into the police station and track all over the rug?"

"The cigarettes were this generic shit, house brand you can't get anywhere around here except at Fill 'n' Fart convenience stores or whatever they call them. Gas 'n' Snak, that's it. They got, what, thirty locations in town. Seven of those carried the candy bar with the lot numbers of the wrapper the police found. They subpoenaed the credit card charges of those stations, ran checks through the DMV, and found the red Cadillac. Ba-bing. This leads them to Mr. Peter Byrne."

"Let me guess. A quiet man, few friends. Neighbors described him as a loner, said he kept to himself, said hello on occasion but seemed decent."

Hitch grinned. "Yeah. But that describes a lot of people, not just the basic psychos you see on the news. Describes most of my family, and they *are* psychos, but they didn't do this, so you can see how your theory falls apart. Anyway, Mr. Byrne is not a psychopath, as we will see. So, the police question Mr. Byrne. He says that on the day in question he got off his job—he worked nights at this plastic extruding company—stopped at the Gas 'n' Snak on Hennepin, and went home."

"Some alibi."

"His alibi includes the fact that he went home and listened to Josh Carlton's show. He was even honest enough to say he didn't know what was on the second hour, because he'd fallen asleep. He never heard of you, so don't get any ideas he had it in for you. From here, it gets worse. The security cameras at the convenience store have pictures of him buying gas, candy, and cigarettes."

"Anything old-fashioned like a motive?"

"The prosecution will try to show he had an unusual fixation with Josh Carlton. Some of the people in the rooming house said they heard him arguing with the show. They said he used to get drunk, listen to the radio, and talk back to it. Wait. Gets more interesting. They found a rifle in the trunk. It matched up with the bullets, and it had his prints. Now here's the interesting part." *Hitch! Hitch!* "They *arrested an innocent man.*"

Pause.

"What do you base that on?" I asked politely.

"Because they found cigarette butts at the site of the shooting."

Another pause.

"And?" asked I.

"He had," said Hitch, with great drama, "given up smoking *two months before.*"

I looked carefully at Hitch, studying him for additional signs of flaming lunacy.

"Maybe he was under some stress," I said slowly. "They say that when you try to quit and something stressful comes up, like changing a job or deciding to kill someone, it's tempting to start up again."

Hitch stood, shaking his head. "Not Peter. Meet him and you'll understand. Quitting smoking was crucial to improving his self-image. He's very proud of it, making for a hard time in the slammer, as you can imagine. Cigarettes are currency there."

"But you said they had him on film buying cigarettes."

"Exactly. *Exactly!* If not for himself, then for whom? If he hated smoking, who would he hate enough to buy cigarettes for? I'll tell you who: Tim."

"Tim."

"Just Tim," he spat. "The mystery man who shot at you. He borrowed Peter's car, took his rifle, availed himself of the candy bars in the glove compartment, climbed the radio tower, waited for you, and shot you as you emerged from the station."

"Do you know any of those silly little details like last name, description, motive? I hate to quibble, but—"

"All we know is his name: Tim. And he's got a Mohawk haircut. And he's probably left town, though we don't *know* that."

"And you believe Peter Byrne is innocent?"

"Completely. Don't worry, Jonathan, we'll get him a fair trial."

"Thanks," I said. "Maybe I'll go down to the jail to talk to Peter myself." Hitch beamed. *And I'll throttle him,* I thought, *until he begs for a cigarette.*

I drifted off to sleep. You'd think I'd be awake for days, given how much rest I'd had. *Tired? Nah! I got a good three months last night!* But I wasn't asleep for five minutes when the phone rang. I sprang awake and immediately checked the window for another change of season in case I'd slipped back into old habits. Still snowing. Sunny day. Okay. I fumbled for the phone.

"Hlo."

"Mr. Simpson?"

"Mm-hmm," I mumbled.

"This is Peter Byrne. You don't know me but I'm, ah, I'm behind bars for shooting you."

I cleared the fog from my head.

"Mr. Marty told me he was coming to see you today and that he'd tell you everything. I wanted to say I'm glad you're okay, and I also want to tell you that I didn't shoot you. It wasn't me."

"No?"

"Uh-uh. I wouldn't shoot a fly."

"They're hard to hit and it brings down the average. Well, who was it then?"

"I can't tell anyone until they get me out of here."

"Why?"

"Because he's still out there and I'm afraid."

Silence from both of us. I could hear angry jailhouse hooting in the background.

"Mr. Carlton? I really liked the first part of that movie about you. I had to go to work and I missed the rest. Can you tell me how it all comes out?"

"I won," I said. "The bad guys either died or drew multiple and concurrent life sentences. Maybe they're in with you. Ask around."

"Hey, are you going to write a movie about this? Because there's this guy I'd like to play me. The one on that cop show in Indianapolis? I like that one. Okay. I got to go now. See you later. Really nice talking with you." And he was gone.

4

POSTCOMA LIFE HAD ALL THE LEISURELY PACE AND GENTEEL character of boot camp, though instead of reveille, there were enemas. I spent the next few days being poked and prodded, drained, and, most importantly, stripped of all body hair. I was shaved by a squat nurse with the posture of a macaque monkey. She used a noisy machine reeking of fried lubricant, the blades trembling on my scalp like a frightened Chihuahua. She slapped on a tonic, massaged my head as though it might leaven and rise, then wheeled me off in my gurney to what she called the brain floor. All the gurneys in the hospital had been shopping carts in their previous lives, so their wheels squeaked in pain and drove me into the walls whenever possible. I arrived at the brain floor with a wretched headache.

Nurse Macaque bashed the gurney through a set of swinging doors marked EKG. She handed me off to a nurse who had narrowly missed a career as a Peter Cushing impersonator and stalked off. I looked around: a spare room, with one machine. Those were the worst kinds, the rooms with one machine. A hopeful sign: The doors were not padded to muffle my screams. There was a large phrenology poster on the wall—a joke, I hoped—displaying the bald head of a complacent, generic nineteenth-century man. The head was mapped according to personality traits that corresponded to the contours of the skull. I noted that Lustfulness occupied an inordinately small area, but it was right on the temple, just where you'd rub if you got a headache.

The spot where the bullet hit my head was called Reflectiveness.

Nurse Cushing explained that we were going to take some readings of my brain waves. It would be painless, she added, her voice suggesting that it would be otherwise if she had anything to say about it. She slapped conducting fluid on my scalp and spread it around; small suction pads like those used to hold novelty items to car windows were placed over the epicenters of brain wave activity. I matched the location of the cups with the characteristics on the poster. I was being tested for Trustworthiness, Godliness, Morbidity, and Hygiene.

Nurse Cushing flicked on the EKG machine, which set a row of pens swinging across a wide roll of paper. The scratching of the pens made my brain sound as though my skull was filled with bored chickens clawing through the gravel for something to eat. But everything checked out, and she pronounced me hale of brain, if a little shy on the volume. Still, there were a few blips that concerned her, and she said they'd be monitoring me from time to time. It would be a while before I could let my hair grow in. I was free to start work on a beard.

In the afternoons I was wheeled down to physical therapy, where a professionally healthy young woman named Heather put me through a series of indignities designed to put starch in my muscles. I wished I was like a golem; no matter how long he'd been sleeping, you just carved some Hebrew in his forehead and he woke up in fighting trim. Not me. I had to struggle to lift weights that were no heavier than a cereal box, stagger along parallel bars on a drunkard's legs. Before the shooting I had been in decent shape, but now I was made mostly of twine and rubber bands. Heather would haul me out of my chair and flop me around like a sack of rags. Whenever I collapsed exhausted into her arms, I felt flesh so firm I wondered if she was made of the same material as those little rubber balls that bounce a mile in the air. I asked her for a date, and she said it would be bad for my health.

After physical therapy, Dr. Oong would come to visit me. He had been assigned to retune my psyche to the common tonalities of everyday living. His face was a parody of his name, one eye a wide capital O and the other squinting in lowercase. It gave him that half-crazed look of a man too long at sea. I disliked him from the start and had begun our sessions by admitting I was naked in all my dreams except for the ones in which I had sex. He nodded and underlined something twice.

At first we played with flash cards. Oong held up a picture and I would identify it. Apparently some who've taken a stern knock to the head lose their ability to tie names to common objects or can't grasp that an object seen from different angles is still the same object. I did not have this problem. I had seen Heather from every angle possible and was able to identify her each time as something I could never have. Then it was Rorschach blots. Dr. Oong told me there was no correct answer, which was, of course, nonsense. Had I insisted that every one of them looked like Mom with Big Castrating Scissors—make that two identical Moms joined at the hips with scissors—they would've paged every Freudian within a three-state radius. I was careful.

"And this?" It looked, as usual, like butterflies copulating.

"A lamb. A happy lamb."

"Fine. And this?"

This one looked like lambs copulating. "Twins sharing a diet soda."

Oong looked skeptical but put his professional face back on and showed me another. "And this?"

I squinted at it. "It looks like Elvis. Two of them. See the hips? The forelock? And it looks like they're grabbing a microphone stand or a—"

"Or what?"

"Nothing." I was not about to say that I had seen twin Elvises jousting with yard-long erections. Next card, please.

He spent the rest of the day plumbing me for anger, depression, anxiety, resentment, feelings of impotence, and found nothing. I was completely normal, and that, to Dr. Oong, was cause for concern. He found promising signs of impatience and boredom, but I insisted on ascribing these to my environs. After a few days the novelty of consciousness had worn off, and I was tired of harsh sheets, slippered feet, and muted voices. But as much as I wanted out, I did not want to rejoin the world. Not yet.

There was work to do. I borrowed an electric

typewriter from the nurse's station and dashed off the philippic on hospital food Fikes had requested. May I quote?

You have to be charitable toward a kitchen whose requests include "Johnson: be advised no colon; broth only." I was served Mr. Johnson's meal the other day, and I can only say the chefs did what they could. It was a meal that did not make a man regret the absence of his colon, and that takes some doing.

But it may be that they shine only when the circumstances are so dire. Normal hospital fare does not so much lean toward the banal as fall into it, arms wide, a kiss-me-you-fool look on its face. Texture—or lack of it—is everything. In the past few days I have been served the following:

A grayish mass of stacked and stiffened tissue paper, slathered with brown mucilage, labeled "sliced turkey breast with gravy."

Vegetables so soft they dissolved upon contact with saliva.

Pasta that did not only yield to the tooth, but positively swooned.

A chicken breast that, upon tasting, appeared to be a trick of the light.

Finally, vanilla pudding, unaccountably stiff, more fit for juveniles to scrawl their initials or plant their footprints in before it set completely.

And so on: my usual arch trouncing of everything served to me. I really have no idea what I'm talking about when it comes to food. I smoke too much to taste it, and I'm rather indiscriminate about what I do like. My palate has been numbed to the point where only a tamale marinated in tabasco and gasoline can get a message through. But as long as I disapprove of everything, of course, I am highly regarded.

What I didn't mention was that I liked what they fed me. Even the pudding. Especially the pudding.

The real world, specifically the part empowered to carry a badge and a weapon, showed up the day before my release. The police had called and said they might drop by, ask a few minor questions. At first I demurred, just on general principle. Police make me nervous. I get that cold-sweat deference that immediately makes policemen ask me to step out of the car and open my trunk.

But I had nothing to fear from the police: I was the guy who'd been shot. I had paid my parking tickets. There was never anything in my trunk anyway.

The nurse brought in the detective, and I groaned.

Detective Harley Bishop looked like the sort of policeman who would beat you once for offering him a bribe and once more because the bribe was too small. His head had the shape of a squat egg. Any normal chicken would have had a cerebral hemorrhage attempting to expel it. His vast stomach was a cemetery of doughnuts, and his fleshy neck and extra chins looked like a store window display of ring bologna. According to his mouth, pursed and puckered, he disapproved of me. But I knew that. We'd met during the food terrorist episode. He had suspected me of complicity half the time, told me nothing until the end, and only brought me on board when it looked like I might get killed instead of one of his officers. He was a run-of-the-mill bastard, and I had amplified that aspect of his character in my book. And now here he was again. Now I knew what was in the trunk: a copy of *Dead Bread.*

"Mr. Simpson," he grunted. I held out my hand for

the customary shake. He looked at it as though it were something he had found crawling in his garden. "Glad to see you're awake. I came to visit you before, but you were out cold." I could imagine him putting pennies on my eyelids and laughing. "We, ah, we got to talk." Bishop sat down on the edge of a chair, laid his huge hands on his knees, and summoned up a hard look.

"I don't know who shot me."

"Hell, son, we know who shot you. We just want to know why." Bishop pulled a folder from his briefcase and laid it on the edge of the bed, gesturing for me to take it. "We went back through the tapes of the Josh Carlton show for a few months, looking for anything that might tie the suspect, Mr. Byrne, to the shooting. We find that he called that show three times, all in the week you were shot. Take a look at those transcripts and tell me if you read anything that strikes your fancy."

I looked at the sheet.

8/12, 4:29 PM KTOK

JOSH CARLTON: And thank you, Bob, for that word on behalf of Steak 'n' Chops in Hopkins. Boy, doesn't a steak sound good now? Nothing like a steak to line your arteries with modeling clay, I always say. Okay, let's go back to the phones, and Peter on line 1. Hi, Peter.

PETER: Hi, Josh. Hey, there's a man here with a gun to my head.

JC: Loaded?

PETER: He looks sober to me.

JC: I mean the gun.

PETER: I'll ask. (*sound of explosives, possibly a gun; phone line disconnected*)

JC: Hah, hah, hah, hah. I can't believe the management is so desperate for ratings that they're forcing people at gunpoint to call this

show. Hah, hah, hah. Let's see who's on line 4.
Hah.

"I actually remember that show," I said to Bishop.
"I watched the news that night expecting them to
announce that someone wearing a KTOK promotion-
al T-shirt had been found slumped dead over his
phone."
"Read the next one."
"It would have been great for the ratings."
"Read."

8/13, 3:21 PM KTOK
    JC: And we have Peter on line 3. Welcome, Pete,
and thanks for holding.
    PETER: How you doing, Josh.
    JC: Bored stiff as ever, Peter; reduced to tossing
out harmless bits of nonsense between the cease-
less flow of shrieking commercials. Did I say that?
I'm kidding! I love my job!
    PETER: There's a man here with a chain saw to
my throat. (*silence for approximately two seconds*)
    JC: Peter, were you the guy who called a few—
(*sound of small engine, possibly a chain saw, being
revved.*)
    PETER: He says if I don't—(*sound of engine,
closer to phone; connection lost*)
    JC: Next time try a little lather and a twin-blade
disposable. You get a closer shave and you don't
have to hose down the walls.

"This is the guy you arrested for shooting me?"
Bishop nodded. "We found a chain saw in his room,
too. Read the third one."

8/15, 5:13 PM KTOK
    JC: One more call before we break for a word

from our sponsors. There's a Pete on line 2. How're you doing, and thanks for calling.

PETER: There's a man with a—

JC: Oh, no, let me guess. He's holding a rabid ferret to your throat. No, he's holding an outboard motor up to your jugular. Or perhaps he has you strapped to the dynamo of a hydroelectric plant this time? What is the point of all this, Peter?

PETER: Well, I don't know. I'm just doing what —(*phone line disconnected*)

"I don't know. Could be another bored idiot who thought he was being funny."

Bishop just stared at me.

"Oh, don't tell me you found an outboard motor in his room."

He shook his head.

"An electrical dynamo?"

"We found this." He pulled a photo from his briefcase and laid it on the bed. It was an old publicity still of Josh Carlton from his early days; written across the bottom were the words THESE ARE THE SMILING LIARS! #1 IN A SERIES. COLLECT THEM ALL.

"Well?" said Bishop.

"What do you want from me? I mean, those are the calls, you found the guy, he's obviously nuts, what do you want?"

"Reassurance," he said slowly. "I want to put my mind at ease."

"So read 'Desiderata.'"

"I don't go in for books."

"It's a poster. Sometimes it's a lacquered piece of wood."

"Shut yourself up now, and tell me something. The

first shot took out the T in that station's sign, which was a good eleven feet above you. And Carlton stood there, didn't move. And when he does get hit—about fifteen seconds later, I'd like to add—he gets shot in the arm, probably the least lethal part of the body aside from the butt. *Now how come he waited.*"

"He probably stood there for the same reason I did: pure terror. I didn't exactly do the jig down the sidewalk after the first shot. What are you getting at?"

"Hell, I don't know. All I know is, this guy wants to shoot him. Why doesn't he do it right? It's a fluke anybody got hit at all."

"So the guy was a bad aim."

"Peter Byrne served three years in the Marines."

"I don't know what he was trying to do! Ask him!"

"I have. I just don't get anywhere. All those prison guards around, it's difficult to whomp the truth out of a guy. See, they get testy if anyone beats their guys—a territory thing."

"Well, go through channels and get written permission to beat them then. Or go talk to Carlton again. I was just there, that's all."

"You tend to appear at the oddest times." He slapped his hands on his thighs. It was like wet bread hitting a ham. "I'll be off. I'll let you know if we find anything."

"That would be a change."

"Bitter, are you?" A humorless smile. "Well, let's get us off on a good start this time. I'll start. Here's a little secret. When we showed up after you'd been popped, we drove right up to the transmitter. Saw two big padlocks hanging off as pretty as you please. How Mr. Byrne got those keys, well, that's a question that would keep me up at night if I drank less." Detective Bishop gave me the smile I had seen every time we had argued about the food terrorists. It was the smile of pleasure of someone who knows the punch lines to jokes you haven't yet heard. And he left whistling.

I left the hospital a week before before Christmas. I still couldn't walk, but I was able to take solid food, and needed no unusual attention. Dr. Phranjari, who had disappeared during my convalescence, showed up on the day I was to leave and gave a stern recitation of my duties: bland diet, physical therapy, and biweekly visits to the brain floor for EKGs.

"Stay bald!" he commanded. "It is a waste and a chore to shave you."

I knew I was fit to leave—I had been demanding release almost since I had emerged from the coma. I was beginning to find the hospital a barrier to recovery. There was the unspoken dislike of other patients on the wing, who resented my ascent to health while they bobbed along in chronic discomfort. The nurses came to see me less as a miracle of the indomitable human body than another collection of orifices to be stoked and swabbed. I was sick of the lurid scent of antiseptics, the flat fluorescent lighting, the guilty looks on the faces of visitors to the ward. I missed the world. I spent hours looking out at the street, watching the cars and buses, like a boy standing on the banks of a tributary and dreaming of wide rivers and limitless oceans.

The world, however, was all a foreign shore. I was not going home exactly. There was no sense in going back to the manor, not yet. There'd be no negotiating that house in a wheelchair, not unless I wanted to crawl up the stairs like a lung fish. It served me right. I'd gotten rid of a little motorized chair that curved up the side of the staircase, built for Aunt Marvel in her declining years. The sight of her swooping down sidesaddle in her whirring little chariot used to terrify me as a kid. The chair was to blame for her demise and my ownership of the house. She caught her dress in it one day, flailed around and hit the up switch, and was dragged—*thonk, thonk, thonk*—up the stairs, receiving, in quick succession, a headache, a concussion, a skull fracture, unconsciousness, and death. Now I needed to reinstall the chair. I called the power company to see if my power had been turned off—it had—and to beg them to turn it on. They agreed with all the friendliness and understanding you find in a regulated monopoly. The swooping-chair company told me my model was out-of-date, and they'd need to order parts. The day I was let out, they hadn't even started yet.

So where to stay? I had, I realized with sadness, no close friends upon whom I could impose. (I thought again of my empty nightstand upon awakening from the coma.) That left strangers.

Tara and her husband, Hank, qualified all too well.

"I won't have you going to a motel! I won't." Tara had called up to see when we could do the obligatory victim-leaves-the-hospital-in-triumph story for the Sunday morning show that no one ever watched. The idea of staying with Tara and her husband, while initially mortifying, had a perverse attractiveness. At least she knew how I liked my eggs. And it would be fun to see close up the gentleman I had cuckolded. "Don't worry about Hank. I really doubt he'll be, like, threatened or anything. We'll tell him you're dead from the waist down. He'll like that. Anyway, we already have kid sister staying upstairs for the holidays, so it'll be a houseful of wonderful loved ones for your holiday season."

"Stop talking like a promo. You're sure it's okay?"

"I'm happy to help, honest. Here's the address. Okay, *capsice.*" I think she thought this meant goodbye.

"*Pontormo,*" I replied and hung up. I still couldn't

believe she was married to a Hank. I said the name to myself, shifting my voice from the diaphragm to the nostrils until it sounded like the allergic reaction of an art gallery owner. Henk. Then I wheeled to my room, gathered my few cards—one from the *Metropole,* another from a local vendor of lighter-alloy wheelchairs—and checked out.

I waited for the cab in the lobby, rolling my chair around the lobby in the convalescent's version of pacing. When my arms tired, I wheeled over to the front door, where an old man shaped like a parenthesis sat in his wheelchair, watching the street for his cab. He cradled an oxygen tank with one hand and had an oxygen mask in the other. A radio sat in his lap.

"But I'm innocent!" came a voice from the radio.

"That's what *you* say," said another voice, deeper than any I had imagined. "You say it every time you call. I got to ask you, friend, isn't phone time somewhat precious in the joint? Shouldn't you be calling your lawyer?"

"I just don't want the listeners to think that I was—"

"And that's your mistake! You're in jail for trying to off the guy who was the most boring talk show host on God's green earth! We're on your side! Stop apologizing! If this audience was your jury, they'd find you guilty and it would be a compliment!" The old man grinned and put the oxygen mask to his face.

"Don't say that, Samurai! Don't!"

"Pete? Keep your back to the wall and and a shiv up your sleeve. I gotta run. Ooookay. *This* is Samurai Stevens, the only reason to listen to AM radio, I mean, the *only* one you got. Spin your dial left and right, what will you find? Brains like a wet match! Music that sounds like it's being broadcast through a rusty soup can! Weather, weather, weather! You want your brain bolted on and pointed where it *ought* to be looking? *Glue* your dial to KTOK or don't even turn the stupid thing *on*, all right? We'll be back."

"Taxi for Jonathan Simpson!" someone called. I turned to the door to see a cabbie standing in the lobby. The old man followed his gaze around the lobby, then shrugged and put the radio closer to his ear. He turned the valve on the cylinder of oxygen, breathed deep, and grinned.

5

A MAN OUGHT TO LIVE HIS LIFE SO HE NEVER FINDS HIMSELF sitting in a wheelchair at the top of the stairs with a professional rival who he has also cuckolded standing right behind him. Or so I decided, looking down the long steep flight.

"I think I'll get out and walk," I said.

"You can walk?" He had already been disappointed to find I was not dead from the hips down. "Why are you in this chair if you can walk?" Indeed, why am I here at all? The whole point of this was to avoid stairs, and now here I was about to be put in the basement like an incontinent dog. But something interesting had compelled me to stay.

His name actually *was* spelled Henk. His mother was Dutch, and the spelling honored her Low Countries heritage. Henk Greusse. It sounded like something that collected in a Belgian fry cooker.

"I can't stand yet," I said. "But here's a page from the cripple's handbook. Watch." I eased myself out of the chair, grabbed on to the banister and began lowering myself down the steps. Heather taught me this trick one afternoon in a stairwell. It had made me wonder right then and there why those who've lost the use of their legs do not learn to walk on their hands to get around.

Henk banged my wheelchair down the steps behind me, grunting more than I did. This was the guy I'd seen Tara maul in public the night we'd met: twig-thin and tall, with mad red hair spiked into tufts and cowlicks, although whether it was from sleeping on it or having it expensively styled, it was difficult to tell. He looked so high-strung that if you ripped off his clothes you'd probably find the body of Reddy Kilowatt. Every new thought sprung alive like a jack-in-the-box. Henk thought a lot of himself and with good reason. He was one of Minneapolis's best-known authors. I hadn't recognized the name when Tara said it because he writes under a pseudonym. Also because my own sense of professional jealousy had strong-armed his presence on earth from my mind. Henk and I had met on a TV panel discussion a year before. He too wrote true crime stories, although much better selling than my own. He came out in hardcover and didn't let anyone forget it. His last book, a five-hundred-page marathon about a small-town honor student who took an ax to his family and ploughed the remains into a bean field, had sold quite well. Not because of the crime—there are plenty of disturbed honor students who disassemble their families each year, although the mulching angle was unique—but because of Henk's writing style. He had a see-Spot-run terseness to his prose that, when combined with sudden outbursts of mawkish pathos, slid down the popular gullet with ease. In the world of daily journalism, he was considered a poet.

The basement was sufficient for a short stay. Like many basements, it was decorated with items that had populated the living room fifteen years before. A mustard-color shag rug covered the floor, and a sofa cunningly designed to look like an old crate sat against the wall. End tables, also from the age of banana-boat chic, flanked the sofa, each with a fake Tiffany lamp bearing the name of a popular soft drink. It was such a perfect diorama of the seventies that I didn't doubt there were Susan B. Anthony dollars and Quaaludes under the sofa cushions.

Tara appeared a few minutes later with drinks and a plate of cookies, some wretched kelp-and-carob things. The juice tasted like the stuff you clean from a mower blade. We talked about how nice it was that I was out of the hospital just in time for a nice Christmas and how nice it would be when I was on my feet again. It was as nice a conversation as three people determined to avoid all the hairy issues romping around the room can be. Then Tara went upstairs and left us alone.

"I realize I'm an imposition," I said. I was trying to roll away from him but was becalmed in the shag. "You're very kind."

"Thank the wife." Henk looked away. "She thinks we'll talk shop. That's why you're here: to inspire me."

"To do what?"

"Write the next book." Henk whipped out an absurdly long cigarette, a mentholated yardstick. He handed one to me. We sat there for a moment, looking as if we were waiting for someone to cry *en garde!* He lit his and tossed me the lighter. "You'll note we've had a drought as far as serial killers go. No sex crimes. No vigorous murderers. Nothing. I frankly appreciate the lull; you don't want to sate the market. But the wife's all big on your story. She intends to pump you dry."

"I'm used to that," I said, instantly, regretting it. Henk went through seven shades of ocher. Play nice, Jonathan. It's his hand on the thermostat. Henk fought his way back to a normal pallor. I wondered when we were going to get around to the fact that I had been wildcatting on his patch for half a year. Maybe he was intending to throw snakes down the stairs and lock the door and leave it at that. Maybe this hadn't been such a great idea.

But a recovered Henk continued. "She sees this as a television thing, naturally. At some point in the story, after her professionalism and objectivity have been firmly established, she'll let it be known that the two of you were old friends." He stubbed out the cigarette and pulled out another. "Which will naturally give a certain tang to the pieces she will continue to do about the case and, of course, your progress. And that will whet interest in the rest of the project."

"The rest?"

"She's doing the TV," he said with breezy nonchalance. "I'm writing the book."

I nodded, gripping the hands of the chair. His presumption was so immense that the effort of keeping my composure made me feel like someone fighting *g*-forces. He was writing a book, eh? Certainly explained my presence here.

"Don't people have to die for a true crime book? I mean, to make it really commercial?"

"Yes."

"I mean, I could see a magazine article, maybe. That's about it. Or I could write a self-help book for coma patients."

"Your target audience would be unconscious."

"Big subliminal tape market."

"That's not what I'm thinking about, Simpson. I'm tired of writing books about awful crimes. I want to examine the effects of small ones. Find the pattern in the lives that are changed by violence. Study the survivors, not the killers. Go legit, in other words."

Nonsense. There wasn't a book in one wounded food reviewer, and he knew it. But apparently he thought I was stupid enough to be flattered. Let him think that for now.

"Fine by me." I grinned at Henk. "Just list me in the acknowledgments." He grinned back. Our relationship was set at that moment. Distrust fortified by iron bars of instinctual dislike.

Hitch came over a few days later to talk when Tara and Henk were at work. He didn't want to talk in the basement, as he found it clammy and claustrophobic, so he insisted on dragging me up the stairs backward while I held tight to the arms of my chair, knuckles white. I kept waiting for him to issue one of his Richter-level twitches and lose his grip, catapulting me down the steps to a broken neck.

"Why they got you in the basement? Doesn't make any sense."

"The guest room is reserved for Henk's sister."

"Is she Jewish?"

We reached the top of the stairs without incident and found ourselves in a small kitchen decorated in a duck motif. I was vaguely appalled to find Tara went in for the country chic, particularly the part that romanticized ill-tempered, incontinent waterfowl. It surely wasn't Henk's idea; he'd have had crows or red-breasted sulkers. Hitch made a pot of coffee, found some mugs (with ducks), and poured himself a cup, which he promptly ruined with some milk and three tablespoons of sugar. One sip and he was twitching like a careless power lineman.

"I told you the basics, right?" he said. "You remember them? You weren't doped up or anything?"

"I was clearheaded enough to know nonsense when

I heard it. You know, Byrne called me that night from jail. Wanted me to know he didn't do it. Did you tell him to do that?"

"Hell, no. Really? He called you? He's a weird guy. So. Anyway. I'm talking to him about this Tim guy."

"The mysterious fictional gentleman with the Mohawk, right?"

"Mysterious no more," Hitch grins. "I got his name: Timothy Obvious. Don't you love it? That's what he signed on the rental agreement. He had the room next to Peter Byrne's in a southeast rooming house. And he was *hardly* fictional. Everyone at the building remembers him. Unfortunately, they only remember his hairstyle. If he'd been living in a building full of mohawks, they'd have remembered his face, but when you got just one mohawk around, that's all you remember."

I took this in. "Okay, so there was a guy who looked like the one Byrne blames for the shooting. Did they know each other? Best friends, bowling buddies, what?"

"Obvious kept to himself for the year he was at the rooming house, but about a month before you get popped, he starts bothering Byrne. Pounding on his wall at night. Following him out the door in the morning to the bus. This is what I get from the other people in the house. They thought Obvious was grade A nuts. Byrne won't say much. He's holding out."

"You get the transcripts of the last week of the radio show?"

"Of course." *Hitch*. "That's why I think he's not telling the whole story. It's Byrne on the radio, but I think it's Obvious doing the sound effects in the background. Of course, when it's time to pop you and Carlton, Obvious makes the call himself." Hitch produced a sheaf of papers, thumbed through it, and pointed to a circled line:

TIM: Aw, I'd rather give you a fun fact. Collect 'em all! So then, did you know that when a man is shot, the impact actually lifts him off his feet?

"Collect 'em all," I said. "The police told me that was written on a photo of Carlton in Byrne's room."

"I got *more.*" He took a videocassette from his backpack and slid it across the table. "Here's a dupe of something I took off the TV a few weeks ago. Give it a look. And there's this." He handed me a sheet of paper. "Byrne's service record. All the papers described him as an ex-Marine, which usually means, y'know, killer wacko. Read that. Drummed out of the corps for idiocy and incompetence. Byrne had such bad aim he couldn't operate a movie projector without showin' the film on the chairs. Now tell me how he hits you and Carlton."

"And the sign. A shot that went wide."

"Maybe. Don't know about that either. That could have been something to get your attention. Like a conductor tappin' the baton. Same difference—too good a shot for Byrne to make."

"Where did they arrest this disaffected, incompetent ex-Marine, a Dallas movie theater? After he shot the cop or before?"

"Only difference between this and the Kennedy frame-up is that you didn't yentz Marilyn Monroe. Plus the Mob didn't do this."

"I thought the CIA killed Kennedy."

Hitch shook his head. "Mob. Although of course maybe this was a Mob hit on Carlton. Who knows. The Outfit's not big in Minnesota. Too cold and virtuous. You see Carlton, ask if he had Mob problems."

"I don't see him. He doesn't call and he doesn't visit. We weren't friends anyway. Getting hit by the same bullet is about all we have in common. I'm rather surprised to find it isn't enough, to tell you the truth."

"Huh." He made a note. "Okay, last piece of news. Byrne is getting out of jail. Someone's bailing him out just in time for Christmas." *Hitch.* "If he calls you, there are some things I want you to ask."

I stiffened. "Who's bailing him out? Why now?"

Hitch. Or perhaps a shrug. Maybe he had economically combined the two. "Don't know. He sure didn't come up with the scratch. His bail's a quarter mill. Here's what I want you to ask him if you ever see him."

"I don't think that will happen."

"Why not? The guy called to apologize, right? He's very sincere. I have no doubt he will find you and want to buy you coffee and talk about this stuff." Hitch gave me another sheet of paper, this one covered margin to margin in a tight neat hand. "There's some BS in there that might not make sense to you. I'm saving you a lot of the hair-up-the-ass theories. Just get his answers down. Call me if you like go to Perkin's or something."

"Of course. Should I find myself sharing a stack of silver dollar pancakes with the man arrested for putting a bullet in my brain, I will most definitely give you a call."

He seemed to take this as a reassurance and drained his cup. He twitched his way into his jacket and left, twitching. He'd driven away before I remembered that I lived downstairs.

Might as well enjoy the above-ground life while I can. There was no one home. I had a mild desire to investigate the bedroom drawers where I would no doubt find an overexposed Polaroid of Henk in lingerie and high heels under a pile of old sweaters, along with dog-eared nudist magazines. Well, let him have his secrets. I wheeled over to the VCR and put in the tape Hitch had given me.

Furry static, rolling picture, credits: "Talk of the Town with P.D. Spaunaugle!" And there he was, rail-thin in a chef's hat, sunglasses a size too small jammed against the blade of his face, staring dispassionately over steepled fingers. "Today, on the finest hour of cable access, one word, and one word only. Let the masses be provoked by: Mohawks." Then the screen showed a street corner—uptown, I could tell, from the brick archway of Calhoun Square in the background. Summertime. A series of people stepped before the camera to give their opinions about Mohawk haircuts.

"Ugly," said one bald, snarling cretin, buckshot with acne. "And not enough! Just not enough!"

"Mohawks?" said a tanned beefy fellow with sunglasses, a regulation-issue moustache; a shirt advertising a Minnetonka marina; and a hard-faced, bronzed, and rather globular blonde on his arm. "Hey, I had one when I was a kid. Everybody did. I'd get one again if it didn't scare away clients!" The camera watched him go, and someone, presumably Spaunaugle, muttered, "Right."

"Ohhhh, Mohawks," said a naked woman. Well, nearly. The smallest of bikini tops, the barest of spandex biking pants. Red hair like a bridal train, the obligatory wayfarer sunglasses. She was accompanied by men with high bristling Mohawks. "Mohawks give me surges." Mutual, I'm sure.

"What?" said Peter Byrne. "I—"

I stopped the tape, backed it up. Yes: Byrne. Saw that mug in the paper. What a loser.

"What?" said Peter Byrne, shocked at the camera's

attention. "Mohawks? I *hate* Mohawks. Mohawks ruin my life, and I don't like it. No sir, don't like them at all."

"Explain, why don't we?" said the off-camera voice. Byrne stared at the pavement.

"Tim," he said in a quiet voice, "Tim, Tim, Tim." And he walked away.

The next woman had a buzz cut. She found Mohawks quite sexy.

At night KTOK ran a promo every fifteen minutes for Josh Carlton's replacement, Samurai Stevens. They had a strident, boastful tone that made Mussolini sound like Bing Crosby. I avoided looking at the radio for fear of seeing the outline of his face, straining to burst free from the grille that covered the speaker.

Josh Carlton now had a two-hour live show from five A.M. to seven. He didn't get many callers; he sounded drunk.

I lay in the dark listening to Josh, fingering the scar on my head. I would have preferred the kind of scar that, when coupled with an eyepatch and a tweed jacket, instills respect in maître d's. Instead I had a small depression that suggested I had gone out hatless into a particularly violent hailstorm. Never mind. I'd drink off this scar for years. Maybe I'd get a little tattoo that said "Ask me about my scar."

Josh hadn't called me. Hadn't said a word.

Whatever lay ahead, it apparently did not include sleep. I was awake all day and all night. My internal clock, like a digital timepiece that has suffered a power interruption, simply blinked the same time over and over again. I lay on Henk's burlap-covered sofa, eyes like the rim of an empty glass, staring at the ceiling. I marked the progress of the sun by the gauzy squares of light that fell through the basement window. When night fell, I watched the headlights of passing cars sweep along the ceiling, hands grabbing for something they couldn't see.

Bankruptcy Talk was followed every night by *Ask the Mortician.*

You can't stay awake forever, of course. Imagine my delight when, one morning a few days before Christmas Eve, I woke up. The sensation was so novel I knew my insomnia had broken. There were other sensations as well: cool tile under my cheek and a chill on my legs. I raised my head to see that I was laying on the floor of the downstairs bathroom. My pants were down around my ankles and the lid to the toilet was up.

I had fallen asleep while relieving myself.

I nearly wept with joy. *I had walked to the bathroom in my sleep.*

"Jonathan?" This was Tara, calling from the top of the stairs. "You up yet?"

"I'm up!" I shouted.

"Listen, we're going downtown to get Mr. Byrne. Be back in a few hours. If Mel shows up, don't worry, she knows you're here. See you when we get back."

"Fine," I hollered, struggling with my pants. "Have a nice drive."

I heard Tara's quick steps on the ceiling and Henk's angry thudding footsteps. A door slammed, then silence.

My eyes opened wide as storm drains.

Going—downtown—to get—Peter Byrne.

Someone's bailing him out just in time for Christmas.

I got my pants on, grabbed the sides of the toilet, and tried to hoist myself up. My muscles trembled like freshly struck tuning forks, but they had enough power to let me swing my knees to the floor. The kneecaps were not entirely pleased with this and sang out a scarlet chord of pain. To hell with them. I grabbed the side of the sink with my left hand, wrapped my right hand around a towel rack, and pulled up.

The towel rack held. The sink crashed to the floor and shattered.

I hung from the towel rack like some monkey indigenous to lavatories and stared at the expanse of porcelain shards that laid before me and the door. A man of hale body could step across it. To me it was as wide as the Atlantic. I grabbed a towel with my free hand and threw it over the broken porcelain. Then I grabbed onto the rack with both hands, prayed, and hoisted myself to my feet.

They held. I willed one leg to move forward. It moved with all the grace of a canned ham falling off a shelf and came down in the middle of the porcelain field.

I saw several colors not yet named by human beings. I let go of the rack and commanded the other leg to swing over the broken field. It evaporated upon landing and I tumbled into the den, banging my head on the thin carpet.

Now what? Get out of here. Before they come back with *him*. Before Mel, whoever the hell she was, oh, yeah, the sister, well, before Sis showed up and held me down in accordance with Henk's wishes. I couldn't call a cab, had no money. The police would laugh— yes, officer, I've recently emerged from a coma and am being held by my ex-girlfriend and her husband in order to further their careers. No, I'd call the competition.

Adrenalin got me up the stairs. I hauled myself up one uncarpeted step after another, pushing with my legs for one step, pulling with my arms for the next. It took me half an hour to get to the top; when I crested the rim of the last stair and flopped onto the floor, I lay there panting, heart knocking on my breastbone like the taxman. Then I rolled over to the phone, pulled it off the hook, and called the *St. Paul Dispatch*.

"City Desk. Bob Brach."

"Hello. This is Jonathan Simpson. I'm—"

"I know who you are."

"I've been held against my will in a basement by a television reporter," I lied. Such gratitude. I could hear the devils stoking the coal for my particular corner of hell. "I'll tell you all about it if you'll send someone to get me."

There was silence. Brach finally spoke.

"Held against your will? By who?"

"Tara Sarnoff. It's a long story."

Pause. Chuckle. "If she held me in a basement, it'd be a long story, too."

"I'm serious. It's too detailed to go into now. She and her husband have just left to pick up the man who shot me and bring him here. And I don't want to know why. I just want to get the hell out of this house." As I gave him the address I heard keys in the door. "Hurry. Someone's coming. Bring photographers. Bring TV. Although not her station. Channel 11. No, 4. See if you can get Dave Moore." He would be excellent with the grim, sorrowful eulogy.

The door upstairs creaked open. I told Brach to move it and pushed the disconnect button on the phone.

There was no way I could wiggle back downstairs nor hang up the phone. It sat by my side and droned the dial tone. I hauled myself up and leaned against a cabinet and tried to look casual.

The door closed. I heard a curse. A few seconds later a figure dressed entirely in black entered the kitchen, face obscured by grocery bags. I saw tight shins, brown skin, a shirt with a hammer and sickle, and the swelling curves of something young and supple.

She set the bags down on the counter, looked at me, and screamed.

"Jonathan Simpson," I said. "How do you do?"

"You scared me," she said.

"Mutual. Can you get me out of this house?" I said. "Now?"

She rolled her eyes and grinned. "Suburbia. I feel *exactly* the same. Especially that basement! Disco cabin fever." She held out a hand to help me up. "I'm Mel," she said, beaming. "Just thrilled when I heard you'd be joining us. Loved your book. Loved your movie. And this coma thing? Sweetheart, that was a *great* touch."

With one strong arm she hauled me to my feet, and this time I stayed there.

I'd never seen a more beautiful face in my life. She was, I should note, completely bald.

6

"HENK IS SUCH A SQUIRTHEAD," SHE SAID, PEERING through the porthole she had scraped in the van's window. The rest of the window was a sheet of ice and snow. We were doing about fifty. "Intellectually, he's a termite. Burrows and gnaws his way through things and can't see anything but the next mouthful of wood, you know? Then the house falls down and he has no idea why."

"I see that, yes . . . Can we slow down? That looks like ice up ahead."

"Of course it's ice. It's winter. How long you been cooped up down there? Has wifey been pouring grass juice down your throat for days, trying to get you to talk? She drives me about eight shades of crazy. Didn't you two used to slam?"

"Slam we did." I said. We were driving in her van, an ancient Ford painted a bright orange that suggested a pumpkin in need of Prozac. I was pasted against in the passenger seat, right where Mel had dumped me. Halfway out to the van my legs had folded like something designed to be packed away in luggage. I had fallen into the snow and nearly impaled myself on a buried lawn sprinkler. She picked me up and shoved me in the van with ease, explaining that most of her friends were drunks, and she was good at this. She picked up my wheelchair with one hand and tossed it in the back.

We hit the ice. Mel took her foot off the gas, tapped the brake, and the back end of the van did a little dance. If the van had been a stripper, it would have men shoving fifties under its windshield wipers. She was grinning wide now.

"You grew up with Henk?" I said, a subject only slightly less unpleasant than her driving.

"He's my brother. Half-bro, really. Same dad. Although I go by Dad's name, Tochter."

"And Mel? Short for Melody?"

"Melodya. The Soviet record label. Mom and Dad were communists."

"Did Henk's mother die or—"

"Divorce." Mel steered the van down the entrance ramp to I-35. "Split over the Brezhnev Doctrine. Probably the first divorce to list 'betrayal of internationalist duty' as grounds for separation." She shouldered her way into the left lane and sped up to seventy. "You want to know where we're going?"

"I want to know why you're bald."

She glanced at me, smiling, and winked. And said nothing.

69

Her scalp shone as though freshly waxed; not a nub or rogue follicle spoiled the effect. Her eyebrows were shaved to two lines the width of a pencil point. She had huge black eyes, pools that swallowed the light of the highway lamps and gave back a deep black glow. Round cheekbones sloped down to a full mouth that would have been best served by a pout. Mel had a face constructed for brooding. But she smiled as though she had no idea what her face wanted her to do.

With a full head of hair, Melodya would make a man pause, groan, and feel a ripe, long peel of regret. Stark bald, she looked she came from the libido of someone far more interesting than myself. Someone with dueling scars and a reputation on three continents. Well, I had the scar. It was a start.

Mel steered the van off the highway onto Thirty-first Street. She took a left, meaning we were bound for Uptown, the entertainment district that laid along Minneapolis's chain of lakes. This was the playground of the young and vacuous in town, full of women who checked the Olympic calendar to see if primping was listed as an exhibition sport yet, full of weightless men in conspicuously labeled clothing. It was a mindless place, hip and brittle. I knew it well, having hung out there since I'd come to town.

"You know the Boomerang?" Mel said. I nodded. Uptown also had a high population of disaffected young people with pierced body parts. The Boomerang was their bar. I'd always been scared to go in after dark.

"Only safe place in Uptown for a skin like you," Mel said. "That's where we're going. It's a fund-raiser for the Anti-Fascist Skinhead Activist League. Have you had a drink since you left the hospital? I'm buying."

"I'm not really a skinhead," I said. "I'm shaved for medicinal reasons."

"Everybody has a reason," she said. "Except me. I just can't grow hair anymore."

"It's not—you're not—you don't have—"

"Do I look like I'm having chemotherapy? With this body? I can crack walnuts with my glutes, buddy. No, I'm just bald. That's all. Can't a woman be bald?"

"She certainly can. I was just wondering, that's all. Shaving your head is supposed to have a political meaning, though. Right?"

"Like *what?*"

"Like you don't head up the local Brownie troop. You don't own any records advertised on late-night television. If you vote, it's not Republican."

Mel grinned. "If you only knew."

She gunned the van through a yellow light, swung into an alley, and parked behind the Boomerang. I got out of the van and promptly tumbled into the snow. Mel sighed and hauled out the wheelchair. I climbed into it under my own power and wheeled toward the door. She strode ahead, opened the back door of the Boomerang, and waved me in with a flourish.

I wheeled into the hallway and was immediately plastered against my chair by the sound of either a band or a power saw in primal scream therapy. My ears felt as though hat pins had been inserted into them. I looked up at Mel, eyes pleading, but she beamed and pointed down the hallway. A man with the girth of a gas pump looked down at me, his hand outstretched for money. Then he saw Mel, nodded, took out a rubber stamp, and hand-canceled my head. Mel cocked her head to receive the stamp, then blew the man a kiss. She grabbed the handles of my wheelchair and pushed me into the maelstrom.

Three bald men stood on the stage, thrashing at their instruments, each one naked to the waist. One was howling into the microphone, veins the thickness of ballpoint pens standing on his forehead, a fine

spray of spittle misting the air around the microphone. I caught a few of the lyrics:

"CHRSTMSDTH!"
"WEDONGRBBBNEXXXXIFICKILIC!"
"BROKNDRMSARGROGGILIDIC!"

The crowd was singing along. And dancing, if that
word fits. The room was seething with bodies, thin,
greasy sticks with flailing arms and angry mouths. It
was like watching discarded chicken bones come to
life. Just as Mel grabbed the handles of the wheelchair
and started to push me away from the edge of the
dance floor, I saw a young man, stripped to show a
torso smothered in tattoos, climb up on the stage and
launch himself into the crowd. Everyone immediately
moved away and the man smashed head first into the
floor. The bartender swore, grabbed a mop, and
headed toward the dance floor.

"Great dance," Mel shouted into my ear. "Really
easy steps."

"That's slam dancing," I yelled. "Ancient history.
Decades old."

"I know. It's nostalgia night."

She tried pushing me through the crowd but got
nowhere. From my level I saw knees and beer bottles
held at waist level. Many belts studded with spikes.
This could be injurious. Mel tried to wheel me
through the crowd, but it had the consistency of fresh
cement.

"Invalid skin!" she shouted. "Have some respect!"

No one moved. Everyone in the aisle was joined
together like a long polymer composed of alcohol and
failure, each molecule staring transfixed at the band,
which had now moved into a new number identical in
chords and tempo but with a whole new set of
unintelligible lyrics. Mel gave up trying to shove me
through the crowd. Instead she hoisted me up with

one arm, grabbed the chair with the other, and muscled her way through the crowd.

I'd seen women like Mel at the gym where I used to work out. Sleek, with all the right bulges plus several additional ones. I found them the most fiercely erotic things I had ever seen. It was a good thing that Mel did not grab me around the hips, or I'd have had no secrets from her at all.

"You got to get walking again soon," she yelled into my ear. "People see me hauling you around, they'll start talking."

Our destination was a corner booth at the far end of the bar, well away from the loudspeakers and the dance floor. There were three skinheads seated at the table, each dressed in black leather jackets. At least three dozen cans of cola sat crumpled on the table as well as an ashtray heaped with butts.

Each of the skins beamed at Mel, then looked me up and down. I was still hanging in her embrace, like a stuffed animal she'd won at the fair.

"Who's the scarecrow?" said one of the skins.

Mel dropped the wheelchair and set me down in the booth. "Guys, this is Jonathan Simpson. The Coma Kid, if you recall the newspaper stories. Johnny, clockwise we got: Ludwig, Stig, Philip."

"Not *the* Jonathan Simpson," the skinhead named Ludwig hollered. I nodded. He beamed and held out his hand. *"Pleased* to meet you!"

"Absofookinlutely!" said Stig. "Fan of yers f' years!"

I looked around the table, saw smiling faces. "You guys are all kidding me, right? Skinheads don't read food columns."

"'Oo said we was skinheads then?" said Stig. He had a huge tattoo of a spider on his scalp, stretching all the way from Lust to Geniality.

73

There was the sound of a boar being impaled on a microphone in the next room and then silence. "We're going to take a break whether you fuckinlikeitornot," the vocalist shouted. I turned to see the crowd loose a barrage of beer bottles at the stage, presumably in appreciation. It was less work than applauding.

"Seriously," I said to the assembled skins, "you guys are not what demographic studies show to be my typical audience."

"Nor are you the typical food critic," said Philip. "You're so patently unqualified for the job it's obviously all a critique of food critiques, right? Hilarious idea. Aggression neatly deflected. None of us read you until we saw you on Spaunaugle's show. You were superb."

"Most people punch 'im in the first fookin' ten minutes," said Stig. "You lasted arf an' hour."

"Such control," said Ludwig. "So pray tell: Who shot you?"

"Guy named Peter Byrne," I said, still a little unsure of my surroundings. And my company. Most of all I was unsure which one of the guys at the table was sleeping with Mel. That was the issue of greatest curiosity. "Although Mel's brother thinks it was someone else."

"Well, *that* figures," said Ludwig. "Some people doubt Pontious Pilate was the one who condemned Christ to hang."

"He was crucified, Lud," said Mel.

"Same thing, gorgeous. Gravity was what killed you in crucifixion. The weight of the body made it impossible to breath."

"I think this is all rather insensitive," said Philip. He was staring into his can of soda, brow furrowed. "The gentleman has survived a rather nasty incident." He looked at me with the grave face of a sophomore who has just decided to major in poetry, and damn the world. "How have you fared? When we heard of your injury, we thought, well, I don't know how to say this—can you, ah, will—"

"I'll be up and jumping head first onto concrete dance floors in no time," I said.

"Ah imagine there was severe emotional dislocation oopon awakenin'," said Stig.

I flicked a look at Mel. She looked bored. Strike Stig.

"Mostly I'm irritated," I said. "It's not like I woke up and discovered Nixon was president again or something."

"Who does Mr. Henk think shot you?" said Philip. He was hunched back in the corner of the booth now, pulling on a Pall Mall.

"Some guy with a Mohawk."

"Ahh, but of course," said Ludwig. *"Cherchez le* Mohawk."

Philip stared at me as though I were a TV program he might be convinced to watch. "And what do you think of that theory?" said Philip.

"More importantly, what do you think of the police?" This was Lud. I was about to tell him about Bishop and his suspicions, but he pointed at the window. "Because here they are. Everyone all paid up on their public urination citations?"

I looked out the window to see a police car, lights revolving, parked outside the Boomerang. A second later, a nondescript white Ford pulled up, and a man I recognized got out. Bob Brach. *St. Paul Dispatch.* Oh, sweet Jesus. I saw it all and liked none of it.

"Mel," I hissed. "Get me out of here."

"You aren't that light," she said. "Let me rest up for a minute, okay?"

Tara's car appeared outside. Henk got out the driver's side. There was a man in the passenger seat: Peter Byrne.

There was the sound of a household pet being hooked up to a car battery—feedback from the band announcing the next set. I had to lean over to Mel and shout in her ear. She smelled of rosewater.

"Listen! It's Tara and Henk! And the guy who shot me! They're outside!"

She turned around in panic and saw Henk standing next to the policeman. I understood in a second. Bob Brach had showed up at Tara and Henk's house looking for me, found Tara and Henk with Tim Byrne, fresh out of prison. And no sign of me, the guy who'd placed the panicked call. All of his alarms went off. Henk must have been frothing about his skinhead sis, and that sent Brach peeling off to the only skinhead bar in town. That explained Brach.

What the police were doing here was, at this point, open to speculation.

The sight of Henk was enough for Melodya. She looked around for exits and escape routes and saw only the same surging mass of people who had greeted us when we entered. I looked around the table: three blankfaced skinheads with no ideas.

"You guys are pitiful," said Mel. Ah: She wasn't sleeping with any of them. Melodya picked up my wheelchair from its place against the wall and kicked it smartly on the side, collapsing it. I hadn't even known it would do that. She shoved her way through the crowd to the bar, shouted something at the bartender, and slid the wheelchair through an opening in the bar. Then she came back to the booth and picked me up again.

"You're not always going to get this kind of treatment," she said into my ear. We plowed through the crowd to the dance floor. People were packed tightly enough for skin grafting here. She deposited me in the middle of the crowd and told me to wait. I started to shout that I couldn't stand for long but soon found that I could. The crowd, bobbing up and down like a convocation of jackhammers, kept me aloft, and my feet only touched the floor every few minutes. I found myself making a slow traverse of the room, like a piece of paper being threaded through a complex series of rollers. I caught glimpses of the lone policeman talking to the skins at Mel's table; I saw Henk angrily interrogating her, with Tara standing off to the side. Then I lost sight of everyone.

The crowd eventually deposited me at the front of the dance floor. The support of the bodies evaporated and I was left to my own feet. They held me for about half a minute, then folded up beneath me. I crashed to the floor, my head banging on the concrete and making the sound of a coconut falling from great height. I looked up to see the bartender standing over me with a mop. Then Mel was at his side, shooing him away.

"Come on, let's go" she shouted. "I got rid of them."

Melodya pulled me up and put her long strong arm around my waist. We went down the hallway we'd entered, the bouncer wishing us a Merry Christmas. Out the door, into the cold sharp air. Mel opened the back doors of the van and slid me in like a sheet of plywood. I saw Ludwig, Philip, and Stig leaning over me, looking down with expressions of concern.

"So who are you?" I cried. Mel put the van in gear and lurched out of the lot. "I've read about skinheads. You're Nazis, fascists, right? Or anarchists? Bomb-throwing radicals? One or the other?"

Philip drew deep on his cigarette. "You can't trust what you read."

"Those are exactly th' attitudes wit' which we struggle," said Stig.

"He thinks we're Nazis!" Melodya laughed. "So which of you is Albert Speer, guys?"

77

"Dear boy," Ludwig said, shaking his head. "We're all graduates of the Institute of Technology of the University of Minnesota, nothing more."

"But you're skinheads."

Ludwig sighed. "How perceptive. Philip? Break the news, will you?"

Philip cracked a smile. "Don't worry, Jonathan. You're in no danger. We're architects."

7

SHE DROPPED STIG OFF SOMEWHERE IN NORTHEAST, AND I never saw him again—something for which he no doubt gives thanks daily, considering what followed. Then Mel drove to the warehouse district and parked next to an immense and ancient building that said RUMLEY CO. on the side. Ludwig pushed me up to the front door while Mel sprinted ahead, ran a card through a security lock, and held open the door. The elevator that took us upstairs moved so slow you could imagine it tied to a horse on the roof, straining at the collar as it tried to haul us up. Whole minutes would pass between floors, so that when the bell chimed to announce you were passing a floor, it came as a complete surprise.

"I don't think I've ever seen an elevator this size," I said. "You could park a car in here."

"Everyone says that," Philip remarked. "And it's true. They used to make cars in this building."

"Cars? This building is ten stories tall. Most assembly lines don't have aircraft warning lights."

"It's the truth," he said, looking around the elevator cab with a look of wonder more appropriate for the Sistine Chapel. "This entire building was an assembly line. Rumley Touring Company. Vertical assembly line, new idea at the time. They'd haul the chassis to the top floor, drop it down, add parts, drop it down again." He pointed to the floor. "See the ruts in the floor? Those lines mark off the wheelbase of the Model D. When we rented the space there was this elevator operator who'd been working here since the twenties. Ancient fellow; he creaked more going up than the elevator did. He said that he never got used to having a car in the elevator. Like walking into a closet and finding a cow, he said."

"He still around?" I asked.

"He died on the job. When they renovated the building for the fiftieth time and had the grand opening, they ran a car up and down the elevators to recall the glorious past. Halfway up, the car slipped out of park." He pointed to a crease in the chrome frame surrounding the doors. "Got him from behind. Never knew what hit him."

"I think he had his suspicions," said Melodya.

"That's awful," I said.

"Rental price went down," said Lud.

The elevator shuddered and stopped; the doors parted slowly, like a curtain opening on a bleak, joyless theater piece. We got out and headed down a hallway paved with linoleum the color and pattern of which was seemingly inspired by the respiratory flu, and ended at a door that read Rumley & Sons.

"None of us are Rumley," Philip said.

"We are all sons," Ludwig added.

"It's sort of faux traditionalism," said Philip. "People see the old Rumley sign on the water tank on the roof and figure we've been here as long as the building." He slid a card through a magnetic reader slot and the door clicked open.

Light filled the room as soon as we entered. I saw a desk the size of Monaco sitting in one corner of the room. In another, a set of leather chairs clustered around a white marble table like beasts at a salt lick. Two windows the size of garage doors displayed a panorama of downtown Minneapolis. The skyscrapers glowed in the night sky, like torches stuck in the ground to warn off bad spirits. In the center of the city stood a thin, silvery building that must have towered a hundred stories.

It hadn't been there three months ago.

"Did I miss something?" I said. "That building wasn't there when I went to sleep."

"That's because you've really been asleep for a hundred years," said Lud. "We've been meaning to bring it up."

"Oh, stop it," said Philip. "I forgot to turn the wall off, that's all. Hold on."

He went next door. I watched a small plane fly across the city, disappearing for a second behind the tall, thin building. There was a distant *click!* and the sky outside lit up. In an instant the night outside changed to day, the silhouettes of the buildings replaced by stone and glass. Sunlight flooded the room.

"Shit." *Click.*

The city went dark again, and soft light flowed from the corners of the room. The tall building was gone.

"Those are TV sets," I said.

"Very good," said Ludwig, smiling. "It's what we use to show clients what their building would look like once it's built. Here's the Mack Tower at sunset. *Phil! Pipe the controls in here.*" He pushed a button on the panel. The window flickered, and the dark sky grew warm with light. The silver column reappeared on the edge of downtown, a smear of fire on its western edge. Ludwig looked at the image with love, running his hand over his smooth head. "Of course, the clients still don't have the financing, let alone tenants, market being what it is."

"You guys designed that?"

"You mean actually draw the buildings fr scratch?" asked Ludwig with mock horror. "No manual labor for us. Too much math."

"We design the computer mock-ups," said Philip from the doorway. "Stig and I wrote a program in college for high-quality graphic reproduction and sold it for many, many millions. That's what finances this place. See, we photograph a model of the building, futz with the picture to add shadows and detail, then we stick it into your basic downtown Minneapolis shot. That gets put up on the video wall. Then whoever's making the building rents this office and trots the prospective tenants through to show them what a landmark they'll be in. Mel here is the charming receptionist who runs the wall."

Melodya curtsied.

"The receptionist from the twenty-third century," I said.

"I have a fine selection of wigs," she said. "One to match each building."

"Red wigs with a brick building really seem to move the merchandise," said Lud.

"You *all* wear wigs?"

"No," said Philip. "We arrive bald. People trust bald artists. They think of us as monks who get laid. Makes them feel hip to be around us."

I chewed on that for a minute. No one spoke. They looked at me as though expecting me to ask another stupid question. I wouldn't. I had given up trying to figure them out, and I told them so.

"You're bald for no apparent reason. You're not skinheads because you enjoy being mistaken for cretinous Hitler-heiling punks, and you're not bald because you think that's how an artist ought to look. There's something about you guys I don't get."

"We're dorks," said Philip. "That what you mean?"

"Well, now we've no secrets at all," Ludwig sighed.

The two men traded nervous looks. One by one they flicked a glance to Melodya. She looked away and shrugged.

"It's like this," said Philip. "She—"

"No," said Lud. "Let me. Shave your head and wear black, and you're instantaneously cool. Doesn't matter a whit if you're a, shall we say, dweeb. All of a sudden we were either feared, admired, or accepted without question."

"Or mistaken for Olympic swimmers," said Philip. "Swimmers undergoing chemotherapy."

"Or lunatics," Mel grunted. "There you have it, Jonathan. These are the *most* unhip guys I have ever met—and they are the toast of the video arts world."

"You grow hair, you lose credibility," said Philip. The others nodded.

"Except me," said Mel. "I don't have to shave my head. Ever heard of alopecia? No? A skin condition. Characterized by hairlessness. I lost it all in high school. I'd have dreams where I was eating my way through a wheat field and wake up with my mouth full of hair. Wasn't until college that I stopped wearing wigs. I had no idea I'd be setting an example for these fellows."

Philip laughed. "We all met Mel in our senior year. One by one we shaved our heads to impress her."

"And they were still wearing their geeky clothes— short-sleeve dress shirts, polyester pants. Looked like Yul Brynner's accountants."

"Gentlemen?" said Lud. "It's ten. News is on. Maybe they shot something outside the Boomerang." He walked over to the desk, pushed some buttons on the keypad, and downtown Minneapolis blinked, then vanished. The wall filled up with the logo of KJGO and the number 3, flying over an aerial shot of the city like a bird returning to the nest to feed a hungry brace of fractions. Then a shot of Bobby Parker, Minneapolis's most beloved anchorperson, raven haired and as putty brained as Tara. She stared grimly into the camera, her expression suggesting that stagehands were underneath the set, tightening vises attached to her ankles. The news was the usual gruel of stupid people killing innocent people and cheery last-minute holiday shopper stories. Nothing on me. Thank God.

By midnight, the skins had wearied and yawned their way out. Philip stayed behind for a few minutes to toy with the bank of computers in the room off the main office, then left with a mild and not unfriendly good-night. Lud said I could sleep in the spare room—a tiny cubicle off the reception room, next to a small kitchen. He bowed and left. Mel stayed behind for a minute to share a cigarette before she left.

"They're good guys," she said. "They need a guiding hand to keep them from diving into their computers and paddling around for the rest of their lives, but they're okay. Impressionable boys, though."

"What are you, the den mother of skinheads?"

Mel laughed. She took the cigarette from my mouth, took a drag, and fitted it back between my lips. She sighed.

"They're all in love with me."

Silence.

"Really?"

"Something I said a long time ago. I refused to sleep with anyone who had more hair than I did, I said. A joke. Ever since, none of them has grown their hair out. Each thinks that another of them is sleeping with me. No one wants to admit they're not."

"Ah."

Mel smiled, shook her head. "Flattering. And scary." She laughed, her eyes wide and dark. "My *favorite* combination."

8

I SPENT THE AFTERNOON OF CHRISTMAS EVE UNDIS-
turbed. No one came, no one called. At first this was
fine with me, I'd had too damn many people barging
through my day lately. Although I'd liked to have seen
Mel again, if only to give her the big, wet eyes and
have her pick me up and cart me around again. A man
could get used to that, particularly one with no pride.

I had breakfast with the newspaper. My disappearance was on page 1 of the metro section, but that
doesn't say a great deal. Pie-baking contests get on
page 1 metro in this town, particularly if there's a
color photo. The article wasn't much—blatherings
from Henk, stern words about the Skinhead Menace,
with a recap of recent racist skinhead mischief. No
quotes from skins inside the bar. Either Bob Brach
was on a tight deadline or, more likely, waddled back
to the office and wrote the thing from clips. I had
picked up the phone and dialed his number before I
remembered I'd told him that I was being held against
my will by Henk and Tara. I hung up the phone.

That hadn't been in the story. Brach had probably
spoken to Henk. Probably good friends. Probably
both in the same serial-killer rotisserie league. Well,
there was one bridge dynamited down to the pilings.

I suddenly felt a vast and vacant gust of self-pity.
No Christmas at the mansion this year, not with
Byrne and Mr. Mohawk running around out there. No
Christmas at *home*. No presents. None of Grunewald's frighteningly large Three Wise Men ginger-
bread cookies, splay legged and spread armed, looking
like a cross between Merlin and an inflatable sex doll.

Christmas alone, the first one. Finally reduced to spending it sitting drunk in front of the TV bawling at *It's a Wonderful Life* as I had always feared. Maybe the film would turn out differently this time. I'd never seen them count up the money that everyone donated. Maybe this year they'd be a few bucks short.

Through most of the afternoon I sat at a window watching snow fall on Minneapolis, quiet and clean. I had a little to drink, pacing myself, working up to a good evening of blurry weeping. By nine I was in that all-things-are-possible mood you get when the bottle content is equal with the name on the label, and I got the glorious idea that I should go up on the roof and survey the slumbering world, bless it with my fierce and solitary presence. I wheeled down to the elevator, waited while it dragged itself up the shaft. When the doors creaked open, I pushed myself in and looked for the button that said Roof. There was, of course, no such button, but it took me a minute to come to this conclusion. The elevator, deciding it had come all this way for nothing, jerked and began its interminable drop to the ground floor. At least I'd brought my bottle.

A few minutes later the door opened; the building's security guard looked at me with no great love and asked if I needed help.

"Just out for a spin," I said, and I pushed the tenth-floor button. The door closed and the car started up again.

It did not make it all the way. When the doors opened, the floor was about seven inches above the floor of the cab, as though the building were now standing on tiptoes. There was no way I could get my wheelchair up that ledge. I was infuriated. Without thinking I stood up and stepped out of the elevator, then turned to haul my chair—

Well, here I was, standing again, completely by accident. Not doing too bad a job of it either. Swaying a little—chalk that up to drink—but definitely stronger. I still felt like an elephant using drinking straws for stilts, though. Better sit down before I get a faceful of linoleum.

I leaned against the wall and put a hand in the elevator—just as the doors closed. The elevator went down, cables screeching and complaining. Jesus. This was like playing tag with a glacier. I pushed the button and waited.

It took five minutes to return. When the doors opened, the cab was flush with the floor. My chair was still there.

With Josh Carlton in its seat.

"Merry Christmas," he said. He gave me a thin and bitter grin. "Santa Claus is here. And he's thirsty."

He stood up, swayed, and patted the gun tucked in his belt.

"Screw 'em all," he said. "Let's get cheerful."

"Is it still snowing?" Josh asked, staring uncertainly at the video wall.

"It's not snowing at all," I replied. I sat in *my* wheelchair. The monitors were playing a tape I'd found, with snow blowing around the beautiful fictional buildings.

"I didn't think so." He peered at the window. "Oh, I get it. It's a TV thing. Can you get a ball game on it? Probably not. Christmas an' all. Old Big Hat from Rome should be getting on any minute now and bless our sinning asses, eh?" He looked at me with bright eyes. "So let's get some sinning in. What do you have to drink here, anyway?"

"Clan Anderson," I said. "I'll pour you a glass if you get rid of that pistol."

"What? Oh. This old thing." He dug in his pants and tossed the gun on the leather sofa. It skidded off the hard cushions, bounced to the floor, and discharged: a loud crack followed by another crack and a hiss and spit of something electric. I ducked, or as much as you can duck in a wheelchair; Carlton stood stock still.

Smoke poured from one of the TV monitors. The rest were snowing away. It looked like someone had punched a hole in that fabric of space science-fiction writers were always talking about, revealing the wires and tubes that powered the universe.

"Jesus!" I shouted.

"Was born on this day," Josh mused.

"What the hell are you doing? Why in Christ's name do guns go off every goddamn time I get near you? Pick up your gun and get out! No, leave it there. Back out of here. Slowly."

"Oh, please." He looked down at the gun. "Be sensible. Think of it from my point. I've been walking around all night with it tucked in my pants with the safety off."

"What are you doing with a gun anyway?"

He smiled. "Someone tried to shoot me a few months ago. You hear about it? In all the papers. Only got me in the arm. Lucky. Made me cautious, though. And what have you been up to?"

"I've been wheeling around in this stupid chair because my brain played catcher's mitt for that very slug, my friend. Which you well know. And might I add I appreciate the cards and the calls at the hospital. How bright were the days. How fleetly they passed."

"Yeah, well, sorry." And he looked instantly contrite. His emotions were coming and going far too quickly for my liking. At this rate, Raving Purple Fury and its faithful sidekick Murderous Pistolwhipping

Rage might show at any moment. "I felt bad since I felt somewhat responsible, sort of. I mean, you can't really blame me, can you?"

That's what he wanted. See me put on the Big Hat and absolve him. Well, it was Christmas.

"No. I don't blame you."

"Fabulous. Just what I wanted to hear. I felt so sick about it all—I mean, I didn't leave the house for a couple weeks, thought someone would try again. Didn't budge."

"I thought they picked up Peter Byrne in a day or two."

"Oh. Right. But that's not, ahh, what I mean. It's the psychological thing." He tapped his head. "You know what I mean?"

I tapped my scar. Nodded.

"I was just all confused. And of course those bastards used that as an excuse to drop me from drive time, even thought they'd been lining up the Samurai behind my back! Behind my back! For months they were planning it!" Here it came, all hot and purple. "Stupid, fucking, lying, motherlicking bastard, swine fucking cowards. Not even the bastard-loving grace to tell me to my face! They left a message on my machine! And I didn't even *own* one! When I didn't answer my phone, they sent someone over with an answering machine, had *him* plug it in, and then they called and *fired me on the tape!*" The whole works: flying spittle, veins on forehead, wide eyes with pinpoint pupils. It was an excellent performance, and I didn't know whether to flee or look for a pail of sand to throw on him.

But—click!—he went instantly calm. "Ahh, thing is, I like the night shift. That's the other reason I didn't visit. I sleep all day now. Haven't seen the sun for two months. I think it was the sun that was making me unhappy. Life's easier when you don't have to squint. You see things more clearly." Josh slapped his hands together and grinned. "Best of all, everyone gets bad ratings at night. You can't take it personally."

The TV shot and his spleen vented, Carlton grew somewhat more normal. He poured himself a tumbler of dessert wine, pronounced it excellent, and let out a great sigh.

"Caaaris'mas. For the first time in my adult life I am not sitting in a small room pretending anyone is paying attention to me."

"You've always worked Christmas?" I sipped at some coffee. "That's awful."

"Oh, yeah. See, the new guy at a station always does holidays, and I usually spent Christmas sitting in front of the turntables, playing holy goop, you know, come in your hat all ye faithful, or putting on jangly ho-ho-ho tunes about sledding and mistletoe and the fat-ass joker with the beard. You don't know how hazardous it was. You just don't find a Christmas song that clocks in over four minutes, and if your bladder or bowels get any ideas, you got to be brisk about it."

He drained his glass, held it out for more. I obliged. If he kept talking and drinking, he would soon pass out.

"Why aren't you working tonight?"

"Best of the Samurai," he said. "Encore presentation. Don't you just love that phrase? Like there's a big, beaming audience on their feet clapping for the whole show to happen again in every detail. And there probably is. *Not that I know.*" He pounded his knees with his fists. *"I can't stand to listen to him!"* he screamed, and I jumped in my chair. He looked at me with wild, raving eyes. An encore presentation of crazy Josh.

"Sorry," he said after a minute. "Professional jealousy! Hah! Anyway. You know I went into radio to impress a woman?" Josh looked at his wine, smiled.

"We were both attending the University of Minnesota. She was a nasty chick, but she had a body that was just a nail gun to the nuts, if you know what I mean. She had a show on the campus radio station. *Songs the Government Doesn't Want You to Hear.* Like the government gives a tin shit what Billy Bragg is saying. But Jesus, did I want to impress her. Those days, anything that ovulated, I wanted to impress. So I joined the campus station. Found out I liked radio. Quit school. The rest is history. Anything you're unclear on yet?"

"Not really."

"My first job was in Grand Forks, North Dakota. Hardcore country, all hollering Okies and weepy Nashville shit. Then a stint in Bozeman, Montana. Fired. Then off to Portland. Fired. Actually did some time in Chicago, but well, you know: fired. Did five years getting fired in your greater Iowan metropolitan areas, then over to New York—I'll admit, I'll admit, the state, not the city. Fired. But by the grace of God I got this shot at KTOK. And it's been good. I don't care what they don't let me do. It's the longest I've ever had a job. And god*damn!*" He grinned and picked up the bottle. "Don't you know I'm going to get fired again and sent back to Iowa." He raised the bottle in a toast. "I don't know who to kill, them, me, or Mar-fucking-coni."

"How did you know I was here?"

"Everybody knows you're here." He gave me a grim and resolute look. "I'd get a gun if I were you. Want mine?"

I declined. He shrugged and picked it up off the floor, where it had been throughout his oral résumé, and put it back in his pants. He drank half his glass of wine and said he had to be off. He stood, wavered slightly, then fell over with the graceful arc of a wrecking ball, cracking his head on the marble table. *Thonk.*

"No problem!" he said, staggering to his feet. "None at all, old boy! You old partner in head wounds, you!" He rubbed his skull and tottered toward the door. "Anyway, you just get the story right when you write about me. Or wrong, I don't care. As long as you spell my name right, as they say. Although I never figured that out. I mean, if they say you're a child molester, spelling the name right wouldn't help you out at all. Bad career move, that." His eyes were half shut now, and when the door opened, he barely gave it a glance.

Melodya walked into the room. Arms full of presents. Her eyes went wide when she saw Josh, and she set down her packages by the door.

"Hello?" she said.

Josh went slack at the sight of her, as though presented with something he would never find in Iowa. Then he hung his head, walked into the door frame, bounced out of the room, and closed the door behind him.

"Friend of yours?" Mel said, staring at the door.

"That was Josh Carlton." I shuddered. "He just sort of showed up. I used to be mad at him for not visiting me in the hospital, but I think I'm glad. We just had a very curious conversation."

"Eeuh," she said. "Well, off to hell with him. I brought you Christmas, and we're going to have Christmas if it—hey, hey, hey, what's this?" She had just discovered the busted tube on the video wall.

"It started hailing," I said. "Cracked the glass." Melodya glared at me. "Josh shot it out."

"Oh. Well. And here I thought it was a malfunction. You want some coffee? I do." And she walked off to the kitchen. As she passed, she kissed her fingers and patted my head. I looked at my watch: In a minute it would be Christmas.

Two hours into Christmas, I was utterly happy, completely drunk once more, staring enraptured at the video snow. Mel and I had knocked back two pots of coffee and banished the liquor from my bloodstream, which she then set about polluting anew with scotch. I foresaw a Christmas Day of heaving guts and a howling brainpan, but ahhh, it was worth it. She was worth it.

First we opened presents. She gave me a copy of *The Fountainhead,* which I greeted with as much enthusiasm as I could muster, having read it once and found it about as interesting as John Stuart Mill's theory of Utilitarianism as performed by members of the Dick, Jane, and Spot primers. Mel explained that I was not to read it but was to get strong enough to rip it in half. "Like ripping a phone book," she said. "But given that it's a bad book, it's much more intellectually satisfying. This is my way of telling you I am in charge of your physical therapy from now on. Don't worry, we'll start gradual. Five sets of tearing chapters in *The Virtues of Selfishness.* But when we're done I'll have you bench pressing *Atlas Shrugged.* Now open this one." It was a set of leg weights. She strapped this to my legs, kneeling like Mary Magdalene, albeit a bald one, then handed me another box. Wrist weights. These went on as well.

"Now stand," she commanded.

I said I'd stood earlier and appeared to have gotten it out of my system, and I didn't feel like—

"Stand."

I stood. The usual madly fibrillating muscles, but they held.

"Walk."

One step. Two. Three. Four. Then gravity's yank. I sunk to the ground, pinned by the weights on my limbs, unable to move.

"And don't think I'm going to pick you up, because I'm not; you got to do it yourself. Okay, let's see what you got for me."

She pulled over two boxes she'd brought in; which of course I'd never seen before. I was curious to see what she thought I'd give her. The first box held a copy of my book *Dead Bread,* well thumbed, too. "Oh! It's just what I wanted. And you *will* autograph it, won't you?" I nodded from the floor. "Good. Now, what's this. Hmmm. A box from Cynthia's Closet. Methinks a floor-length flannel gown, mayhap."

"Were you by chance ever in one of those Renaissance festivals?"

"Ahh, yeah. Couple of summers. Does it still show? I was a dancing wench for the king. I see what you mean, though. I'll keep the mayhaps to a minimum. Ah! Perforce, what be this?" And she held up a garment that couldn't have weighed more than half a gram, less a negligee than an ambitious cat's cradle. "You know, I was just saying today how I needed something new for the office. Let me go put it on." And I watched her dance off to the studio. Within the minute she'd put on some music and piped it into the office speakers: something fierce and precise and ass-grabbingly randy, a well-bothered clavichord. I wanted to get up, make something of myself, but I was tired and half drunk and pinioned by the weights, too helpless to get up. Not that I needed to try, really: If she actually came back wearing that thing, I would rise like a Minuteman.

She came back wearing it, all right, and I swear I heard the sound of my brain liquefying and streaming out my ears. It consisted of a simple cinch an inch wide across the most spectacular breasts I had ever seen, firm high planets kissed brown by some lucky sun. Another strip of fabric swept down between her legs, broadening to an inch and quarter for modesty's sake. She spun around *en point.* Theoretically, it was clothing. But if she'd worn it in Rio during Carnivale, someone would have thrown a blanket over her lest she corrupt the public morals. It being in Minnesota in the winter I merely lay there and hyperventilated.

Melodya laughed and sprang over to where I was laying. "It's perfect," she said, straddling me and grabbing my hands. "Let's dance." And she hauled me up, flopped my arms over her shoulder, and began dragging me around. Trust me: never in my life have I wanted to burrow lap first into a woman than I did then, but I might as well have been a scarecrow for all I could do. The most I could manage was to twitch my hands, unable to lift my wrists. My legs were pails of concrete, dangling in the air: She had lifted me a few inches off the floor to make the dance easier.

That was our first dance. I think I would have fallen for her completely then, instead of later, if only— If only there hadn't been something detached about her dance—perfunctory, rote. It smote your retinas to smoking ruins to watch it, I imagine, given that incredible body, and being bounced by that taut and curvy physique made your very marrow dissolve to constituent elements. Or would have if— If it hadn't felt so damned innocent.

Which is what it was. From the shine on her face, you'd think I'd bought her a pinafore for her First Communion. She was having too much fun, that was it. Melodya was, I realized, one of those women who have the sexual impact of a firehose, know it, and find it convenient to overlook that all the men around are flat on their backs, dripping wet. It made life simpler. I understood that. It didn't go with wearing *that* and doing *this,* but Jesus! I think too much. Enjoy, Jonathan, enjoy.

The song ended as these thumping dance songs always end: by gradually becoming another song, barely distinguishable from the last. Melodya set me down on the sofa, and I slid to the floor with what I hoped was grace and refinement.

"Could you take these weights off?" I said. "I'd like a drink, and I don't think I could manage."

"Let me change first," she said.

"No. Please. Keep it on. *Please.*"

"Hmm. Maybe you don't need a drink."

"It was my gift to you. Only fair. 'S ungrateful of you."

"You *definitely* don't need a drink. But who am I to read the dram shop law? You're not driving tonight." She put a foot on the chair of my wheelchair and pushed it into the corner. "Be right back."

She returned wearing a man's shirt and found me gaping at the snow. She said we needed new scenery and went back to studio. A huge roaring fire leaped from the wall, and I must have screamed. She yelled "Sorry!" and called up another program. It must have been the camera pointed at downtown, for there was the Norwest tower, lit with red and green, and a string of lights draped over the obelisk of the Foshay tower. My town. I was filled with great love for it, for everything, for Melodya. Even Josh. Even Peter Byrne, damn his bodkin, mayhap. God, was I drunk.

Mel returned and put my glass in my hand. I drained it and I leaned over and kissed her on the cheek.

"Why that?"

"It's Christmas, and I have company, and I like my company."

"I mean why the cheek? Plenty of lips nearby. Open for business."

So I kissed her again. Nice. Warm, wet, soft. I was still too drunk to gauge what the kiss meant, I just wanted to do it.

Melodya's kiss made me think of someone trying on a new perfume at a counter, salesclerk looking on. I had the feeling this was another gift, and that the wrapping on this one had been used many times. I pulled back, saw two Melodyas, and commanded the incredibly thick and rusty pulleys in charge of my eyes to focus.

"You're *really* hammered," she said.

"'S the decaf," I said, pointing to my long-evaporated coffee cup.

"You've had too much. You're three sheets to the old wind, boy."

"More than that," I said. "We have to send out for more sheets." Melodya helped me up, smoothed my hair.

"I can stand," I said. And I did. With the weights off, I felt light and limber. "I'm not as drunk as you think I am. You know the spoonerism that goes 'I am not as thunk as you drink I am'? I just spoonerized a spoonerism. For ironic effect."

"You're *really* drunk."

"It's *intentional.*"

"I don't doubt you. How many fingers?" She held up a hand.

"Many." I said. I smiled. "Okay, four. Really, I'm just a little . . . exhilarated. Will you go to bed with me?" Ah, *vino* and *veritas,* old friends and cohorts.

"You're sure you're not too drunk?"

"How do you think I'm going to answer that *now?* No, I'm just fine. I just think we should go to bed. For Christmas's sake."

"I thought you'd never ask."

"I'm not asking. I'm pleading."

"Shut up," she grinned. "Come here. I'll try not to break anything."

If she did, I didn't notice. The only thing I remember is that the phone kept ringing. I think it was the phone. It had a soft metal trill, and I knew that wasn't Mel. The sounds she made I'd never mistake for anything else.

9

IT WAS THE PHONE. OR HAD BEEN. THE MORNING PAPER told me straight away that someone had been trying to call Mel last night.

MURDER SUSPECT BEATS MAN, ESCAPES
"BLOOD ON THE TURKEY" SAY WITNESSES
by Robert Brach, Staff Writer

Henk wasn't dead, damn the luck. Just lacerated in the head and humiliated in the paper.

It was hard to read the headline; the letters were ill behaved, refusing to come to attention. Everything was moving. The world looked jittery, like a cheap VCR paused between frames. If I'd had a hangover this bad before, I had forgotten it, just as women forget the pain of childbirth. It's nature's way of making sure you drink again.

I put the paper on the table, braced it with both hands. The room made a few desultory carnival-ride dips, then settled down. I read.

An act of Christmas charity turned into a gruesome melee Thursday night, as Peter Byrne, the man police believe shot talkshow host Josh

Carlton, assaulted the man responsible for his holiday release.

Byrne, 27, had been released on bail and was spending the holidays with Henk Gruesse, reporter for the *Minneapolis Times,* his wife Tara Sarnoff Gruesse, and guests. Witnesses say the trouble began when Byrne was asked to carve the turkey. He allegedly took the electric carving knife and struck Henk Gruesse on the head, knocking Mr. Gruesse, 34, against the wall. The blow not only knocked Gruesse unconscious, it activated the carving knife, and as Byrne was grasping the knife by the blade, substantial damage was done to his hand.

"He swore a lot at that point," said Harriet Hohauser, a guest. "But he picked up the knife and threatened us with it, said we had to give him the keys to our cars. Everyone just backed up a little—I mean, the cord on that knife was only so long. But then he held it up against Henk's throat and turned it on high, the setting you use for really thin slices, and we knew he was serious."

Byrne escaped in a 1983 tan Ford Escort owned by Ms. Hohauser. Detective Harley Bishop, who led the police team that arrested Byrne several months ago, had no comment. Police confirm that the blood taken from the turkey matched Byrne's type.

This guy was so stupid he beat someone with a knife. Probably graduate to slitting his wrists with a pistol.

There was a mug shot of Byrne, grinning, holding up the card with his name and number as though it was a particularly good report card. He had long, thin hair the color of used sandpaper, eyes as dull as cueballs, icepick chin. One of those downy moustaches favored by kids who kill themselves after listening to heavy metal music.

There was nothing else on Peter Byrne's rush for glory, but there was an interesting little clip several pages later: a radio announcer for KSIS radio, Sacramento, had been slightly wounded when a pipe bomb exploded outside the station, hidden in the first S of the sign. They knew it was a pipe bomb, because half the pipe had shot through the door of a car across the street and ended up in the leg of a man waiting for his wife. There's one man who looked around expecting to see King Kong waving a nail gun, I thought. I could commiserate.

The story had been circled in red.

Someone at the house picked up the phone on the fourth ring. I heard loud whining drills and shouts in the background, as though I had called a dentist's office for Brobdingnagians. The man who answered the phone said they'd be finishing my stair chair installation this afternoon, and I was welcome to come by and try it out. I gathered my things, called a cab, and left the loft with a little regret. It had been a wonderful night, I was sure of that. I wished I could remember it, just to be certain. On the other hand, I was now free to make it the best night of my life.

I hadn't heard her leave the loft that morning. She'd probably read the paper, left it out for me to see, and sprinted off to tend to her brother. I was sure she'd kissed me good-bye. It did neither of us any good to assume otherwise.

The manor was as ugly as it had been three months before, except now it looked ugly and abandoned. All the gargoyles wore skullcaps of snow. I wheeled up the walk, or where the walk would have been had it not been snowed under, panting as I ploughed through the drifts, occasionally hitting patches of ice that would either spin me out or send me sliding down the walk. It was like skiing uphill. When I got to the steps, I stood up, pulled the chair to the top, and sat down again, wheezing and spitting like I'd just won the Tubercular Olympics. God, I had to stop smoking. The workmen had obviously been using the servant's entrance, for the lock was frozen shut and would have nothing to do with the key. Never met it, didn't like it. I took out my lighter and warmed up the key, thinking, *Good thing I still smoke.* The key went into the slot with a sizzle, and the tumblers fell into place.

I wheeled in, looked around, breathed deep.

Home.

Home, where the electricity had been off for three months.

Home with a lot of meat in the long-disconnected fridge.

I revved up the furnace, heard it thunder to life downstairs. Good. I spent an hour hauling dead stinking green things out of the fridge, all the windows open to displace the high ripe air in the house. Needed to get some air in the place. To hell with the heating bill, the place smelled like a crypt. I went to wait in the den, shivering, gagging on the ripe air.

On the table in the dining room, neatly stacked: letters, three months' worth. I looked back to the front door and charted the distance from the mail slot to the table at perhaps sixty feet. Either the mailman used tongs or had unusual strength whipping them through the slot. Good thing we weren't home, or these letters could have taken someone's head off. Odd. Well, the workmen probably did it.

Ah! Speaking of which: the chair. There it was,

idling at the foot of the steps. Grim and utilitarian as ever. I wheeled over, eased myself into it, and gave it a spin; it jerked and bore me up grudgingly, clanking every few steps as the chain played over some unhappy gear, moving with great deliberation and drama. *I'm not ready for my close-up, Mr. DeMille,* I thought. *I'll be down in a minute.*

When I got to the top of the steps, I was wondering how the hell I was going to get around up here without my wheelchair, when I noticed a change in the local decor: Standing along the balcony on the second floor were tables—gray metal tables about five feet tall. Six of them. They looked like TV stands from a high school.

What in Christ's name was this all about? I stared at the tables, wondering if they'd always been there and Phranjari had scooped out their sole appearance in my memory. No. These were new—I could see wood shavings curled at the base where the tables were bolted into the ground.

Bolted? Someone breaks into my house, bolts five ugly tables to the floor, and straightens up my mail? This bore a closer look. I'd have to get the wheelchair, though. Back down in the motorized chariot. I grabbed my wheelchair with both hands and pulled it up as I rode up the chariot, holding on tight—lose it now, and the wheelchair would bounce down the stairs and flee across the room, and there'd be a twenty-minute interval imitating a lung fish as I dragged myself after it. How people who had to live like this forever managed without sudden and fierce insanity, I had no idea.

I made it to the top, manhandled the wheelchair to the landing, giving thanks unto Heather for upper body strength, and wheeled over to the tables. There were TV stands. Each read CENTRAL HIGH on its side.

I'd been hit by a rogue audiovisual department. Or their alumni: Central, I remembered, was knocked down for apartments ten years before.

CAUTION! said a strip of tape on the bottom rung. EXPLODING BOLTS.

It said that on all of the tables, except for the last one. That read: WELCOME HOME.

A police car, its siren making that sound car alarms want to when they grow up, screamed up the drive a few minutes later. It skidded to a stop. All that commotion was apparently intended to impress everyone but me: Once in my driveway, the officer switched off his siren, took a clipboard, and began making notes. Then he carefully stubbed out his cigarette. He got out, locked his door, checked it twice. He then walked slowly up the sidewalk, stopped, and looked at the house like he was thinking of buying one just like it. I opened the door just as he rang the bell. He was a standard-issue Minneapolis policeman—a Swede in his late twenties, sandy moustache, slightly bald, waistline heading leisurely toward Bishopian dimensions. His nameplate identified A. Slensk. (He was that if he was anything.)

He looked down at me—a man in a wheelchair in a dark gothic house—and performed the neat cop trick of filing me into the category of people to be dealt with very, very carefully.

"You called about some stolen bolts?" he said. Standard flat policeman's voice.

"Explosive bolts," I said. "This way."

"May I ask what you had these explosive bolts for, sir?"

"I didn't have any explosive bolts," I said, wheeling ahead. "Let's start again, officer. I recently returned to my house after a few months away. I was shot in the head and went into a coma. I wake up and discover someone had broken in. That's crime number one."

He took out a notebook, one of those sad dime-store spirals policemen always use. "Anything taken?"

"Not that I can tell. Whoever broke in moved my mail from the front hallway and installed several gray metal tables. That's crime number two. Not the mail part, just the tables. I felt straightening the mail was rather thoughtful."

"Is it possible, sir, that before you went away you told a neighbor to look in on the place, and that's what all this is about?"

A. Slensk wasn't joking. "Did you hear me? I was shot. If I'd been prescient enough to tell a neighbor about it in advance, I think I would have known enough to duck when someone shot at me. This is a break-in. I have few neighbors besides the charming Mrs. MacPhereson. There's a hospital to the north and a funeral parlor to the south. I generally don't see my neighbors except when they're headed underground. I'm hesitant to impose on them. Someone broke in here and bolted six tables to the floor upstairs, and would you please go upstairs and look at them before I call 911 and tell them the cop they sent is broken and I'd like a refund?"

Somehow in this peroration I had gotten worked up enough to stand. I realized what I was doing and sat back down, then gestured curtly at the stairs. Slensk gave me a frank look that told me I'd be the talk of the station house today.

"I'll just take a look upstairs then."

He came back down after ten minutes, and I apologized for getting excited. "It's been a rough year," I said. "What with the coma and all. Shorter year than average, but rough."

"I finally placed you," he said. "You're that

Sampson writer fellow." I said I was. "Few guys weren't altogether sad you got hit after that book you wrote," he chuckled. "I personally enjoyed it." The book or me getting hit, he didn't say. "Anyway, it looks like you have bolts, all right. I don't think it's serious, but I'm going to call in the bomb squad anyway. I'll be back."

The bomb squad was much quieter on arrival, almost on tiptoe, something that told me that the fanatics of the world had developed a trigger that went off at the sound of a siren. Of course, if a trigger was able to sense pomposity, the arrival of these guys would have turned the whole block into a bucket of chum. They swept past me, all stern black jackets and mirrored sunglasses. There were three, each with a big metal box. I only had time to see them throw a gray quilt over the first TV table before we were all herded outside and bade to wait in the snow. They emerged an hour later, conferred briefly with Slensk, threw me a look of indifference I was supposed to take as professional assurance, then sped off, clearly headed for bigger and better false alarms.

"No explosives," Slensk said. "Just ordinary old bolts, it looks like. Do you have any idea why someone would break into your house and bolt tables to your floor?"

I didn't.

"Well, I'll file a report."

"And what should I do now?"

Slensk thought hard for a moment.

"Tablecloths," he finally said. "Maybe some vases."

10

IF I WAS GOING TO BE HANDICAPPED, NO MATTER HOW temporarily, I was going to make a big deal of it. Food reviewers never spend much time talking about whether a restaurant accommodates the folks who bring their own chair to the place, so now I could gain great moral points by dishing some dudgeon on behalf of the disabled.

It had been a few weeks since I'd returned home, and I was growing stronger. Credit Melodya. She had been dropping by to supervise my rehabilitation, sitting in a chair and smoking cigarettes while instructing me what to do. She brought me various heavy objects and had me lift them. I could now lift a big tin of honey-smoked Virginia ham with my legs thirty times. For upper body strength, she arm-wrestled me. Every session ended at seven-thirty sharp with a nice long kiss on the lips. That left me more sore than anything else. I never had any energy to walk her to her car, so I just stood at the window and waved. She was driving a blue Bel-Air convertible now. No room for my chair in the trunk, she said. I'd have to hoist ham more often if I wanted a ride.

I was doubly handicapped: not just a bad case of gummy legs, but cursed with a flare-up of recurring Carltonitis. Josh had called me and said he had something of Utmost Importance to show me, and I was curious enough to agree. But I wasn't looking forward to any of it. We were going to That Mango Place, a faux-Caribbean restaurant in the warehouse district I'd reviewed before. They had previously given me such a fabulous case of food poisoning I had calluses on my esophagus from throwing up. I had written a punitive review that would have driven them out of business if anyone thought I knew what I was talking about. It couldn't have been less accessible for the wheelchair-bound if you'd had to reach it by walking a balance beam. You sat in chairs made from steel drums bolted into the floor. There was no way to accommodate a wheelchair.

Even better: It was set at the bottom of an inclined street and the adjoining sidewalk glistened with fresh ice. Carlton held on to my chair's handles and steered me down with the grace of a drunk piloting a dolly with a stuck wheel. Twice, I banged into the wall. He finally slipped on the ice and let go entirely, and I went skidding down toward two posts embedded in the concrete, placed there decades ago to keep errant carts from flying into traffic. I grabbed hold of one of the posts as I flew past, and the wheelchair shot out from under me, clattering down the hill and smashing into a Porsche. Its alarm promptly whooped like a robot faking an orgasm. Carlton skidded by a second later. I found my feet and slid my way down the sidewalk holding on to the building. I retrieved my chair again and waited for Carlton to get up and push me the rest of the way.

That Mango Place was on the second floor. There was no elevator. Carlton was wheezing by the time we got to the landing and had to call for help. Two waiters with the cumulative physique of two blades of grass huffed me up the rest of the way. The door was too small for my chair. I had to get out and lean against the wall while they Laurel-and-Hardied the chair through the door. The host saw what his staff had dragged in and nearly wept. Not just a food critic back for a fresh savaging, but a food critic in a wheelchair.

"Mr. Simpson. How nice. Come to give us a second chance?"

"Actually," I said with a smile, "I was in an accident, as you can see, and lost parts of my memory. All I know is that this café left quite an impression on me, and I want to know why. May we have a table?"

The host looked around the café, desperately wishing to conjure patrons at every table. But it was nearly empty. "Smoking or non?"

"Smoking," Carlton panted.

"Right this way."

We were placed near the window at a small table with two seats, each, of course, bolted to the ground. The table was made of lacquered wicker, with sharp little points frozen in plastic sticking up everywhere you wanted to rest your hand. Palm trees, sand, netting, and the rest of the merry accoutrements of impoverished island nations were painted on the wall. Since I couldn't sit at the table, I had to hang in the aisle, a big chrome indictment of their inaccessible policies. We were handed menus the size of board games, and our waiter (Bill) began rattling off the day's abominations. When he finished, I asked where I might find the bathroom. He blanched. They were, as I knew, downstairs.

"Don't you know there are codes requiring this whole place to be handicapped accessible?" I snapped. "What if I have another of your jerked salmonella specials and have to go sprinting off to the lavatory?"

"We'll stand by," he said and rushed off.

Carlton watched all this with disinterest. "How long are you going to be in that stupid thing anyway?" he said.

"If Melodya has her way, about two more days. She's quite the physical therapist."

Carlton's face darkened. "Isn't she just, though."

"Do you know her from somewhere? The other night when she came in—"

"I don't know her socially," he said. "Professionally, that's all. Doubt she recalls me, though. Anyway." The sudden grin again. "New twist here for the Josh Carlton story. Radio history made while you watch." He reached into his pocket and pulled out a cellular phone. Set it on the table. Looked at it like something he'd smuggled from behind enemy lines.

"It's a phone," I ventured. "Right?"

"It's a satellite phone. Direct connection to KTOK."

"Via satellite? That's like going around the world to cross the street, isn't it?"

"Don't know how it works exactly. It's the concept. See, I'm their man on the street now, right? The ultimate free agent. KTOK has total liberty to call me up at any time of the day and have me go live. Wherever I am—the crapper, the laundry room, whatever. I gotta do a show from wherever I am—find people to put on the air, describe something. I could be at a meal, in the shower, in bed, and I do mean in bed, and bang! I'm live."

"I see."

"It's a conceptual thing. Idea is, I'm always doing a show. My life is a show. They cut in on other people's show to check out the Josh Carlton Life Story Show, already in progress. It's never been done before! No set up, no test one, two, three, just ring! and I go."

"And this is in addition to the night show? They've got you working night and—"

"Oh, that's done with. They've cut me loose. Freed me."

He appeared happy, but who could tell? He patted the phone with love. "Today's the first day. Supposed to cut in during the Samurai's show. Back in drive time again, son. Samurai has been instructed to make room for *me*. That's why you're here. I want you to see this from the beginning. You can get something about this in the paper, can't you? 'The chicken went well with a cool red wine and a few observations from the Josh Carlton Show. You're the only media guy I could think of. Can't you? Do something?'"

I checked my watch: three o'clock. The Samurai Stevens show was just starting. The waiter came by, and I ordered the daily special, which turned out to be withered chicken under a flood of gingery spices. I had one bite and pushed the plate away. Carlton had a Mangoburger with Island Fries. He ate it all and drank three glasses of cool red wine. We watched the phone.

Four o'clock. Carlton relaxed. "News time. Bastard wanted the first hour all to himself." I ordered more coffee.

Four-thirty. I was regretting that coffee, as Carlton had forbade me to use the restroom. "I need a guest," he said, gesturing to the empty restaurant. He made a call to make sure the phone was working. It was. Five o'clock. No calls. My bladder was now a tight, hot basketball that demanded deflating, and I insisted Carlton at least accompany me to the rest room in case I needed help. He snapped that I should have a cane like normal crippled people but went along sullenly, phone in hand. I was in the bathroom, leaning up against the wall and pounding my stream into the urinal when the phone rang. Carlton swore, coughed, and answered: "Josh Carlton!"

"No," he said evenly. "This is not the symphony box office. You have—ma'am? Ma'am, I don't know what's playing tonight. I have to—"

"Mahler's *Kindertotenlieder,*" I shouted from the stall. I had season tickets. I intended to go.

"Kinderwhat?"

"Songs on the Death of Children."

"Ma'am? Norman Mailer tonight, singing about dead kids. Now get the fuck off my phone." And with that he left the bathroom, slamming the door behind him. I staggered back to the table, past the hateful gaze of the host, who was clearly beginning to question just how serious my severed spine was. Carlton sat at the table with his hands crossed at his chest, staring hot, spiky lightning at the phone. I took out a notebook and began to jot down a few lines.

"Don't take this down," he snarled. "This is not history. Wait for history."

"I'm taking notes on the restaurant," I said. "For the review. Noting how the place is empty and we haven't been served in forty minutes." Unfair, of course, seeing as it was five in the afternoon and we had paid our bill an hour and half before. But I had a lot of regurgitation to avenge. In fact, it looked like there might be more: Carlton, in addition to having brimful of hate, was beginning to green slightly. He gave his stomach slight massages, swallowing gently. By five-thirty he appeared to be more distressed than usual. The phone did not ring. It was dark outside.

When six o'clock came and went, it was apparent Samurai had no intention of inaugurating Josh Carlton's life on his program. We left the restaurant. Carlton by now had that bleary cast to his eyes that presages a stern vacating of the stomach. He was unable to help me down the steps. I took the first flight on foot, the second flight bouncing down on my rump. We stood at the bottom of the incline, looking up; Carlton groaned and started pushing. His breath came in shallow pants, and he muttered about That Damn Mangoburger, it wouldn't stay still. I looked back in alarm, realizing that should he shout out the Mango anthem, I'd be directly in line of whatever gouts he produced. We reached the top of the incline.

Carlton bent over, puffing. The phone rang. He straightened like someone had kicked him in the rump, whipped out his phone, said "Hello, Twin Cities!" and promptly threw up. He doubled over, orating to the sidewalk; the phone fell from his hands and skidded down the incline. "HELLO? HELlo? Hello?" I heard it say as it slid away.

Ah, Christ on a stick, this man was impossible. I eased myself out of the chair and slid down the incline, grabbing at the pole in the sidewalk as I passed. The phone sat in a gutter. "HELLO! HEL-LO!" it shouted. I picked it up and said hello, who was this?

"It's Doctor Neil!" said a bright voice. "It's the Doctor Neil Sims Show, on KTOK AM 1510, and we're checking in with Josh Carlton, man about town! How are you, Josh?"

"This isn't Josh. He's . . . unwell at the moment. I'm a friend. Can I help you?"

Momentary panic at the other end. We were off the unscripted script. I could hear Josh at the top of the incline, who, from the sound of it, was bringing up Zwieback he'd been fed as a child while teething. "He's, ahh, unwell? Sick? Is that what I hear? I'm Doctor Neil, maybe I can diagno—"

"It's food poisoning," I said grimly. "Bad hamburger meat."

"Ah," said Dr. Neil. "I think you'd better call a doctor."

"A doctor called *him,* for heaven's sakes," I said. "In midboot no less. Any advice? Seltzer water? Soda crackers?"

"Those are all good remedies, yes. With rest and plenty of fluids. But I strongly advise he seek medical attention, though."

"Anything else, Dr. Neil?"

"I, ah, I don't believe so."

"Right, then, and thanks for calling." I hung up. I

made my way back up the incline, flopping around like a seal. I had two goals. One, find a cab. Two, never, ever set eyes on Josh Carlton again.

The cabbie was surly and had body odor that surged out and thrust its thumbs up our nostrils. This meant we had to stop the cab while Carlton leaned out the window and went *arrrrrgh* at the ground. When the cab dropped him off, I told him I never wanted to see him again.

"I don't like you," I said.

"I understand."

"I've been on the fence on the matter, but that did it."

"Wasn't my fault. Blame the meat."

"It's you. You're generally unpleasant and strange. Please leave me alone."

"What about the article?"

"Josh, drop it. I'm not writing an article about you and you know it. It's all I can do to keep my stupid food job."

"Don't mention food!"

I told the cabbie to go and we did, the three of us: me, the cabbie, and his body odor. He made no move to help me up the manor steps, but by then I was so charged full of anger and adrenaline that I walked it myself, kicking my chair as I went.

There was mail by the door slot. I picked it up, dropped into a chair, and read. A birth announcement from someone named Jane. I had no idea who that was, perhaps a resident of my excised brain part. The second was a thick letter with a gold-embossed return address. Another lawsuit from the lackeys of my Scottish nemesis next door. I almost threw it away, then had an awful thought. Had she been filing small claims suits while I was away in Comaland? I ripped the envelope over and scanned the first paragraph: Moneys owed . . . Judgment not contested . . . Liens will be placed . . . Please respond . . . File she had. Three suits, all rubber-stamped by the court when I failed to appear to contest them. I owed her $4,500. Failure to pay within thirty days would mean a bench warrant issued for my arrest.

I crumpled the letter and threw it across the room. It wasn't the money. It was the humiliation of going to my butler when he got back and asking him to write me a check from the vast pool he had accumulated through inheritance and lottery playing. Made me feel dissolute and prodigal, the family rake. So dreadful sorry old man, couldn't control the X-ray vision, don't you know. Damnedest thing. Be a sport and help me out.

The third letter was postmarked Sacramento. It was originally sent to KTOK, and according to the stickers on the envelope, it had been rerouted to the hospital and then Henk's place. Someone had handwritten my address on the bottom of the letter.

Sacramento?

The letter was printed in generic dot-matrix letters.

```
DEAR JONATHAN SIMPSON. TOO BAD
ABOUT ALL THAT WITH THE HEAD AND ALL.
NOTHING PERSONAL. UNDERSTAND THINGS
ARE BETTER NOW. APOLOGIES EXTENDED.
REGARDS TIM. PS DONT REMOVE TABLES
OR HOUSE WILL BLOW UP IN OH SEVER-
AL MILLION PIECES. MAYBE. AT LEAST
ONE BOLT MIGHT LIVE UP TO BILLING.
PLS DO NOT REMOVE IF CURIOUS AS REA-
SONS EXPLAINED EVENTUALLY. LOVE TIM.
```

I went cold all over.

The radio station recently bombed was in Sacramento.

My head started to ache—something it hadn't done

since I woke up. My legs started to shake, then my arms, then my head seemed to be full of fizzing bees and I became mad, madder, maddest. I pounded the table, then kicked my wheelchair across the room.

Nothing personal. Apologies extended.

11

"HUH." *HITCH.* "WELL, THAT'S IT, THEN. CLARIFIES A lot, lemme tell you." He sat at the dining room table at the manor, holding up the letters as though a secret message might be hidden in the watermark.

"Maybe if you hold it over a flame," I said. He gave me a look. "If he wrote something in lemon juice, it would be visible if you held the letter over a flame."

"You got a guy who shot you, blew up another station with a pipe bomb, sends taunting letters, and you think he's taking hints from the fuckin' Hardy Boys?" Hitch was excited.

"You think Tim did the dirty in Sacramento?"

"Uh-huh." *Hitch.* "I know it. Knew it soon as I saw the story."

"Based on what? That's a thin conclusion to draw from two incidents."

He grinned. "It would be. If there weren't four more between them."

The room felt cold and big and empty.

"What four more?"

"All across the country, I'm talking north, south, east, west. I did a wire scan this morning; no one's picked up on it yet. We got a nut out there blowin' up personalities."

"Where? Jesus, Murray, tell me!"

"I will, provided you tell me some things. Like

whether that book deal you signed had an option for your next."

Option, hell. The publisher had paid for it and I'd spent the money long ago. I just nodded.

"Tell me whether you're going to write about your experience here. And whether what I just told you makes it a, y'know, more marketable proposition." I nodded again. "Okay. Now, you're the writer here. I can't write these like book people want. You know, colorful. That's your department. But cut me in and I'll do the legwork you can't." He reddened. "Sorry, *sorry.* You know what I mean. Whaddaya say? Deal? Partners?"

"You're on," I said, half meaning it, half hoping it wouldn't hold up legally. You never know.

"Great." *Hitch.* "Here's the skinny. We got to move fast. Someone is going to figure this out soon if they haven't already. Friend of mine over the *Times* tells me that asshole Henk is heading off to Sacramento this week, so he obviously thinks something's up. We don't have the money to fly all over and dig up shit, so we'll have to make up in style what we lack in topicality."

"Box scores could beat Henk in style," I said. "Now tell me about the other stations."

Hitch stood. "Show me a contract I can sign, and we'll talk. And how we'll talk!" He looked around. "Nice house. You book guys live nice."

Valentine's day was two weeks away, but I wanted to send Mel a card earlier than her other nameless swains.

I walked to the mailbox at the end of the street to do it. I'd come far since December. Heather, my official physical therapist, said so, although she correctly suspected I was seeing another therapist on the side.

She'd grown chilly lately, had warned me of the dangers of training with amateurs and left it at that. I think she had a vision of me trolling the street in my wheelchair, luridly painted physical therapists leaning from doorways.

Thanks to Mel's instruction I was out of the chair most of the time now, banging around the house in a walker. Melodya had helped me paint it—glossy black with hot pink accents. It looked like a jungle gym for preadolescent pygmy girls. Mel hung some fuzzy dice from the crossbar, giving it a reckless hot-rodder look. It was all very happy and merry and friendly, which was just what I didn't want. Well, I wanted that and more. The opportunity to cleave and twitch and moan together, ending up months later spitting withering dismissals of each other, was rapidly passing. At this rate we'd be nothing more than close and lifelong friends. I understood, sort of. I was still a bag of twigs who needed ten pounds of pipes to hold me up, and she was a big, glowing beauty of neoprene and steel. Surely she had boyfriends.

Dozens. Thousands.

Odd how she never got around to mentioning any of them.

The *Metropole* was in the warehouse district, like just about everything else contentious in my life lately. The building was a hollowed-out brown brick hulk originally used to store construction material.

I had been summoned to a meeting with my editor, never a merry prospect. Fikes was on the phone when I entered his office. He nodded for me to sit. My walker stood there black and pink, its pendulous dice looking like something a juvenile delinquent would use to dry fine washables. Fikes said "damn you" to the phone and hung up. He looked at me with a blank look, and smiled.

"Simpson. *Mrrrgm.* What have you done for me? Not even lately. Not even within the span of human memory. Within, oh, say, the span of recorded time. No, time immemorial."

"Well." I hated these talks. I seemed to get them at every job I held. "I've met my deadlines with the reviews. As per my contract."

"You don't have a contract. Unless we went union overnight and I missed it. Tell me now so I can phone some scabs."

"Verbal contract," I said, suddenly very much in favor of quasi-legal agreements. "One review a week plus the occasional feature."

"Ahh, occasional. Well. We've certainly stretched the operative definition of that word, haven't we? I consent, because that's the kind of man I am: gentle, yielding, understanding. But my gentle understanding arse has been reamed thrice and sideways by your inertia. Are you following me?"

"I should get moving on a piece?"

"That is the pith of my gist. Here's what I want. I want you to work with Hitch on the next piece. Strikes me that as long as I have one of the victims in my employ I might as well mine him for his sagacious observations. Give me all you can on Peter Byrne: daring escape of, concerted hunt for. Give me something on this pathetic Carlton fellow. Christ, have you seen what they have him doing now?"

I nodded. "He seems happy."

"So did Son of Sam if I recall the photos." He tossed a cigarette in the ashtray, hawked a nugget of expectorant into his wastebasket, and groped another cigarette from his pack.

To placate him, I wrote a typical alternative newspaper story, too long by half and self-indulgent. I discussed the letter from Sacramento. (This would be no news to the authorities. I had given Bishop the letter a few days after I received it, and he had regarded it with the enthusiasm usually reserved for dental appointment reminders.) There was plenty about the New Josh Carlton, now a full-blown local curiosity. His man-about-town stints on KTOK had lasted two weeks and been the subject of vicious little snipes by the Tuber, the *Metropole's* media critic. The station had awoken him in a bar once, absolutely hammered, and another time had found him at three in the morning grunting rhythmically while someone made pro forma grunts of delight in the background. The grunts came faster and faster until Carlton pressed on the pound key, and the phone sang out in joy. Three times he'd been called up at a strip club, or so he said. Odd man with an odd life. No doubt the station wanted to can him, but word got around that this debaucher was out there rutting and boozing and ogling for all he was worth, and people began listening for his reports. The station, smelling a ratings increase went to him. They must have told him to spend his days shuttling between the museum and the sacristy, for the more he appeared, the more he seemed to behave. The duller he became.

When he was finally earnest, boring, and back to his old smooth pasteurized self, KTOK ended the radio career of Josh Carlton. They handed him over to KJGO, their parent company's TV station. They made him the Man about Town for *Great Day! With Stan and Cindy,* an inane afternoon talk show hosted by a raw-boned former newscaster busted down in rank for being too intelligent and a hard-eyed block of ice with black hair and the personality of a dental pick. Every afternoon show has a guy like Josh, someone goofy who goes out among the community, puts himself in silly situations, like bronco riding or windsurfing or brain surgery, fails at whatever he does, and then makes lame japes with the unimpressed but courteous professionals. This was Josh's job, and given that he was unstable, violent, drunk, and manic-depressive, he was lucky to get it.

But then they made him wear the Harness.

It was the TV version of the satellite phone—a wire cage that fitted over his head, rested on his shoulders, was anchored to his back by rubber tubes, and contained three pencil TV cameras. One was pointed at him, the other looked at him from the side, and the third looked out at the world. When he was doing something spectacularly silly like rappelling the huge neon GRAIN BELT sign on Hennepin, the cameras fed into little eight-millimeter videorecorders. Not a bad idea, really.

But he had to wear it all the time.

He couldn't be the Man about Town if no one knew he was. The idea was to spark the citzenry's curiosity, come up to him, engage him, perform, all the while capturing Josh's reaction through the goggling fish eye of the camera. Day and night he had to wear the Harness. It got him a lot of publicity for a week, and I watched a few installments. He looked absolutely humiliated. This was the reverse of his goal as the talk show host supreme. Instead of standing apart from creation, unseen, casting his voice down among the masses like manna, now the world was peering at him every second, front and side, never giving him a moment's peace.

There was a little hinge in the front of his cage to feed himself.

Josh, Peter Byrne, Detective Bishop, Dr. Phranjari, Heather, the mean nurse in the EKG room, Henk, my own humble self, were all tossed into my piece and stirred with rote enthusiasm. It was 145 inches when finished. I had no idea what any of it meant. Worse yet, there was no grand context in which to place it: Hitch, still after the nationwide angle, had extracted travel money from Fikes and disappeared, telling us he'd file when he knew the answers. He sent expense reports from all over the nation, bills from bars and motels with garish names that brought to mind burnt-out neon letters. Every week he submitted expense accounts from barbers, which gave me a shudder. I imagined Hitch with a Mohawk, inauthenticity screaming in his every mannerism, penetrating fringe communities who regarded him as a figure from the pop-up version of *The Protocols of the Elders of Zion*. He faxed back twenty pages a day—all of it written in his unintelligible hand. On my trips to the *Metropole* I paged through the faxes, curling like ancient scrolls awakened from a millenia-long rest in a cave. I wanted to know what they said. I wanted to hear his voice perform the translation.

There was a blizzard the day my piece came out and the copies were late getting to the stand, and what did make it was soon blown away by the wind or trodden by snow-crusted overshoes. The peril of working for a paper given away in the entryways of bars. That same day my work was blowing high over roofs and getting shoveled up by janitors, someone else was at work far away in Piquot, Oregon. That day—February 14, a Saturday; Melodya should have long ago gotten my card—someone put a bullet through the shoulder of the weatherman for KPQO as he pulling up into his driveway.

Police arrested the boyfriend of his ex-wife. He was later released for lack of evidence.

I checked the expense report Hitch had filed a few days before and got out a map. He'd stayed at the Murmuring Pines Motel in Piquot, Oregon, the day before the shooting.

But no faxes came whirring through the machine that day.

12

March 3:

IS A SERIAL KILLER STALKING AMERICA'S MEDIA?
By Henk Gruesse, Staff Writer

SACRAMENTO—Pete "Wildman" Richards stands outside the radio station where he used to work and thoughtfully rubs his thigh. He wants to talk about the pipe bomb.

"I can't get it out of mind," he says. His hands rub his thigh again. "One day I was just sitting in my car looking for a spare pack of cigarettes, then there was . . . the explosion."

For the duration of his radio career, Pete "Wildman" Richards has garnered a reputation as someone who will do anything for ratings.

There was the Wildman Godiva incident in which he drove a car naked down the street.

There was the Wildman for a Day contest, where Wildman exchanged places with the winner—a crack dealer whose on-air tirades nearly lost the station its license and whose house was raided while Wildman was taking the winner's place. (Wildman spent the day in jail, leading to the Free the Wildman One protest by nearly ten loyal listeners.) And there was the time Wildman responded to management complaints about his style by staging a mock crucifixion on the station's transmitting tower on Good Friday.

People have come to expect anything from Wildman.

"He did it to himself," said Hilda Jorgenson, a spokesperson for a local church group that tried to get Wildman removed from the air after the crucifixion incident. "It's the sort of cheap ploy we've come to expect."

Sid McClaren, a Wildman fan, surprisingly agrees.

"Anytime someone gets wounded and it's only a flesh thing, I'm suspicious," said McClaren, 24, a bicycle messenger. "I mean, look at all the publicity."

The Wildman replies by pointing out he is Wild no more. While recuperating, the station declined to renew his contract.

"I'm the victim here," says Wildman. "I'd like anyone to tell me how I could rig a pipe bomb to hit me across the street. Tell me that. Just tell me that."

The police agree, and say that Richards is not a suspect in the investigation. Beyond that, they say little, for there is little to say. They have no suspect and no leads. Whoever planted the pipe bomb has not stepped forward to claim responsibility. They may even have left town.

Perhaps to do the same thing somewhere else.

A check of recent news stories points out a disturb ing fact: In the last six weeks, three radio or television personalities have been the target of violence.

Sacramento, California. A pipe bomb explodes in the station's sign, wounding Pete "Wildman" Rich ards.

Piquot, Oregon. A station's weatherman is shot in the shoulder as he leaves the station. Shots are also fired at the station's sign.

Las Vegas, Nevada. Shots are fired at the van of KVGS in the station's parking lot.

Each episode took place on a Friday exactly two weeks apart.

In each case, authorities seem quick to say they regard it as a local matter. In the Piquot case, a relative of the weatherman was arrested but released without charges. In Las Vegas, police blame vandals. In Sacramento, police are investigating the possibility that hate groups incensed by Wildman's on-air taunt ing of racial supremacists may be to blame.

Perhaps. But add to this the curious and still unsolved case of Josh Carlton, a talk show host in St. Paul, Minnesota. Carlton was shot as he left the station seven months ago. (A bystander was also wounded.)

The FBI refused to comment for this article, and local authorities declined to say whether they had been contacted by the FBI. For now, media figures around the country can only wait until the next Friday and take precautions.

"If it can happen to me, it can happen to anyone," says the Wildman. "You sit in that booth all day with the outside world far away, and you never think that the craziness that comes in your headphones can be waiting for you when you leave. But it can. It can."

And he rubs his thigh once more.

March 14:

RADIO HOST SHOT IN OMAHA

(AP) Radio personality Tom Stewart of KETE, Omaha, was wounded in the leg Friday by an unknown gunman.

He is in stable condition.

The station's sign also suffered damage in the attack.

Stewart, 56, was the host of the popular "Rummage Hour," a program that allowed people to advertise unwanted goods.

"He had concluded the show and stepped outside to have a smoke," said station manager Stu Thomas. "We heard the shots and ran outside."

It is the third shooting of a radio host in the United States in the last eight months. Additionally, one disc jockey has been the target of a pipe bomb attack. Authorities are investigating the incident as unrelated to the previous shooting.

"People get disgruntled sometimes," says Sergeant Charles Selbesynski. "They buy a lawn mower on the show, and it doesn't work, and they take it out on the host. He has some hate mail to that effect, and we're looking into it."

March 28:

TELEVISION REPORTER SHOT IN FLORIDA

(AP) L'fitta D'Naka, a consumer-affairs reporter for WAHK-TV in Simminee, Florida, was shot Friday as she prepared to do a story outside a local mall.

She was shot in the shoulder and is in stable condition in a local hospital.

Bystanders reported seeing a black van drive away from the scene, but no connection has been made and police efforts to find the van have been so far fruitless.

Ms. D'Naka was the fourth media personality to be shot since . . .

April 4:

DISC JOCKEY SHOT IN MONTANA

(AP) In the latest in what authorities are now calling a baffling series of shootings of media figures, Rick Harry, a late-night disc jockey for KREE radio, was seriously wounded Friday as he stood outside the station during a break.

April 8:

NEWSCASTER KILLED IN IOWA SHOOTING
By Henk Gruesse, Staff Writer

IOWA CITY, IOWA—This time, they saw him.

Paul Bruce of TV station WERE-4 was walking to his car with the weatherman, chatting about the evening's broadcast. Bruce had been giving the weatherman a hard time on the air. They did that from time to time: kid each other. They liked their jobs. They liked each other. Bruce had been complaining about the weatherman's tie.

Then the shots rang out.

Paul Bruce lay dead on the pavement, a bullet wound to his head.

When police arrived they found the weatherman cradling his friend. His tie—the one Bruce had complained about—was wrapped around the dead man's head in a fruitless attempt to stop the flow of blood.

Paramedics removed it, and the tie lay on the blood-soaked pavement—a terribly sad reminder of a friendship now destroyed by the man who seems to be stalking the airwaves of America.

Fifteen people now bear his scars.

One is dead.

But we have a name for him now. The Man

with the Mohawk. As the weatherman held his dying friend, he saw a man with a Mohawk-style haircut across the road from the station, shoving a long cylindrical package into a white van. The van sped off into the empty countryside, down one of a dozen narrow roads that thread through this heartland like the capillaries of an immense, grain-filled body. . . .

Roadblocks and state patrol searches have failed to find the van or its driver. But now they know what he looks like. The next deadly Friday may bear fruit of a different kind. The fruit, perhaps, of justice . . .

April 13: "DEADLY FRIDAY" PASSES WITH NO SHOOTING

April 20: AUTHORITIES WONDER IF MOHAWK KILLER HAS STOPPED HIS DEADLY WORK

May 15: FRIDAY JUST ANOTHER DAY FOR RE-LIEVED RADIO PERSONALITY

Daily Iowan, May 16:

JOURNALIST FOUND DEAD IN CORALVILLE MOTEL ROOM

Minnesotan strangled, then given a haircut, police say.

13

HITCH'S ONLY SURVIVING RELATIVE WAS A SISTER, AND SHE arrived the day of his funeral. She spent the ceremony alternating between a stunned look of utter horror or mad hysterical laugh. In Jewish ceremonies the coffin is closed, but she'd no doubt seen the body. I'd heard what his body had looked like when he'd been found: eyes closed in peace, glasses tucked in his jacket pocket, his hair done up in a freshly laundered Mohawk.

When the funeral was over, I slipped out and walked across Hennepin Avenue to Gelpe's Bakery, ordered a coffee, and smoothed out the faxes that had whined out of the machine for the last few months. Hitch's faxes were consistently indecipherable, but I was determined to crack his handwriting code. There seemed to be some sort of a key: Several pages had one capital letter at the top: S.T.E.E.H.A.E.R. Another page had NEA? at the top, with exclamation marks scattered throughout. Steeahernea? Sounded like a groin infection. During my second espresso, I realized I would never decipher this, for there was no deciphering to be done. Hitch simply had poor penmanship. He wrote in that fluid scrawl of one who is merely making marks to fix the information in his brain. The letters would remind him of the specifics. It was the script of someone who was cautious of libel suits and subpoenas. He could get up in court and read his notebooks and no one could tell him it wasn't what was written.

Hitch had been found tied to a bed in a motel room in a suburb of Iowa City. Ropes had been lashed around his limbs and wound tightly around the legs of the bed, with poor Hitch on his stomach. He had been shaved in that position; his hair all over the pillow. According to police interviews, he'd died around midnight. A couple in the adjacent room had heard urgent grunts and the squealing mattress springs through the thin wall and had ascribed it to the standard ambient noise of a motel. When they heard the gruesome sounds of someone being sick, they'd considered asking for another room, but the sounds had ceased shortly thereafter.

He probably wasn't supposed to die. There were no drugs in his blood, no bruises or wounds. Poor Hitch had been so frightened he had simultaneously vomited and hyperventilated, drowning in his vomit. Asphyxiation was the cause of death.

The agent of his exit, of course, was obvious, which made the faxes all the more infuriating. Buried somewhere in his scrawl was the story of Hitch not just figuring something out, but tipping his hand somehow, making someone follow him back, tie him up, and steal his notes. Had Hitch walked in while his room was being tossed? Why tie him up if you're cover's blown, your identity known?

I paid for my coffee and left and walked down the block to the motorscooter I'd bought last week as a refutation of months of immobility. I loved dashing about town, feeling the wind in my inch-and-a-half long hair. (Well, it was a start.) Summer stirred in the margins, and I looked forward to it with inordinate gratitude. Happy to be walking; happier to be alive. Worried about everything, but happy.

Samurai Stevens beamed from a poster on a nearby bus shelter, all two hundred pounds of him. Maybe half a pound of that was fat, perhaps less was brain matter. The rest was muscle and attitude. His picture had the look of a man who'd already had the summer I wanted. He was probably having it as I looked at him.

This was not a guess. They were running TV spots for his show, emphasizing what a hip, with-it, happening guy he was. He was driving his blue Bel-Air, grinning, with a gorgeous and familiar blonde in the backseat, her arms draped around him, a yard of hair rippling in the wind. I didn't know Melodya had a wig that color; she usually wore black ones when I saw her. The woman in the commercial said, "He's a happening human!" in a dumb, breathy voice. Maybe that was her voice too, or maybe they'd dubbed in someone else's. It certainly didn't sound like the woman I knew.

14

"HEY. HEY." THIS WAS FROM A MAN LEANING FROM HIS CAR window at the stoplight, frowning as though he had been trapped in his car for many years and could only now tell someone about it. "What kinda mileage you get?"

"Five hundred miles to the gallon," I said, smiling. I heard this question at every stoplight and kept upping the mileage: a test of people's credulity. "And it never needs oil. Just daub some Vaseline on the cylinders."

"Five hunert miles? Get outta here," the man said. The light changed, and I obliged.

June. A hot, dry time, the sun like a fist, blasted lawns struggling to green. I was on my way to a gym in St. Paul to meet Melodya. She'd left a message on my answering machine saying she had something for me and I'd better come and get it—the sort of words that would make a man chew his way out of Folsom prison.

I slowed for the turn into the club, checking my rearview mirror. A truck was thundering up the road, MEAT written in backward letters above the grille, as though this was an ambulance. Maybe it was, albeit a large and rather matter-of-fact one. I pulled into the parking lot and trolled for a spot, ending up at the far end of the lot, next to a Bel-Air parked illegally, half up on the grass. There was a sick lurch in my stomach. That's what she had to show me: her big boyfriend, perhaps a wedding ring, a tummy large with children, a certificate testifying to joint plots in the cemetery.

Maybe it was a different car.

It wasn't.

The gym, like all gyms, had its own unique stink. Not as vile as some. I used to go to a gym that smelled like someone had taken a cat in heat, dipped it in roofing tar, and waved it around the room like a censor at a Catholic mass. That was, I think, the smell of steroids. Everyone at that gym sweated steroids. I worried that my nose would become huge and ornately muscular from breathing the sweat.

This gym had the usual acrid tang in the air, with a note of healthy diets, topped off by a roiling cloud of musky hormones. It was all mirrors and chrome and thin, haughty people ignoring each other. One room was given over to the machines—exquisitely designed instruments probably bought when the KGB held its going-out-of-business sale. A vast, glass-walled room held the aerobics classes, which consisted alternately of pudgy people dancing as though responding to gunfire at their feet and thin, grim beauties joylessly flailing, hollering *Whooo* when the instructor asked if they were having a good time. Ridiculous.

The free weights, as they are called, were stuck in a corner of the gym, like chunks of meat set aside to keep the dangerous beasts from terrorizing the innocent. Mel was laying on a bench, legs parted, hoisting a bar and two metal plates the size of tractor tires. Ah: It would be pectorals today. Her chest was hard enough already, firm breasts atop a bed of stern muscle. It was hard not to imagine her hoisting you up and down on top of her, as though you too were an implement of greater fitness.

"Aaawwwgh," she bellowed. The bar went up halfway, stayed there. *"Hmrg! Rhgrwh! Hhhhhraaaa!"* The bar was now straight up in the air, her arms as stiff as phone poles.

"You're pitiful!" said a man standing over her. "Weak! Gutless, small, weak, weak, weak!"

"Rrrrgghr!"

"Drop that bar now and you're a Girl Scout! Merit badge in Failure! Can't even lift a box of cookies!" He was about nine feet tall, golden hair, golden skin, a catalog of all available muscles. He put his bus shelter pictures to shame.

Mel screamed something that included several brand-new vowels and somehow pushed the bar higher. Then her arms trembled, and the man who was shouting at her leaned down and took the bar with one hand.

"Good girl." He set the bar down. "Strong girl. Bad girl, and I mean that sincerely." He strolled up to a mirror, scowled, stabbed his hair with his hands until satisfied, then clapped a small and overbuilt man on the back with such velocity that the man fell off his bench. He wandered away.

Mel was still on her back, exhaling like a quitting-time whistle. She was dressed in a few shards of black fabric, sopping wet around the clavicle. Somehow she'd coaxed a tan from the spring sun. It went well with her short, inky-black wig.

"You have too many prominent arteries," I said.

"Jonathan," she exhaled. She gave me a smile from a billboard: ten feet wide, affixed with paste. We'd hadn't seen each other in a couple of months. The last time she'd called me up late at night from the office, tears in her voice, and asked me to come over and visit. All smiles once I got there, no clue as to the problems that made her decide I was the right man to be with. The night ended up on the roof where we talked until daylight, arguing about the mannerists and rococo until a fine cobalt Giotto dawn came up and shamed us both. Such a kiss she gave me then. A kiss and—how to put this?—permission to artfully grope. If I'd thought it was leading anywhere, I'd have been excited. As it was I was alternately surly and uncommonly randy.

But I was here for a reason other than pointlessly stoking my loins and groaning my way home again, shifting with pain on the seat of my scooter. "You said you had something for me," I said.

"Right. 'S in my locker. Meet me in the lobby."

I waited in the lobby, watching the colossi pass, feeling small. A TV set was tuned to *Great Day! With Stan and Cindy.* They were about to interview a manager for an indoor theme park featuring inordinately large cartoon dogs, and Stan was attempting to be sufficiently thrilled about the matter. And, of course, later there'd be Josh Carlton, Man About Town. Stan announced that Josh would be visiting with the Twin Cities's latest family: falcons nesting in a skyscraper! Vigorous, pro-falcon applause from the audience.

"Here," said Mel. She stood, mopping her brow with a towel, holding out a letter. "This is for you. Josh Carlton came by to work yesterday and dropped it off. Said you weren't to read it until after today's show for some reason or other."

"From Josh?" I looked at the letter, apprehensive. "Why couldn't he give it to me himself?"

"I asked that very question. He said you'd banished him from your presence." She tugged at a lucky pink ribbon of spandex that held her in a sort of sling, if you know what I mean. "Anyway, I was supposed to deliver it in person, and I sort of missed you anyway. So here you are and there it is. Want to take a sauna?"

"Is Goldilocks coming?"

"Goldi—oh, Sam. No, sir. Probably has an invite to the women's showers by now." She was looking past me at the TV set, pointing.

"There he is."

There was an inset picture of Josh in the corner of the screen, surrounded by squiggles of color that were no doubt meant to indicate he was a crazy sort of fellow and anything could happen.

"And let's just look in on Josh Carlton, Man about Town. Cindy, I understand Josh is up on the Multi-foods building today, looking in on a family of peregrine falcons!"

"That's right, Stan. You know, peregrine falcons are an endangered species, and as part of this station's EarthCare program, we've adopted a family nesting on top of one of the city's highest buildings."

"But no one's talking of naming the baby falcons after the *Live at Five* guys," said Stan. Moderate ripple of laughter from studio audience.

"Not unless the daddy falcon starts wearing plaid jackets!" said Cindy. A reference to the station's venerable and amiable drunken sportscaster. Ho, ho, ho. "Anyway, here's Josh, high in the peaks and crags of downtown Minneapolis. Josh, what's the bird's-eye view up there?"

Split screen: Josh's fish-eye face on one side, the view from his external camera on the other. He had a baby falcon in his hand.

"I can't get them to fly," he said. And he heaved the baby bird over the side of the building.

Gasps from the audience. Josh wandered over to the side of the building and looked down. The screen showed a little brown thing fluttering down fifty stories, hitting the atrium roof of the shopping center below with a faint *punk!* Good microphone. "They just don't want to fly," he repeated. "Maybe they need altitude." He walked over to the nest, picked out another cheeping innocent, and aimed it at the sun. It arced over the roof. It dropped like a rock.

"Boy, Josh," said Stan's voice, "it's a good thing

those are just little stuffed animals. And we appreciate the demonstration on how a bird just isn't born flying, it has to learn it from Mom and Dad—" We were back to the studio now, Stan making frantic throat-cutting gestures to someone in the wings. Then he straightened up and grinned mercilessly. "We'll check back with Josh as soon as the mommy and daddy come back. But first, these important—"

"I'm going to fly," said Josh's disembodied voice. Then his face was back on screen. "It's about time I learned."

His face was slack and his eyes were flat, and I knew he was absolutely serious. He was going to fly. I was out the door and on my scooter in a minute. If Mel called after me, I didn't hear.

The police had blocked off the street by the time I arrived. Channel 11 was just setting up, and channel 4 was already swiveling its cameras up at Josh, swaying on the lip of the building fifty stories above. I couldn't get close. Police were setting up barricades on the sidewalk, shooing away the morbid. Entrance was likewise banned into the City Center shopping mall below the building. If Josh dived off the roof on this side, he'd go through the atrium, and no one wanted shoppers to end their excursion with the memory of that. I tried using my press badge at each of the entrances and got nowhere; the reputation of the *Metropole* had preceded me. But I knew another way into the building via the parking ramp and snuck into the mall by an elevator. Once inside I found some TV cameramen setting up in case Josh belly flopped this away. I stood nearby, press card in hand, wishing to hell I had a hatband to stick it in.

And wishing Josh would sober up and come down. This was stupid. This was wrong. This was probably going to happen.

Henk, stood a few yards away, madly scribbling on his notepad. He looked up, spotted me, and strode over. He looked at me hard for a second, then said, "You get a letter, too?" I nodded, waiting for the full flame in the face. Didn't come. "What a sack of bullshit," he said. "Or so I'm assuming." He gave me an appraising look, then shrugged. "Although who knows?"

"Who knows?" I said.

"Well, we'll talk," said Henk. He walked away. I overheard a cameraman trying to lay a bet on Josh's trajectory with the soundman, who gave him a ferocious glare in return, although whether from distaste or from having his levels ruined I couldn't say.

There was a monitor set up, tuned to Josh. He wasn't saying much, just pacing the rim of the building, occasionally looking over at the scene below, panning over to nearby office buildings, where you could see people at every other window, faces pressed to the glass. Then the picture jerked violently and half the press people swore, but it turned out to be Josh looking up at a helicopter thrashing overhead.

Then he spoke: low and calm and dead sober.

"I won't say anything stupid here, for a change. None of you drove me to this. This job pays $42,350 plus benefits, with a liberal vacation policy and medical-dental for my wife, if I had one. I am lucky to have this job, I suppose. I am not good at it, though. I'm not the right kind of stupid. But that's irrelevant. I'm doing this for personal reasons. Nothing more. Please continue to watch and enjoy the fine programming on KJGO TV and KTOK AM 1510. I'm Josh Carlton, and I thank you. I'm going to plug into my VCRs here, and I hope you enjoy the view."

The picture wavered, cut out, then flickered back in.

"Oh, Jesus," the cameraman groaned. "He's still hot. How long a cord does he have on that thing."

"Fifty feet," someone called, "if that."

I couldn't see him from where we stood. We were under a balcony by the ground-floor bookstore, and police forbade us to step out and gaze up. So we watched the monitors. Josh, expressionless. Josh, the skyline level at his back. Josh, eyes cast down, then closed.

The world wheeled around in the background, as though the building had thrown itself backward. Then the sky poured over the screen and smothered all. We saw the side of the building spin by, rough beige aggregate, windows with faces flashing past, Josh in the center of the picture, shouting something. The wind whipped his words to shreds and nothing could be made out. Then the picture jerked up and the screen went black.

"Cord's pulled," said the cameraman.

It would have been better somehow if there had been silence. No one was speaking, no one was moving, but the Muzak, of course, played on, the B-52s, I think.

Then the horrible cymbal crash from above as he hit the atrium roof. Glass rained down and a dull sack streaked past, snagged on one of the banners hanging from the roof, ripping it from its mooring and smashing into the ground with the flat wet slap of a kicked pumpkin. Josh was fifteen, twenty feet in front of us. Something splashed up and I went down on my knees, gorge bolting. But I couldn't look away. No one could.

A red thing in a white shirt. Twisted metal tubes strewn around the head of the stain, one piece of tubing skidding across the marble floor. The banner fluttered down with theatrical grace and settled on the ground. It missed the body altogether.

I stayed at the scene for the next five hours. It took two to identify, isolate, and collect the various portions of Josh Carlton distributed about the shopping mall. It was a wretched and grisly affair, the low point hearing a man on the roof who was examining the hole in the glass ceiling lean down and shout "Got hair here." The rest of them on the ground were marking off the Rorschach blot of Josh with adhesive tape. From the third floor I had a full view of the impact pattern. There were little circles of adhesive tape fifty feet from the body, like a connect-the-dots picture. I had called the *Metropole* and had them send Sol the photographer down and learned he had been on the spot before me. Fikes had been ecstatic I was there. Now I was acting like a journalist! Had I got splattered? I said I had and he sighed with gratitude and hung up.

Eventually the police let the reporters get close to the mess and take notes. I stood there feeling green, knees quavering. When they pulled back the sheet and I saw that pat of jam that used to be . . . I turned and, perhaps in tribute to the last time I saw Josh, geysered my revulsion all over the floor of the mall. I staggered off to the bathroom and, when I returned, saw a policeman solemnly putting a circle of tape around my mess. I sat in a corner and took notes for the next few hours. The Muzak never quit, incidentally. Got positively jaunty toward the end.

When I left, Henk was up on the atrium roof, poking at some samples not yet scraped and bagged by the police. Such a thorough man. I took the parking ramp stairs to my scooter, regretting my own lack of rigorous reporting. Henk's piece tomorrow would be as dry as cigarettes in the back of a drawer, but it would have all the facts. My article would be lively and gaseous. Maybe we could be put together into a particle accelerator and combined at high speed into a decent journalist. Better yet, have him stand in the street and let me aim my scooter at him.

My scooter!

I stood there in the ramp, heart thumping anew. I found my scooter on its side, storage compartment flapping open. Goddammit all to stinking bubbling sulfurous hell! Someone had punched through the lock on the compartment, took nothing, as there was nothing to take. They had also punched out the windows of the cars on either side. Of course, what better time to rob than when the police were occupied topside on spatula duty? I set the scooter upright, with dark hateful thoughts of the city's riffraff and mentally sat each down in the electric chair and turned on the juice. The engine whined to life.

The seat would not go down completely, so I had to ride poised like someone crouched on a high-dive board. Jesus, what a day. Drown it in Clan Anderson, bury it with ice, shovel it over, say some Latin, and send it away for good.

I took Sixth Street through deserted downtown streets. This was the best time to scooter around downtown, and it restored a measure of peace to my heart. I looked up at the Norwest Tower just as the rooftop floodlights kicked in and got that feeling, common to my first year in the city but, oh, so rare as I got older: that things were occasionally arranged entirely for my benefit.

I should have been paying attention to my rearview mirror, of course. As it was I only saw the van with MEAT written backward the final few seconds before it hit me from behind. Not too hard. Not too fast. The baby bear of collisions. But I flew off the bike, helmet banging hard on the ground, sparks and flowers springing up before my eyes. I skidded a few yards and came to rest in a gutter. I heard tires screech, and the van pulled up to where I lay. A door slammed shut. I saw someone set my scooter upright, which did not exactly seem to be the first order of business. Then a face was staring down at me. It was Spiderman. A super hero had hit me. I expected him to pick me up and take us via web slinging to Dr. Phranjari's house, but no. The masked man briskly set about going through my pockets. From my back pocket he pulled the letter I hadn't yet opened from Josh Carlton.

"Ah," said Spiderman in a muffled voice. "You wonderful, inattentive little dick, you."

Spidey had a Mohawk.

He left, and the van went away, and I laid there for a while. Nothing appeared broken. My limbs reacted to my signals like radiator pipes on the first day of cold weather, all angry clanks and hisses. After a while, I sat up. Dusk had passed and the sky was black. Spiderman's mask lay next to me on the street, empty eyes staring up at the dark. A car passed, and the breeze made the mask dance away. I laid back down in the gutter, disappointed.

When I was a kid, Spidey was my hero.

Melodya

1

You TRY CARRYING A COFFIN WHEN YOU HAVE TO WALK with a cane. The only other chap from the station shuffling alongside the old wooden overcoat was that Dagler fellow. The rest of the pallbearers were funeral home professionals who, from their expressions, charged extra for bereavement.

If I looked choked up, I was. My leg was killing me. I had broken nothing in my tumble to the ground, but I'd be hobbling around with a cane for the next week. I would have made an excellent riddle for the Sphinx to pose Oedipus: What walks on four legs, then two, then four wheels, then six (the walker phase, remember), then two, then three? That idiot over there. The one pretending to help out as the coffin is taken from the car and borne to the ground. The one who sat through the funeral twisting his program, alternately feeling dreadful for not being nicer to Josh and feeling angry for not slamming the door the moment he started pretending we were friends. Just because we'd shared a bullet. Man watched too many old war movies.

Recrimination got the best of the match, as it usually does with me. Well, he was dead and that was that.

It was like every other funeral I'd attended, a musty snuffling affair that made me nauseated with dread, that shiny oak slab set on a pedestal like yet another Warhol print at an auction house. The preacher gave a gaseous eulogy so broad and ecumenical you couldn't figure out if Josh was going to be reunited with God, the Great Spirit, solar wind, or one of Newton's laws of physics.

After the burial, I winced my way onto my scooter and drove downtown to the New French Bar. A pretentious place, but with my favorite pretensions. White walls and Billie Holliday on the speakers. In the old days you could see from its windows the northern part of the old warehouse district, back before it all started to get cute. There used to be a sign on a furniture showroom that blinked the time and temperature. It had fallen dark a few years ago. Perhaps we should have thanked it from time to time. Beyond, the dark stocky warehouses as yet unrenovated, dreaming like bears with full stomachs.

Then up went the parking ramps, and now you can't see anything. Says the crank. Says the old-timer at the New French bar. I had a big frosty scotch and was unhappily smearing garlicky mayo on a piece of bread, looking around the room at the chattering idiotic multitude. I ordered another, drank it with no joy, and realized at this rate I would soon be drunk. I considered a cab ride, but in Minneapolis that practically requires two-week advance notice. A walk, then, to clear the head. I tottered up to Hennepin, past a shuttered little hut that had belonged to a hamburger chain, White Castle or White Tower or White Hovel or Cairn or White Casket, couldn't recall. Then I saw the strip joint where I'd watched a friend of mine choke to death on a poisoned brownie, given to him, innocently enough, by me. I looked at it blearily, wondering what page in *Dead Bread* that scene was on. Before or after the Many True Photos?

The strip bar was empty, the booths filled with half a dozen wattled old spuds, the lights of the stage winking on the beads of sweat on their heads. The same bartender who'd been there the night I'd killed my friend was still standing in the same spot, punishing the same glass with the same filthy rag. No, a different rag. This one was a lighter shade of gray.

I took a seat at the bar and ordered coffee. The bartender said there was a two-drink minimum, so I told him to pour two shots in a coffee cup, dump it down the drain, and refill it with coffee.

"You've seen *Five Easy Pieces* too many times, brother," he said. "Why don't I just charge you for two drinks and give you the coffee. I don't want to pour this stuff down the drain. It's hard on the pipes."

I drank the coffee and watched the stripper.

"You're hitting it pretty hard," said the bartender, nodding at my empty coffee cup. "Another?" I nodded and he filled the cup. "Ten dollars."

"Now, wait a minute."

"Just kidding," he said, but at that moment I didn't care. I was looking over his shoulder at the photographs on the wall. There were various faded celebrity pictures, most in bad checked jackets, leering a la Vegas at the camera. But one photo was more recent and familiar. I pointed to it.

"I was at his funeral today," I said.

"Dean Martin died?" said the bartender, aghast.

"No, to the left of Dean, him."

"Josh Carlton?" Instant frost. "No kiddin'. Friend of his?"

"Sort of. I was with him when he was shot."

"Shot? I heard he did the big dive off the Multifoods over there."

"He did. But before that he got shot. One of the bullets hit me. It was in all the papers."

"Oh, that." He looked at the glass he was drying, decided perhaps that the fingerprints might be needed for evidence, and put it down. "How was the funeral?"

"Sad. Did he come here a lot? I remember once the radio station called him on the air and he was at some strip joint."

"Didn't happen here. He hadn't been around for a long time. In fact he wasn't allowed. Got attached to a dancer, a big blonde named Anna. And I mean a real blonde. You could check for roots if you know what I mean. Now, I don't mind guys hooting and hollering but jumping on stage to examine the merch is not in the house rules. Eighty-sixed him. Still, he was a funny guy when he had a few in him." This said with no love.

The conversation lapsed. I went back to enjoying the show, and the bartender picked up the glass and resumed rubbing, presumably to a razor-sharp edge. After a while I went and sat down at the Table, faced the wall, just as I had that night.

I couldn't look down at the floor, couldn't. I took my coffee cup to the bar and traded it in for a scotch. Returned to the Table.

I drank off the scotch, looked at the floor.

There were little bits of tape. A line here. Semicircle there. Dirty brown, beaten into the linoleum.

The police had outlined my friend's body with tape, procedure in a homicide. The management had never removed it—just let it be worn away by feet and chair legs. I stared disbelieving, eyes tearing—surely that little curve described the swell of his gut, that line over there his arm. I stood and knocked my chair over, fell on my knees, and started scraping it from the floor. I had half an inch of filthy sticky tape in my hands when the bartender appeared over me, tapping a foot and motioning at the door. I walked out with bits of a dead man's last silhouette under my nails. Josh's ghost smiled at me from the bar as I left.

I stood outside the Rumley building, swaying, full of dark plans and ocher grudges. Something had been gnawing at me for a week, something I couldn't kick under the rug. It was the look that flowed between Melodya and Carlton the night he barged up to the office. *Do you know him? Only professionally.* Josh Carlton did not strike me as a man in need of a high-rise office suite, which is what Mel sold.

It all made for a good excuse to demand Melodya's company again. I'd called her apartment, had her paged at the gym, hadn't found her anywhere. Granted, this did not cover all the possibilities: She could have been at some lingerie store in Southdale wriggling into something small and pink. Atop the Rumley building, I saw lights in the skinheads' suite.

A strange shimmering light played across the blocks —either the videowall was on, displaying some bizarre effect, or the janitors were amusing themselves by opening up gateways to Lovecraftian dimensions, and I would find giant, evil worms oozing throughout the suite. I doubted any of the skinheads would be there; they were probably down at the Boomerang for Wet Hairshirt Night or Nipple-Ring Night or whatever sort of self-flagellation was popular this week. I went in. Judging from Josh's Christmas visit, the security guard's job seemed not to prevent intruders, but rather to let them know they had a friend in this cold, hard world. He gave me a wave of his hand without looking up. I took the elevator, studying the crease in the door.

Voices fencing in fast dispute sounded from behind the door. I heard Melodya, aggravated and tired. The other voice was somewhat less familiar. Still, I knew that high, nervy sound: petulant and condescending, a child who can prove through calculus why he is entitled to the ice cream. Henk.

I knocked. Melodya swore. Her shoes clacked across the floor. I'm guessing they were hers. Henk didn't seem the sort for high heels. The door flew open, and there was that perfect Slavic face, hard and dark.

"Ah, you." She stepped back and waved me in. "Great. Fine. Perfect. Well, come on." She turned and walked into the reception room and dropped onto a sofa.

Static played on the videowall. She wore her black dress; a red wig sat in another chair like a fox pelt. The light from the TV played on her bald head. For a second it seemed her skull was opaque, and I could see her thoughts.

Henk stood in a corner of the room, hands folded tight across his chest, red hair swirling as though he had been expelled from a frozen dessert machine.

I picked up the wig, put it on the sofa, and sat down. "Just out for a walk."

"A stagger more like," said Henk. "I can smell you from here."

"It's been a hard day, Henk. Had pallbearer duty at Carlton's funeral."

"Hardly qualifies as heavy lifting." He looked away.

"Didn't see you at the funeral." I lit a cigarette and leaned back.

"How was it?"

"At least the casket was closed."

Henk barked a bitter laugh. "They could have put Josh in an envelope and mailed him to the cemetery."

"So much for speaking ill of the dead."

"What does he expect? Does a grand Knievel off the goddamn roof. It's his own stupid fault he's dead."

"I don't think you're exactly the expert on Josh Carlton," I snapped. "I spent some time with the guy, and he was troubled about something."

"And when will we see your brilliant take on Mr. Carlton?" Henk sneered.

"Top of the hour," cried a tinny voice in the next room.

"Pay no attention to the silicon chip behind the curtain," Mel said. "That's just Ludwig's computer. He has it rigged to call out the time."

But Henk was paying attention. His eyes grew wide, and he stared at Melodya. "The computer is here?"

I had walked into something odd.

Henk hurried to the computer room. Mel growled and got up to follow. I stamped along behind.

"This one?" said Henk, pointing to a Macintosh. Mel nodded. Henk sat down and hit a key. The screen displayed a row of gray folders: SCRIBBLE, PHRAK, OBVIOUS.

"What's this?" said Henk, pointing to OBVIOUS.

"Never you mind," Mel said. She ran a hand over her head. "Probably empty anyway. You shouldn't do this. They'll be back any time now."

Henk clicked on the folder, and it sprang open. There was a file sitting in the folder, a colorful icon of a book with the name T written beneath it in tiny script.

"Is that what you were talking about?" Henk demanded. "Is it?"

Mel looked at me and shook her head. "Henk," she said with great patience, "please."

"Give me a disc. I want to copy this."

"You can't. I don't know who it belongs to. You can't just—"

"Give me a disc."

"Henk," I said, "if Melodya doesn't—"

"Simpson? Shut up. You might not recognize it, but this is actual journalism at work. Mel, give me a disc."

She sighed and moved over to an adjacent table where computer supplies sat piled. I watched her legs, how they moved. One moved gracefully beneath the table, extended a toe, and hit a switch on an outlet strip. *Click!* The computer screen collapsed to a single white point, then winked out. By the time Henk had spun around, already in full combustion, Mel had reached around the back of a putty-colored box on the table and yanked out some cords. She held the box in her hands.

"Okay, now go. All right? I can drop this now, and the heads aren't parked, okay? Which means the needle that reads the file is swinging as loose as your dick in those silly boxer shorts your wife likes you to wear. Press the issue further, and I drop it. Data gone to data afterlife. Now please go home."

Silence. An entire minute of charged mute fury, the monitors in the next room hissing their melody of static.

"Fine. Keep it." He stood. "I think I have a pretty good idea what's on that disc. Expect a subpoena."

Henk slammed the door with the vigor of someone who thinks people are impressed, if not swayed to a previously unthinkable course of action, by the decibel level you can attain through the immature abuse of hinges and frames.

Melodya watched him go with her chin high, eyes blazing. Then she started to cry. She put the disc drive down with great care and sat down, wrapped her arms around my waist, and sobbed.

"Get me out of here," she said. "Take me with you." She looked up, cheeks wet. "Don't ask any questions."

"What questions?" I asked.

"Shut up." Melodya daubed at her eyes with the sleeve of her sweater. "Do you have a spare room?"

"I have twelve spare rooms. What's going on here? Why is everyone telling me to shut up and do something?"

"It's complicated."

"Good. I'd like to think that the decision to make me shut up is one not easily reached."

"You talk too much." Her tears ceased. "All right, I'll show you what I can. Then we get out of here, and I get to live with you for a while. Is that okay? Please?"

I tightened my grip on my grip on my cane and tapped it on the floor as if thinking. I was actually trying to will away an erection grand enough to moor airships on. "Okay," I finally said. "But only for a while." She nodded. I wondered where I could get the mortar and bricks to seal up the house once we were inside together.

They could airdrop food and wine down the chimney.

"Don't worry," she said. We were at the computer, drinking coffee. Mel had just finished plugging the disc drive back into the Macintosh. The tears and drama were over now. "Everyone is out at the Boomerang for a while. Warheads reunion concert tonight. They'll be there till closing."

"And then go to Embers for an evening of sneering at everyone else not sweaty and tattooed," I said. "I know the drill."

"That's my boys. Watch this." She turned on the

computer. "I was going to work on something a few hours ago—"

"What?" I said.

"Very bad poetry. Don't ask to see it because I know you like me and you'd feel compelled to lie about how interesting you find it."

"Let me read it."

"No."

"If it's that bad, I probably won't like you anymore, so I won't lie."

"Bullshit. You'd praise a limerick for its innovative form if it meant you could sleep with me."

"Not true. Would you like to hear my haiku? It's about intellectually precocious women who don't even allow a guy the possibility of hope but prefer to poke them in the nuts with a sharp stick."

"Too many syllables. Okay, so I turn on the computer. I go to open my folder, SCRIBBLE. But I'm kinda bad with the mouse, and I open OBVIOUS by mistake. I see this." She opened the folder and revealed the same file we'd seen before: T.

"It's a little book," I said. "Meaning what?"

"That little picture tells you what kind of program it is. This is something called Notebook. You can dump anything in it—pictures, text, noises, whatever you want. Like a scrapbook except your kids probably won't be able to look through it because by then this computer will be obsolete ten times over. Anyway, it's handy. Let's take a look at what is in this volume, eh?"

Melodya clicked on the little book. The screen blinked, and the disc drive gnawed at itself. Then a picture came on the screen.

"That's—that's—that's—"

"That's before you were shot."

Josh and I stood on the steps of KTOK, unlit cigarettes in both our hands. It was a grainy picture, with a white line running along its bottom.

"The line's video static. This was taken from a camcorder." Her hands, I noticed, shook slightly. "Give me a cigarette." I gave her one. "Note the angle."

The photo's vantage point was not that of someone high on a tower. It was taken by someone who had to look *up* to get the picture.

They were in a ditch across the road from the station.

"Act now and you get much, much, more." Her fingers flew across the keyboard, a movement as quick as an owl plucking prey from the forest. Mel gave me a grisly slideshow: the exploding sign, Josh getting hit, knocking me over. It looked like war footage: fallen comrade, smoke, and blood.

"Where the hell did this come from?" I said.

"From someone with a nice, fancy computer. It takes a lot of tips to pay for a video board, and that's what made this." She tapped a long, pink fingernail on the screen. "Someone hooked their camcorder up to their computer, made a digital copy, and—here's my guess—shipped it into this computer here over the phone lines."

"How do you know it wasn't Lud or Stig?"

"I don't."

We sat for a minute and worried that one down to the nub.

"But I don't think it was them," she said. "If they had pictures like this, I don't think they'd leave them where I could so easily find them. I mean, this might as well be left on the coffee table. Besides, I did a check on the file info"—*tap, tap, tap, tap*—"and the file was created at 8:04 P.M. tonight. The guys have probably been gone all night. I think this came in over the phone, if what I—" She was interrupted by a high whistling sound from the computer, sort of a mechanized attempt at lechery, followed by a burst of static that sounded like a rainstorm in a tin cup. The noise computers made when they talked to one another over phone lines. Someone was calling in.

"Well, well," said Melodya said. Laughed once. "What timing. Just what I was talking about. The guys have a bulletin board for professional architects, people swapping preliminary designs, badmouthing other buildings, that sort of thing. This could be someone calling it. Or it could be *him.*"

"Who?"

"Whoever sent the dark and foreboding T."

"We can watch what they're doing, can't we?"

Pink fingernails clattered over the keys, and the bulletin board program filled the screen.

CONNECT 9600, the screen said and typed, THIS BOARD IS INVITATION ONLY. PLEASE ENTER YOUR NAME.

O, someone typed, then slowly: B V I O S.

SORRY NO RECORD OF OBVIOS. TRY AGAIN?

O B V I U O S.

SORRY NO RECORD OF OBVIUOS. TRY AGAIN?

"Bad shot, bad speller," I said. "A pattern is starting to emerge."

"They get three chances," said Mel, and the hands on the other end of the phone line were trying again. O B V I—

Come on, I thought, *O U S. You can do it.*

O U S

WELCOME OBVIOUS. PASSWORD?

"I hope it's not Nebuchednezzar," Mel said.

XXXXXXXXXXX

"It's masked on this end," said Mel. "Damn." She held out her hand, fingers V'd for a cigarette. They were trembling slightly again.

LOG-ON SUCCESSFUL. WELCOME TO RIGOR MORTICE, THE RUMLEY BOYS' BULLETIN BOARD FOR ARCHITECTS AND DESIGNERS. WHAT NOW?

A) GO TO FILES

B) GO TO DISCUSSION

C) GO TO MAIL

The hand on the other end typed A. Mel lit her cigarette, sucking deep.

WELCOME TO THE FILES. WHAT NOW?

A) LIST FILES

B) UPLOAD FILE

C) DELETE FILE

The hand typed C, for delete. I stiffened. Another menu duly rolled down the screen.

DELETE PRIVILEGE LIMITED TO SYSTEM AIDES. IF YOU ARE NOT AN AIDE, FORGET ABOUT IT, PAL. ENTER Q TO EXIT TO MAIN FILE MENU OR <CR> TO CONTINUE.

"Make or break time," said Mel. CR, I knew, was carriage return.

The screen scrolled up one line. CR it was.

NAME OF FILE TO DELETE? it said. Mel stared at the screen, cigarette smoldering, forgotten between her long fingers.

T, the hand typed.

"Stop it!" I said. "Turn it off!"

"No. I made a copy. If we turn it off, he'll know we're watching. Let him go."

The disc drive growled and whined, grinding the magnetized ones and zeros that made up the photo of my shooting into fine atoms. OK! said the screen and presented the same menu: LIST, UPLOAD, DELETE. It was Upload this time.

NAME OF FILE?

T

30298K AVAILABLE. READY TO RECEIVE. Then the disc drive light started flashing with the quick irregular dartings, like the eyelids of someone in REM sleep. "Why is he sending it again?"

"Because," Mel said softly, "he forgot something the first time."

"What? Credits?"

"A way to keep us out."

We sat in silence for exactly three minutes and thirty-two seconds, after which the computer beeped. UPLOAD COMPLETE. XM94+!R% NO CARRIER.

"He's gone."

Melodya exited the bulletin board and went back to the folders. OBVIOUS was empty. She scowled, pulled down a menu, and opened a program called FINDIT and typed T with one peck of a pink fingernail. The computer thought about it for a moment, then beeped: NO MATCHING FILES WERE FOUND.

"Now where in hell did he—*aaah!*" She jerked her hand up and the cigarette, now a smoldering stub, flew in the air.

"Park them in the ashtray from time to time, Mel."

She got up to fetch the butt, burning a mark on the scarred wood floor. "Where did that stupid T file go?"

"It's somewhere. We saw him load it." But that wasn't what bothered me. THIS BOARD IS INVITATION ONLY. DELETE PRIVILEGE LIMITED TO SYSTEM AIDES. Whoever was calling was a person not unacquainted with the Lords of Rumley.

Ludwig lived in a small building by Loring Park half a mile from Lake of the Isles. We parked and buzzed him.

"Speak your piece," said Lud's voice on the intercom.

"Jonathan and Mel. Let us up, Lud."

"But of course. You two haven't been having sex, have you?"

"Since dawn," Mel said. "Who cares? Let us up."

"Promise you won't be all happy and glowing."

"Don't worry," I said a bit too churlishly. The buzzer sounded.

Ludwig opened the door with a vast and insincere smile and waved us into his apartment. Bare walls, black metal furniture. "To what do I owe the pleasure and at what interest rate? Let me offer you a chair." He kicked the wall hard. It swung inward, and a musty-smelling Murphy bed swung out and fell to the floor with a crash. Black sheets.

"I'll make cocktails. I'm hiding out this week. I didn't expect company."

"Hiding from who?" Mel said.

"From you," he said from the kitchen. "Whiskey all around?" He appeared in a minute with drinks, each in a glass decorated with cartoon characters. "Is this a social visit or are we here to worry about odd pictures appearing on the bulletin board?"

"You've seen them," I said.

"I see everything. Your drink all right, Jonathan? That's spring water in the ice cubes. You'll have a purer, *cleaner* hangover tomorrow." He took a steep draught of whiskey. "And what of the pictures?"

"Someone who knows you," Mel said slowly, "took them. Or at least put them into the computer. Neither of us think it's you."

"Well, aren't you the trusting idiots then?" He gave a wan smile.

"I know you, Lud. There's no way you'd have anything to do with shooting anyone."

"Thank you for your faith." He took another sip, not as large. "You're right, of course, I have nothing to do with this, whatsoever it might be. I was up at the office today when that file came in. It had no name aside from T, which made me curious. And it was absolutely huge, which made me doubly piqued. You know, there are bad folk out there who amuse themselves by uploading huge piles of garbage just to tie up your system and eat up your drive space. So I opened the file as it came in. Frightened me to death and back again, I needn't tell you. I think, what little, wormy fellow has snuck into my system and dropped off pictures of senseless violence? So I go into the system myself and see who owns this account. There's nothing there, my friends. The files only say the account has complete system privileges; it doesn't say who set it up or when. I didn't set it up, and you don't know how to. Which leaves Stig or Philip or one of a hundred hackers with a devil dialer. But then, thinks I: *We all meet Mr. Simpson, tragic gunfire victim, and a few months later, pictures of his little drama come gushing into our computer.* Coincidence? Fate? Cloudy, as the ball says; try later." He gave me a furtive look.

Mel stood and took the glass from Ludwig's hand. "You're coming home with us. Jonathan has plenty of room, and I need your help. I klepted copies of the files, Lud. Maybe they're full of mystery files I can't get at it."

"There's more?" he said, dismayed.

"That's what we have to find out."

Ludwig stared at Mel, then glanced at me. "You're not going to act happy with him, are you?"

"I promise."

"See that you don't." And he smiled at her with love.

2

"WHY? I'M SURE I CAN'T TELL YOU," LUDWIG SNIFFED. "Us boys are generally obtuse about things. On those odd moments when we have happened to share a moment of personal revelation or two, the rationale for shooting a minor media figure never came up." He peered at the computer screen. "We'll know more in a moment."

I'd come home from work to find Mel and Lud

working at the computer, the disc from the skinheads' office sitting atop my dictionary. Hunks of styrofoam like amputated limbs of some inelegant, clumsy animal were scattered around the room. I had a momentary pang of fear. They were both in on it and were busy destroying the incriminating data. But Lud merely looked up, saw me, and waved me over. The drive still worked, he explained. He had been able to get a copy of the T file with a recovery utility and was now dredging up some interesting files we hadn't noticed the night before.

Someone had indeed sent the pictures over the phone lines but had also constructed a program that would hide the file's presence. "It's like putting a book in a library," Lud said, "only the card catalog is written in invisible ink. From what dear Melodya says, your mystery man sent a file without hiding it and remembered his error. Last night he called up, deleted the old file, and inserted a new invisible model. Simple stuff, really. I just want you to know I am certainly not going to explain any of this to any police. Not with my haircut."

"You would look better with a Mohawk," I said.

"That's outré," Lud murmured, staring at the screen. "All right, pay attention, because I don't want you dragging me over every time you get the twitch to crash our precious bulletin board. Right? I'm using—"

"Wait a minute. What if he tries to call in and finds the board is down? Won't he get suspicious?"

"Indeed. Ergo, *la nécessité* of rerouting our computer phone line to your house, which I have done." Ludwig bowed to accept our acclaim.

"You what?" I cried. "Jesus! That's against the law, Ludwig." I remembered a story about some hackers who had amused themselves by redirecting calls to different locations just by changing the code in the phone company's computers. Two of them were now doing community service—teaching computers to high schoolers, as it turns out, probably teaching them all how to bankrupt pizza delivery businesses by sending the calls to the county morgue. *Yeah, I want the meat-lover's special.* "The phone company can trace that sort of stuff. And they'll trace it to my number, not yours!"

Ludwig nodded. "That's true. If I'd hacked it, you would be in trouble. As it was, I used call forwarding. Shows up on my bill every month, so I believe it's legal."

"Oh."

"Anyway. Whoever sent this stuff could have tried to get into the system last night but wouldn't have been able to. That wouldn't necessarily be suspicious. These things crash and hang or shut down for house-cleaning or to powder their nose from time to time. An overnight delay would be naught of importance. Now look. This program here"—Lud tapped the screen, pointing at a tiny icon of a sheeted ghost, arms out in a BOO posture—"this program looks for invisible files on the computer's card catalog. I have gone over this drive sector by sector and found—drumroll if you think it appropriate—these!" He pointed to three little book icons. "And if we examine our first and bestest friend T, we learn it was sent June 1."

"The day Josh Carlton jumped. And the day Spiderman in the meat truck took my letter."

Lud looked at me and lofted an eyebrow. "Spiderman in a meat truck?"

"Didn't you read my story in the *Metropole?* I was coming back from the suicide when I got bumped in the butt by a truck. Knocked me off my scooter. A guy with a Mohawk and a Spiderman mask took a letter Josh Carlton had sent me."

"The man with the Mohawk was driving a meat truck?"

"An old ambulance. It said MEAT in reverse over the grille, so you could read it in your rearview mirror."

Melodya seemed to stifle a laugh. I glanced at her and saw her staring wide-eyed at the floor.

"I didn't tell you that?" I asked her. "I guess no one reads the *Metropole*."

"All very interesting," said Lud, turning back to the screen. "So let's see what *l'homme de* Mohawk has sent us." He clicked on one of the little books, and the screen went black.

PASSWORD? came on the screen.

"Goddamn." Lud sat back, ran his hand over his head. "Let's think."

"It's obvious," croaked Mel. Her voice was so strangled both Lud and I looked to make sure someone wasn't standing there throttling her.

"What is?"

"Obvious."

"Spell it out, okay, sweetness? I can't read your—"

"O-B-V-I-O-U-S."

Lud shrugged and typed OBVIOUS. The computer beeped, did nothing.

"Predictable," Mel said in the same pinched voice.

"What's predict—?"

"Type *predictable!*" she shouted. Ludwig flinched but did as he was told. The computer beeped, did nothing.

"Thoroughly," she said.

Ludwig stared at her until their eyes met. Then he turned around and tapped in THOROUGHLY.

The screen went blank once more. Then OK! came on the screen. The disc drive whirred angrily.

"Wow," said Lud.

"Christ." Mel blanched, clutching the nearby bedpost. I would have gone to help her but I felt weak myself.

On the monitor's screen was a picture of a radio station's marquee. The next picture, taken a second later, showed a different view, a shot of a car with a pole sticking into its door.

"Try the next one," she said in a voice from somewhere over the horizon. Lud called up the next notebook and was greeted with PASSWORD?

"Despicable," said Mel. She was seated on the bed now, one hand gripping the bedpost so tight I expected the post to cry uncle and buy the next round of drinks.

Lud typed, sang tonelessly: "It's obvious, predictable, it's thoroughly despicable, it's—"

OK!

One picture this time: A man wore a trench coat, a microphone at his feet. He had begun to duck, his hands frozen en route to covering his head. Behind him stood four letters that appeared to have been carved from blocks of ice: W Y C. The fourth letter was in the process of blowing up.

No one spoke. Finally Lud turned around and looked at Mel with an expression as sharp as a tattoo needle. Mel looked away.

"Pathetic," they both said.

Lud called up the third file and typed it in at the password request.

A close-up of a billboard for KSTP television news. The S was riddled with small holes. A big red X covered the smiling face of the anchorman.

"How do you know?" I hissed, looking at my feet. "Why do you know the goddamn right words?"

Melodya's jaw quivered. There was mad panic in her eyes. She stood and walked from the room.

"Let her go, Jonathan," Lud said sadly, but I went

after her. She was walking down the stairs with careful poise, one hand gripping the balustrade for support. I put a hand on her shoulder, and she shrugged it off. I walked in front of her, and she pushed me aside.

"Melodya. For God's sake, you've got to tell me—"

"Go away, Jonathan. Forget about it." She looked me up and down. "And get out of my way."

I started to say I wouldn't, but she shoved me aside again. She crossed the main hall, heels clacking on the tile. I persisted. When she reached the door, I grabbed her wrist and pulled. I'd meant to pull her off balance —not difficult when someone's in high heels—but Melodya spun around as though she made her living on high heels, drew back a fist, and slugged me flush on the mouth. It would have hurt more if it hadn't been for the subsequent pain of cracking first my tailbone and then my head on the floor. I heard the door creak open, slam shut. The hallway had assumed the look of a set from a German expressionist movie, towering malevolently above me. Then it decided to behave and assumed its usual posture. I put a hand to my mouth, just to make sure my blood was still red. It was.

Ludwig stood over me.

"Oh, fuck the lot of you," I shouted. "Miserable, bald, stinking, lying bastards." I sat up, the back of my head now a pealing carillon. Something modern, with no melody.

Ludwig looked down at me in silence.

"Listen," he said eventually. "Let's just forget about this, all right? Erase all files, take our numbers out of your Rolodex. I think we've seen enough to know it would be wise to see no more." Ludwig stepped over me and opened the door. "Don't go looking for me, because you won't find me. I plan to become invisible. Well, translucent, more visually interesting." He tipped an invisible hat, winked gravely, and walked out.

He paused at the door.

"I will say this: *Cherchez le* meat." He left.

3

"SIT," SAID DETECTIVE BISHOP. "TELL ME SOMETHING I don't know." He leaned back in his chair, his body like a garbage bag full of tires. A cigar the size of prepackaged cookie dough idled in the ashtray. "I suppose you're going to drop a bomb like, ah, it really is the man with the Mohawk who shot you, and you have proof that one of those baldies you met the other night is mixed up in it. That right?"

"It smells like burned fingernail shavings in here," I said.

"Not for long. I had Mexican for lunch." He took a deep pull on his cigar. "So what vital piece of information have you today? Let me guess. Christ is dead and you suspect the Romans."

I set Mel's disc drive on his desk. "It's a disk drive from a computer," I said. "On it are several pictures of media people getting shot or shot at. Josh Carlton is one of them. Whoever did the shooting probably took those pictures. Plug that in and take a look."

"Plug it into what? Where did you get this?"

"Plug it into a Macintosh computer. As for where I got it, don't worry, I didn't steal it. It was left at my house by its owner. I'm just passing it along with my love and best wishes."

Bishop gave a low whistle.

"So if I read you right, the cueballs had pictures of Carlton getting whacked? And there's other pictures? Of who?"

"I don't know. I figure you know who to give this to. Maybe the FBI or something—if these pictures were taken in other states, it's a federal case."

"Not that they'd tell me," Bishop said bitterly. He picked up his cigar. "They eat cooperation and shit condescension. Thanks for this." He patted the drive. "Give me a leg up. All right, you gave me something, I'll give you something. Only fair. Those skinhead sunzabitches? They give you some line about why they have shaved heads?" I nodded. "Me, too. I say, You're really Hare Krishnas? Show me the fuckin' saffron robes. 'At the cleaners,' they say. Yeah, right."

"I run some pictures through the files, and *whoa,* there they are. Fresh shots, last year. They all got Mohawks. And do you know why I have pictures of them, Mr. Investigative Journalist? Well, about eight months ago all three were picked up in a bar fight. Charged and booked, although charges were later dropped. I remembered a couple of 'em, though, 'cause they slung some lip when they came through the station. Downright disrespectful."

"But they told me they've been bald since college."

"Well, like I say, you're the investigative journalist. If they told you that, then my mug files and fingerprint records must be all balled up." Bishop smiled. "I'll go kick some butts down in records."

"It's because of her," I said, confused. "Melodya. She's bald from a disease, and they're all bald . . . out of, ah, sympathy." It all suddenly seemed very stupid.

"Well, maybe they were wearing toupees that night. Hair Club for Deviates." Bishop squinted at me, ran his tongue around inside his mouth, like someone looking for something in sofa cushions. "I'm going to let you in on a secret if you promise not to tell." I nodded. "No, I mean really. Flap your mouth, and your life will become one long series of random traffic stops and Breathalyzer tests, okay? I'm serious."

I nodded and looked appropriately worried.

"Because I need you to do something for me. You ever get up to that skinhead place?" I said I had occasion to visit. "Next time you're up there, go prowl around in the bathroom. You find any bleach, peroxide, or anything else that would lighten hair color, tell me."

"Why?"

"This is the part you don't mention. The guy with the Mohawk that Peter Byrne kept yammering about? He had a white stripe down the middle of it. That's not something we've let on about. One of those little details we like keeping to ourselves."

"So you can weed out all the people with Mohawks who show up and want to confess."

"There've been a few. Now, do that for me and I will actually start to like you again *and* give you more information. You will be so in my debt you'll dedicate your next book to me."

"What makes you think I'm writing a book about this?"

Bishop barked a laugh. "You are just remarkably thick," he said. "Don't you wonder why those charges were dropped against the brawling Mohawkers?"

"Well, now that you mention it."

"See, there was this brawl, bunch of 'em teamed up on some guy who was giving them trouble about their hair. After the fight, he said he couldn't identify who punched him. Couldn't tell 'em apart. Had to drop the charges."

"So? That's not particularly dramatic information, Bishop."

"Guy they beat was Josh Carlton." Bishop folded his hands across his stomach. "But then I suppose Queen Baldie already told you that."

* * *

So what other lies have they told me?

I lay outside the Hennepin County Government Building, stretched out on a bench. It was a humid Minnesota summer day, sun hammering down like the world was a nail in a knotty block of wood. The standard procession of grim sweating Swedes staggered past, collars open, mouths agape. A tiny Hmong woman sat on the adjacent bench, accepting the heat with unquestioning compliance. She wore a wide straw hat that looked like a cymbal stolen from a drum kit. She looked comfortable. I imagined every one of the miserable Scandinavians around me in big, flat straw hats and almost laughed. No, a Swede was never happy unless he was keeping some tidy misery to himself. The Hmong woman couldn't have given that hat away.

Had Mel lied, too?

I wore my standard summer garb: shorts, tank top, big blousy shirt, sneakers. Since I so rarely showed up at the paper, there was no need for grown-up clothing. I peeled off my shirt, felt the warm wood of the bench on my back. *I am thirty-five,* I thought, *and I have a tan that says "waiter with a night shift."* Maybe life was all right.

I watched a jet fly high above, etching a groove in the sky. There were no clouds, nothing to see save the feathery trail of steam and haste. I watched the wind nibble indifferently at the line, pull it apart.

Had she been lying to me when we did all that kissing?

I closed my eyes. A breeze picked up water from the fountain and cast a mist over my body, making me shiver with gratitude. I decided to stay on that bench for the rest of my life. Nothing would ever happen, nothing but the small incidental gestures of the world. It would be a safe place. I could get a portable computer and send in my stories from this bench. I could use a cellular phone to order meals. And my tan would be George Hamiltonesque.

It's one of them sending in pictures by portable, I realized. Out there, armed with a gun and a modem. I could see the headline now: Information Super-highwaymen.

It was all clear, except for two minor details: who and why? Other than that, damn! I had this down.

4

DOUG GORDON, FORMER HIGH SCHOOL FOOTBALL HERO, local television reporter, and all-around pride of Blue Earth, Minnesota, was shot right in the call letters. The bullet entered in the *E,* right above the word *LIVE* superimposed on his image, and exited off camera, according to my sources. That's the kind of ear-to-the-ground journalist I am. I have a network of sources deployed around town, all of which conveniently report over the television at six o'clock every day.

Back to business. Fikes summoned me and yelled some simple instructions: Go there.

"Can I stay overnight?" I love motels.

"Take out a mortgage and settle down for all I care. Just give me something I don't read in the dailies. And don't make it up for once. Despite what you believe, I am not running a short-story periodical."

"I like to think of them as essays."

"Mrrrrghgmhm," he responded.

I left for Blue Earth the next day, Lake Street to Highway 169. Half an hour out of town, the road pared itself down to two thin lanes, each with a thin, unpaved shoulder. Flat, treeless farmland flowed over the horizon. I rolled down the window and breathed in the sweet thick scent of the crops.

This was a mess. Nothing but bit players, everybody speaking lines from a play different than the one I was watching. Everybody seemed connected. I wouldn't be surprised if I talked to my parents and heard that they hired Henk to trim their shrubs and that he'd brought Ludwig along to sharpen his blades.

I talked out loud, taking it one person at a time.

Melodya. Sister of Henk. No, that would be too tidy: half sister. She's bald and good-looking, A-Number One fun in the sun, more so after dark, open and friendly until the day when she gives out passwords for secret files, then goes frigid, decks me, and disappears. Knows plenty.

Peter Byrne. Textbook loner and loser. Elisha Cook Jr. would have played him in the movies. Arrested for shooting Josh Carlton, he is bailed out and escapes by waving an electric carving knife given to him by—

Henk Gruesse. Half brudder of Melodya. Bad feature writer doing a yeoman's job of running circles around me on this story and probably using the material for another of his execrable true-crime books.

The Rumley Boys. Skinheads with a lot of money, an apparently thriving architecture/design firm, and no good reason to be skinheads. Said they all shaved their heads in homage to Melodya, who is naturally bald, but according to the police, they had Mohawks last year. Which might make one of them:

The Man with a Mohawk. The person Peter Byrne said shot Josh. I suspect Byrne is right about this since Byrne couldn't figure out which end of a pencil to use without written instructions. The MWTM (Man with et cetera) could be one of the Rumley Boys, although Bishop said he had a skunkish white streak in his Mohawk. Or he could be a friend of theirs. Probably the latter: Whoever has been taking those pictures, and presumably doing the shooting, has been out of town for a long while, and the boys were pretty much present and accounted for. I'd inquired about Stig, and he was showing up nightly at his dishwashing job.

Unless they worked their collective crimes in shifts.

Finally: Josh Carlton. The one part of this story bricked up and mortared over. If he lied about how he met the skinheads, God knew what else he lied about. My guess: He knew something, and someone tried to kill him for it. The old standard.

So why didn't he say so when he survived the first attack? Why keep quiet and kill himself? And who the hell knows what was in that letter.

It all needed someone to bring it all together. Well, there was me. *Of course! I was the common link! It was I that was guilty!* If only. At least I might able to figure out my motives.

Well, it was in the hands of the police now. I'd write the piece on the Blue Earth shooting and return to the smooth, glossy boredom that had characterized my life before this mess. How I wanted life to be boring again. (Maybe slightly more exciting than my coma, though.)

Why so much happened to someone with so few ambitions was a mystery I'd solve after this one. When I got around to it.

I had checked in at a motel by the interstate, a place that sat in the shadow of a sixty-foot-tall statue of the Jolly Green Giant. The giant, dressed entirely in vegetation, looked north, hands on his hips, laughing, as though he could see Canada from here and found it unaccountably amusing. The statue was erected years ago to honor the corporate symbol of the town's largest employer, but it looked like a pagan worship site or something built to scare away lesser green men.

The motel advertised itself as the World's Only Hand-Painted Motel. Don't ask. Retired couple. Time on their hands. A mural of Scandinavian history that stretched the length of the hallway, with a bloody Viking battle taking place around my door.

"That's the berserkers there," said the old man as he showed me to my room. "See, when they got good and fired up, they'd light their beards on fire and run into town. Scare hell out of folks."

"There seems no dearth of berserkers in Norse history," I said, looking down the hall.

"They all point you to the fire extinguisher at the end of the hall. In case of fire, follow the berserkers. It's art, but it's practical." He opened the door and admitted me to the Edvard Grieg suite. The mural on the wall showed the composer sitting at a piano, which was incorporated into my headboard. His hands were up as though to strike a ghastly fortissimo chord. I would not sleep tonight.

I drove into town and found the chief of police, a jowly slab of German heartiness. He drove me to the edge of town, then back to the giant.

"See up there, by his bicep?" I looked and saw what appeared to be a bandage. "That's a temporary patch, keep the rain from getting in and rotting him out from the inside."

"He's made of vegetation," I said. "He's been standing in the sun for ten years. I'd think if he was going to rot, he'd have done it by now."

"Ha!" said the policeman. "I like that one. I used to think the same thing. After a couple years of wearing a salad bar for underwear, he ought to be getting a little high. But that's the miracle of Fiberglas. The first bullet entered the statue in the bicep. The second entered the anchorman in the bicep."

"I heard there were three shots."

"Four. The third hit the giant in the forehead. The

fourth hit the giant in the ankle—see?—right by whatever that foot bone is called. If the anchorman had still been standing, he would have caught it right in the head."

"And the shots were fired from—"

"Don't know. Somewhere out there." He gestured at the state of Minnesota all around us. "The angle suggests somewhere to the right by that highway sign, but we can't tell for certain. No one saw anyone. If he was on the highway, we figure he's long gone. You got Montana over there, and Iowa down there. Be easy to just vanish."

"Into trackless Iowa."

"Exactly. Now you're wondering why there was a reporter standing here, right? Good. We had a report of a bomb planted here at the giant and came by to investigate."

"Any idea who called it in?"

"First thought was the Winnebago Chamber of Commerce. They'd love to see this thing blow up. Don't print that, just kidding. No, I had no idea then, but it's in the job description to check up on these matters. TV station must have heard the scanner traffic and came over. Not much news around here, and they get what they can."

"First the giant in the bicep, then the reporter in the bicep," I said. "Would you say that was intentional?"

"Someone was trying to make a point, certainly," said the policeman. "They're both bigger than life, smile a lot, and are totally hollow. If it wasn't a crime, I'd appreciate the symbolism." He smiled. I liked him. I smiled back. The giant smiled down on both of us.

Chet's Place was the smallest bar in the world. There was a mounted squirrel head above the door, next to a horseshoe from a miniature pony. The bar was a foot deep; at one end sat a tiny plastic pinball machine. A row of bottles of the size usually found on airplanes lined the wall behind the bar. The bartender, of course, weighed about eight hundred pounds and probably had to be lowered in by block and tackle. He never moved, didn't have to. Everything in this bar was within reach. He could drive you home without moving.

I ended the night at Chet's, intending to talk to the locals, look over my notes. I wanted to write down everything that had occurred to me in the car and make sense of it.

After I ate.

"Do you have a kitchen?" I asked the bartender. He nodded and jerked a fat thumb at a microwave on a shelf behind him.

"Good. A menu, please."

"Kitchen's closed."

"What do you mean? It's a microwave."

"Kitchen closes at eight."

"It doesn't look closed."

Without taking his eyes off me, he reached over and unplugged the microwave. "Closed."

Fine. I ate seven sacks of peanuts and drank my scotch. Aside from the bartender and a man in a gimme cap (Swenson's Feed Fertilizer and Video), I was alone.

An hour passed in silence. There was no jukebox. A sign over the radio said they'd turn it on for ten minutes for a quarter. Bartender's choice of station.

"Quite a thing about that anchorman getting shot," the man next to me finally said. An hour and a half had elapsed with nary a word passing between us. When I ordered my third scotch, he must have decided I was worthy of conversation. He did not look promising. Glasses thick as manhole covers and one of those fecund untrimmed beards that usually spells an interest in science fiction or ham radio.

"It was a thing all right," I said. I had my notebook on the bar, and I flipped to a fresh page. Reached for my pen. Local color. "I guess people around here are pretty upset."

"You could say that. Don't see much murder here, much less on television. Well, no, actually all the murder we see is on the TV. It's just unique to have someone real get shot. Although I'm not sure a TV reporter qualifies as real, if you know what I mean. He's on TV, and lots of people get shot on TV. So it doesn't really come as a surprise, given the medium and all. But yeah, people were startled. I was."

"So you were watching the evening news, and boom, the guy gets it?"

"No. I was there."

I clicked my ballpoint, unsheathed the point. "Really. Boy, I imagine the newspapers have interviewed you a dozen times over."

"You'd be the first." He nodded at my notebook. "You know, no good ever comes of talking to people with a small notebook. Policemen. Reporters. Insurance men. They all have these small notebooks."

"Lawyers have big legal pads."

"You have a point. But I think that's an ego thing, and that changes the complexion of the matter considerably. Name's Stan Wopzenscriski. Yours?"

I introduced myself, asked him to spell his name.

"Tell you what." He took a sip of his scotch. "You call me back when you've written your story and read me everything that pertains to me. Then I'll spell my name for you. I guarantee you'll get it wrong if you do otherwise."

"Don't you trust me?"

"Can't say I trust everyone who sits next to me for an hour and doesn't say word one."

"You haven't exactly been a bubbling font of conversation."

"Etiquette," he said, sipping. "Don't bother a stranger. He might just have a reason to want to drink in peace."

"That's me. Believe me."

"Oh, well, then I'll leave you be."

"No! I just mean that I have reasons to drink in peace."

"You done being in peace?" I nodded yes. "You sure?" More nods. "Okay. So ask away."

"Tell me it was a man with a Mohawk," I said under my breath, looking down at my notes.

"Oh?" Stan looked surprised. "He did it?"

"What? Don't tell me you—"

"Saw him the day before the shooting. I work up at the Gas 'n' Gullet by the motel. The hand-painted one? It's famous. Anyhow, there was a guy on the self-serv. Had a van, filled it up. I remember him 'cause first off, there aren't many of the Mohawk persuasion this way. Never mind the Indian name of the town."

"Blue Earth is Indian?"

"Well, it's translated."

"What is it in Indian?"

"Something that means blue earth. Anyway, he was just your ordinary off-the-interstate customer, but I noted him for a couple of reasons. One, he used the intercom on the island to ask if I'd come out and take his money. Odd. Two, and this is what I said earlier was my first reason for remembering him, he had this Mohawk. Under a cap. When I was giving him his change, he dropped some coins and bent to pick them up. Hat fell off. A fedora. There's this tidy little

Mohawk, all white in the center. Most unusual thing you'd ever see. Like a skunk was in love with his head."

I was writing furiously. "Why," I said, "do you think he asked you to come out for the money?"

"Can't think of a reason," Stan said. He took a sip of his drink. "Unless, of course, was a fugitive of sorts and didn't want his picture taken by our security camera."

"How would he know you had a camera inside?"

"There is a large sign to that effect posted on the islands."

"What did you say he was driving?"

"A white van. Smoked windows. Couldn't tell you where the plates were from—they were plain black and white, like state government plates. You really think he was in on that shooting?"

"I *know* he was."

"Well, then, we'd best get down to the gas station."

"Why?"

"We tell them about the cameras in the cashier's window," Stan smiled. "We don't tell them about the ones on the island."

"You can't tell anything from this," I said. We were in the back room of the Gas 'n' Gullet, squinting at a video of the Man with a Mohawk.

"You can tell it's him. See—" Stan froze the picture. "There's that curious white stripe there. And you can see the taillights of his vehicle, which spell out F-O-R-D to anyone who knows a thing about taillight profiles. And there are three numbers on his license plate visible."

"Eight—"

"Or three. Could have used mud to change the look of the number."

"And a three—"

"Or eight." He shrugged. "Stands to reason."

"And a zero."

"Or an eight or a three."

"Forget the plates," I sighed. "At least we got a fabulous look at the guy's back. Well, at least it's proof he was here. Can I have a copy of this?"

"Will do. I'll dub one off at home. You staying around tonight?"

"Motel 90."

"Where they put you, the Torvald Sugeruvuld room?"

"Who the hell is he?"

"Called the father of Norwegian meatpacking. You'd know if you were there."

"I got the Grieg room."

"Oh. C major."

"What?"

"I've been in that room. Opening chord of his piano concerto is C major, and I imagine that's what he's preparing to play."

5

BACK IN MINNEAPOLIS THE WOMAN WHO ANSWERED THE phone said, "Uckack." I paused, waiting for her to dislodge the chicken bone she had apparently swallowed before taking my call. "Uckack, hello?" she said. "Hello?"

"Hi. Sorry. I must have the wrong— What did you say this number was? I'm looking for the Uptown Cable Access."

"That's what you got. Uckack."

I looked at the listing in the phone book for Uptown Community Cable Access Center. Uckack, indeed.

"Wouldn't it be better with a soft *c?*" I said. "Like Youssie-sac, maybe."

"We used to do that, but everyone called us U-Suck, so we stopped. Can I *help* you?"

"Yes, Sorry. I'm looking for some tapes of a show. The *Talk of the Town* show?"

"We don't do that one anymore. Sorry."

"I know. I'm just looking for tape of some old shows." I hoped she didn't ask why. Because the tape I wanted, the tape Hitch gave me, was at Henk's house, and I didn't want him to know why I wanted it. Because then they'd look, and they'd see what I dimly remembered seeing. "It's for a piece in the *Metropole,*" I added.

"On a show we don't do anymore? Hold on, let me give you to a producer."

Click. Music. An old 45 by the Clams, an all-female band that used to play the Boomerang before it went utterly skin. I hadn't heard it in a while and was irritated when someone clicked in. "Hello, We-Suck production."

"Ah—I was looking for some back tapes of *Talk of the Town,* and they gave me to you."

"Back tapes? Sure. Any show in particular?"

"It was one where the host did one of those man-on-street things. The word for the week was *Mohawk.*"

There was a pause.

"The word for the week was always *Mohawk.*"

"Oh. I didn't see many shows."

"You can come down and look through the tapes if you want. We're not doing anything this afternoon anyway." I thanked him and said I'd be down.

The cable-access studio was located in a building on the corner of Hennepin and Lake, right across from where they'd taped the shot of Peter Byrne damning Tim for his Mohawkedness, a block up from the

Boomerang. The proximity of these events might be cause for suspicion in, say, New York, but in Minneapolis, these few blocks were the nexus of skin and punkdom and general disaffected youth. It made no sense for them to congregate here. Aside from the Boomerang, the neighborhood was filled with shops that prostrated themselves before the affluent and gorgeously silly. Most of the skins and punks were too young for the bars and were always getting kicked out of the McDonald's up the street, so they sat on the sidewalk scowling at everyone, like Muslims in Vatican City. The punks still wore the florid toxic-rooster hairstyles that were au courant in 1976. They looked as pitiful and dated to me as hippies had fifteen years before. The skins milled around a block down the street, the peaceable ones congregating in the shade of a movie marquee, the rough element glaring at them from across the street. Once a year they all got together to protest some aspect of U.S. foreign policy and would heave a bowling ball through a window and rock a few Saabs. The rest of the time they were good, dutiful anarchists: colorful, powerless, irrelevant.

There were two of them sitting in the entrance of the door that led to UCCAC. I expected to be dunned for spare change, but they nodded and moved aside. I took a creaking flight of stairs, leg aching halfway up, and found the door. Knocked, entered. Inside, a young man in a flannel shirt was talking to the receptionist; he looked up and recognition flickered on his face.

"Johnny Simp," he said. "Right?"

"Simpson." He looked vaguely familiar, sounded familiar. "I was here to look at some old *Talk of the Town* tapes?"

"Sure. I'm the guy you talked to. Bob. We met when you did that *Talk of the Town*, remember? I was the producer."

"Sure." We shook. He was a thin guy in his twenties, limp brown hair with purple tips, the pallor of someone long in the editing booth, wiry fingers. "You should have said it was you. I'd have found that tape in a second. Come on back."

We passed through a narrow hallway, smudged and battered walls painted a sad beige. The place had the quiet, bitter air common to all grudgingly funded public agencies. Halfway down the corridor he opened a door that read ARBEITRON MACH FRIE and motioned me inside. It was an editing suite, with two walls crammed with videocassettes. "D'you like that show you did with us?" he said. "I called to thank you for coming, but you were, y'know, in a coma."

I said I had a fine time but hadn't seen the final product.

"Really? Nooo. Well, let me dupe you off a copy just to be neighborly. Only take a minute."

"Actually, I'm here for something else. I want to take a look at the man-in-the-street tapes. The Mohawk thing. It's for research."

"On Mohawks?"

"Public attitude toward same."

He shrugged. "Whatever. I can give you the highlight reel we did when we got the grant. That's got most of the man-on-the-street stuff. Otherwise you're going to have to sit through about thirty shows." I said I'd start with the highlight reel, and he began to search through the tapes, humming. "Ah." He pulled out a tape and fed it to the machine, gave me a brief course in running it. Then he slid another tape from the shelf and waved it in the air. "This is your show. I'll dupe while you watch that. Yell if you screw anything up or something."

The VCR whirred to life, displayed those color bars that always look like the flag for a country with no sense of style, then went black. The *Talk of the Town* theme song came on—cheesy sing-a-long organ music. A cartoon of P.D. Spaunaugle, grinning, chef's hat at a jaunty angle, appeared in the left-hand corner and moved around jerkily. "He's wonderful! He's marvelous!" sang a woman. I hit the fast-forward button. Ploughed through a dozen interviews, most ending in slapping matches and spittle-flecked exchanges. Then the words VOX POPULI: MOHAWKS. I slowed the tape and waited.

And saw exactly what I expected to see.

"Oh," said Bob when he returned. I had the VCR paused and was staring at the screen. "I can see why you were looking for that. You want a copy? I can add it to your reel here." I said I did, and he inserted a tape in the drive. A few twists of some knobs, and the pictures flowed from one deck to another.

"I notice I'm not on the highlight reel," I said. "I don't mind, but given that our interview ended in more strife than any of these—"

"He was pretty pissed about the tooth getting cracked on the camera," Bob said. "You wouldn't think a guy in a chef's hat would be vain, but he was. Also, I don't think it looked good on the grant proposal. Too much violence, he said."

"Did you get the grant?"

"No." Bob said. "Went to a show about ducks at the Lake of the Isles."

"Well, that's sweet."

"That's what the board thought. We got infrared of ducks doin' the nasty. It's a revisionist approach." He hit a button on the VCR. "Here you go. Sweet dreams." And he winked.

I had planned to go home and pour myself something clear and cold and look at the tape over and over until inspiration flowed from the heavens and splashed in my lap.

I would have done it, too, right then. Would have saved time and a truly gruesome evening. But . . .

Ludwig had not unforwarded his calls. My computer was still pretending to be the bulletin board. I heard the modem whining when I entered the house and found the screen full of angry messages from people trying to download files. I pulled the plug on someone named OMNIPEST and took a look at my drive with Ludwig's magic invisible file program just to see if any more mayhem was sitting on the drive.

There was a Notebook file.

READ ME JS the file was called. I clicked. It opened. A picture.

Melodya.

Sitting with her arms around the man who shot me in the head.

She looked happy. He had a Mohawk with a white stripe. His face was blurred in each picture—and I don't mean the blur you get when someone moves when the shutter is moved. His face had been airbrushed from each picture. Simple trick nowadays. *Be Your Own Stalin!* they ought to say on the software box. *Remove People From History, Obscure Identities to Fit Your Agenda!*

There was a row of books behind Mel and Mr. Mohawk. I took a look at the titles.

How to Convince a Wolverine to Play Shuffleboard by A. Obvious.

Expert's Guide to Identifying Wood-Grained Plastic by A. Pathetic

Finding Veins the Parole Officer Doesn't Know About: A Memoir by Queen Elizabeth, as told to A. Clumsy

And several more, all written in tiny type and pasted on the books on the shelf. The passwords to the files, in other words. Mel had given us the first three; now I had a digitized bookshelf full of passwords.

This was a password key sent directly to me: READ ME JS it was called. Ludwig. Or Melodya. Or Mr. Mohawk, continuing his taunting-maniac routine. All I had to do was wait for the other programs to come in over the phone.

And there were many. Thanks to Lud's rerouting, the board had been up and running while I was in Blue Earth. I had received several requests for access to the board, about twenty-five pieces of loose traffic—conversations, uploads of blueprints—and an angry letter from an architect in San Francisco who demanded to know why no one had replied to his daring critique of Helmut Jahn.

Someone had also uploaded another Notebook file that demanded a password.

I checked the picture again. The next book on the bookshelf after PATHETIC—the last word Mel had given before she decked me and stalked out—was *How to Skydive in Hell* by M.E. Malignant.

PASSWORD?

M A L I G N A N T

OK!

As I figured. Doug Gordon of KEEL, turning to look upward, a small spurt of red emerging from his arm. Next picture: more blood, his face blanching, mouth starting to draw back, eyes on their way to closing. That was all.

The wound had the station call letters, KEEL, superimposed over it. This shot had been taken right off the TV.

Thought: Mr. Mohawk hadn't been aiming for the bicep, he'd been aiming for the station letter as it would appear on TV. He'd phoned in a bomb threat, probably told the TV station about it. Then he lay in the dark at the edge of the interstate with a portable TV—probably a little LCD unit, something you can fit in your hand—and watched to see where the station's call letters lined up. And then he'd shot the man right in the call letters.

What was the point of this endeavor?

He'd shot or blown up over a dozen insignificant newspeople and shot or incinerated a bunch of other stuff—neon signs, trucks?

Aiming at letters.

Oh, sweet Jesus. I bolted out of my chair and grabbed the stack of Hitch's faxes. I hadn't seen it before, because I hadn't been looking. Who would? I arranged the faxes in the order they'd come in, according to the dates the fax machine stamped on each page. S. T. E. E. H. A. E. R. The letters on the top of the pages. Hitch had been coding his notes according to the letter that had been targeted by Mr. Mohawk. But he'd shown up at the locations in a different order than Mr. Mohawk had planned, gotten the order all wrong.

S. T. E. E. H. A. E. R.

Think.

The. You could get *THE* out of it . . . as well as THESE, which left ARE.

What was the order in which the Notebook programs came into the computer? I called up each file and did a GET INFO. Rearranged the faxes as I examined each file, came up with THE SMIL

These are the smil. What was Smil, an ethnic group? Smil forces attacked the airport today. Smil guerillas have vowed to fight to the death. No. These are the Smile. But *smile* is singular, *are* means plural—

I stood up, ran downstairs to the recycling bin, where I hoped a copy of my first roundup on the shooting was still residing. It was. I was too lazy to actually gather the papers and put them on the curb and threw them in the recycling rack as a sign of my theoretical solidarity. I found the part where I described Detective Bishop's ridiculous hospital-bed convocation.

We found this picture of Josh Carlton at Peter Byrne's place, he'd said.

Scrawled across Carlton's face: THESE ARE THE SMILING LIARS!

I thought again of the video I'd seen that afternoon. Three Mohawked men, grinning, draped around a luscious redhead. Ludwig, Stig, and Philip. Mel in a wondrous wig, the red mane I'd seen draped over the chair the night I barged in on her at the Rumley office.

Followed by Peter Byrne, declaiming that Mohawks ruled his life.

I spent the rest of the night in the dark—lights off, doors locked—sitting upstairs chain-smoking, waiting for the phone to ring and for whoever to ship more mayhem into my system. Wishing Hitch were here to share theories.

Theories? He knew. He *knew.*

6

WHEN I OPENED THE DOOR, HALF ASLEEP, I HAD THE SUDden belief that the Green Giant had paid a visit. Climbed off his pedestal, tromped north, and dropped by to discuss his shooting. Maybe he was standing on my lawn, hands on hips, grinning. Crouched down on all fours, peering in the door with the same hideous leer. A high, wide man walked into the room and stood looking at the ceiling. He was wearing pink underwear and a lime green tank top so bright it felt like someone had attached jumper cables to my optic nerves. His hair was blond, unnaturally so. It appeared to have been surgically enhanced, as though every strand had been bleached by laser. He was six feet tall plus change and had so many finely defined muscles he looked like a parts catalog for the human body.

The last time I saw him, he'd towered over Melodya at the gym, dripping sweat and abuse.

"Simpson," he bellowed. He took my hand, wrung it dry, grinned a smile that would shame a lighthouse. "What *are* you doing?"

"Talking to a stranger in my hallway."

"Stranger?" The eyes clouded over. "You haven't seen me in every bus shelter in town?"

"You're bigger in life," I said. "More, ahh, vivid."

"Tell me about it! Large as a barge and cut like a scut!" He struck a weight lifter's pose. "You do know a scut is a ship." I nodded. "You would. You're the word man. I write some, too. As you can tell from the show. Hey! *Let's* do the formal thing! Samurai Stevens." Out went the catcher's mitt of a hand again. "And you're Simpson of course. We need to talk."

"We do?"

"Well, maybe *I'll* just talk. You take notes. That's how *I* usually operate. I mean, it's not like you've said anything interesting *yet*, right? We have the basis for our relationship *clearly* established." Samurai laid a hand my shoulder. "You can deviate from the rules if you show promise. Otherwise, shut up. Shall we go?"

"Go where? I—"

"Hot and haughty strippers with surgically implanted breasts await. We have time to kill and G-strings to fill. Let's go."

"Dress code," said the Samurai. He stood in a parking lot, putting on a pair of pants. "Never go to a strip club that doesn't have a dress code. If they don't make you wear pants, the liquor is *watered*. Guaranteed. Not that I drink." He stopped pulling on his pants and struck a lecturer's pose. "That's behind me. That man is *gone*. I take a drink, I become the Tasmanian devil. Rip up! Fall down! You like old Warner Brothers' cartoons?" I nodded. "Always wanted to see him go up against Foghorn Leghorn, but no! The *one* combination they never got around to doing. Hey! You know what I love about the modern age?" I shook my head. "Check it out. I have been running around all day in my underwear. These pink briefs, technically, they're underwear. But the lines have been blurred between underwear and street clothing. Context is everything. I walk around in my underwear and I have the right amount of—of—of—of, damn!"

"Elan?"

"Elan! You *are* the word man. Right, élan. My whole posture, my ability to project élan, says these are shorts. *No one* says this is underwear. But the minute I start to put on pants, they become underwear. Amazing. Context *is* everything."

"Should I be taking this down?"

"God no, I hand this stuff out for free." He pulled a T-shirt from his trunk and put it on. "Okay. Now that I'm dressed, let's pay money to see someone else take it off."

The club, which occupied the ground floor of an old bank building on the edge of downtown, was called Body Works. Great controversy had attended its opening. Feminists had rallied in protest accompanied by a starched and thin-lipped delegation from the religious community. They had ended up in a fistfight over abortion rights, broken up by bouncers from the bar, who pummeled all with happy abandon.

Samurai presented a membership card to the bouncer, a quiescent Holstein in a tuxedo, and was bowed in. The bouncer gave me a nod meant to convey both greetings and the speed with which I could be evicted. We proceeded to the bar.

"Wheat juice," Samurai cried. "What will you have, my small friend?"

"Coffee."

"Please. As Ingrid said to Humphrey in *Casablanca,* you have to do the drinking for both of us. I *radiate* sobriety. It's up to you to throw a wet towel over that emanation, or everyone in this bar will feel ashamed. You'll ruin the mood of—of—" He looked around the empty club. "Of nearly a *dozen* men. Bartender? Whiskey and wheat juice for the little man."

"Whiskey and wheat juice? Are you—"

"It was my transitional drink when I was in midflight 'tween drunkenness and the *happening* species of manhood I am today. Trust me."

It was an awful drink. It was like licking the grass stain on a Scotsman's kilt. I took one deep drink, nearly spewed it onto the bald head of a man at the bar, and managed to spill the rest as we walked to our table. There were no strippers on stage at present. A placard announced that the next show was in twenty minutes.

But things were generally nude, anyway. We were just pulling out our stools from our table when a waitress, nude from the waist onward and upward, appeared. "What would you like?" she said.

"Genes like your parents!" Samurai pronounced. "That we might issue such wham*digious* infants." She gave us an instant smile, like a blank movie screen suddenly coming alive with the coming-attractions reel.

"No, I mean, really," she said. I suddenly wanted to know her name and by instinct looked to where her nametag would have been had she not been predominately nude. I was greeted with nipple—flaccid but possibly open to suggestion. "What were you having?" she said to me, her smile now downshifting to a promo for a G-rated movie.

A *bleakly obvious fantasy*. "Whiskey," I said. Samurai cocked a bleached-blond eyebrow. "With a water back. Spring water."

"Nothing for me," said Samurai. "I'm high on life." The waitress gave a grin as deep as a shoebox lid and left. "Don't know why I said something that stupid," said Samurai. "Should be obvious."

"So," I said, "now that we're friends and all, tell me about yourself."

"Former arms merchant turned talk show host. What more is there? Grew up in California. Spent my youth doing drugs and demon rum and making *mucho dinero* supplying armaments to various social organizations in Los Angeles. There are fourteen years of which I have no recollection, none, but I know it must have been *happening*. In 1985 I mistakenly found myself sober through no fault of my own, understand. I then discovered, wow! I have a weird tattoo, a drug habit, and a criminal record! Scary." Samurai gave a shudder, which consisted of twitching each of the several thousand muscles in his torso and sipped his wheat juice. "I was at the beach when this roving camera crew came along to sample opinion of the citizens, and I, being all weirded from the galvanizing impact of not being stoned, gave an oration of such consummate peculiarity it was put on network news as an example of how odd people in California can be," he spat with great bitterness. "After that, it was cable access, which is purgatory, then local commercials, which is like heaven for the nearsighted, then talk radio. I was hired as a curiosity, but I caught on like Velcro. And so I do this happening thing here now in this medium-sized market."

"And you've been sober for—"

"Seven years. It's been tough. This body, for example. I have no idea where its unique and *in*contestable fabulousness and magnificence comes from. Last I knew, I was a tall geek. I sober up and find out I've been working out. Went down to Venice to Muscle Beach, asked if they knew me. Nobody did. Couldn't find, like, a gym membership card or anything. How I got this body equals mystery numero uno. So there you have it. Ergo me. Enter the Samurai. Now, about you. You slept with Melodya, right?"

"Ah, no. We never, ah. You and her . . . I'm guessing, you—"

"On occasion, yes. After the photo shoot for the ads you no doubt saw all over town. We did hit it off, as superior structures like ourselves are bound to. Then I got an inkling of the basic makeup of that damaged little unit. Melodya needs a secretary to keep track of her lies. Should have had a stenographer walking around at her side, one of those court reporters. Hey, ever wonder how those people type so fast and get it all down? I mean, what if your life depended on one of them, you're in court, right, and the prosecutor asks the court reporter to read back the transcript, and he says 'Defendant said Melodya did not have an orgasm' when you know she did?"

"She did?"

"I certainly hope so." Samurai squared his shoulders. It was like watching Hoover Dam get comfortable. "Drilled that well longer than a wildcat oilman on his last lease. Damn and a half. Stung in the shower for two days. She's the kind of woman who bounces between decent normal gentleman, such as present company, and ratbutt mothers like our predecessor."

"Wait. Stop. Go back. Who was the predecessor? When did you—"

"Only saw him once. Thin guy, but wiry. I could have killed him, but I would have cracked a sweat doing so. And I'd just showered. He came into the gym once, before I knew Melodya. Stood there looking dank and unhealthy, *skull*fucking her."

There was an ugly word I hadn't heard in a while. "Marines?" I said. Samurai looked confused. "That, ah, skull word. Had an old roommate who was in the Marines, used the word on occasion as a synonym for lascivious looks. Never heard it from anyone not in the Marines."

He thought for a moment. "It's entirely possible I was in the Marines," he said. "That would explain several burns and at least one tattoo." He smiled broadly. "Thank you! So as I was saying. I was just looking her over, and she was doing likewise—woman has eyes like dental picks, you know? Never spoke, just watched each other on a daily basis. Halfway through one of our little preening sessions, in comes Mr. Hair."

Throw deep, Jonathan. "Mohawk. White stripe."

"You know him, right? So he comes in and gives me this grin, all the while looking at her with that way that says 'my property,' you know, you can tour the open house but you can't move in. Really sick look. Unwise, too, given that I have about a hundred fifty pounds of drop-forged steel in my hands at the time. He leaves. I walk over to Mel and say, 'Listen. You need a new boyfriend.' 'I know,' she says. And here's the line: 'I'm looking for the right kind of bad,' she says. Fine. I tell her I'm the momma bear of bad. Not too hot, not too small. You see that cartoon?"

"No."

"Bugs Bunny waxes the three bears. One of the best. So, we leave the club later. Back to my place, *shazam* for hours and hours."

"When was this? This spring?"

"Hell, no. A year ago, and then for a few months only. You have a thing for her? Don't be ashamed; all men have a thing for her. It's whether or not she lets them use it. Eventually she and I were cold porridge, albeit with the old physical familiarity you have between two people who parted smiling. I shuffled *her* off, let me make that clear. Mr. Hair kept coming around, and I could see he'd dropped anchor deep in her particular harbor."

"One more thing."

"Shoot. No, don't, I'm a media figure." He downed the last of his wheat juice. "Forgot."

"Why did you bring me here?"

"We needed to talk. What better place?"

"Who goes to a strip joint to talk?"

"Depends what you want to talk about." The waitress returned with our drinks. I tried not to look at her breasts; seemed insulting. But her breasts seemed so bored with all this.

"Dammit, I said dammit boy," said Foghorn Samurai. "I paid, ah said ah paid for you to have the right to look at nekkid women. Pay attention, son."

"I don't know. I'd like to. Seems demeaning to them."

"Wrong. They're making money here. Their income depends on you getting all goggle-eyed and giving them huge, undeserved gratuities. Play along, boy. They won't think less of you for looking, and they most definitely won't think more of you if you don't."

"I still don't know why we're here. And how did you know Mel and I were, were—" Were nothing. "That I was, ah, interested in her?"

"She said as much. Often. And with a smile." He sipped his wheat juice. "Here's to clean blood and happy intestines. Here's to having something in common. Best of all"—Samurai raised his glass—"here's to me knowing some things you don't."

* * *

"Let's have a round of applause for Johnny Simpson!" said the DJ. "Our lucky, lucky groom of the evening!" Applause, halfhearted and resentful, sounded from the crowd. It was two hours later, and I was somewhat drunk. Samurai had remained cagey about his reasons for our meeting, but his presence was bright and magnetic. Just sitting at the same table made me feel like I was getting a tan. We had spoken no more of Mel nor of Carlton. What we had talked about, I can't remember. Perhaps his amnesia was infectious.

I found myself on the stage on a wooden chair, blinking at the lights, the evening's star groom. From what I could deduce, the Groom Show was a special event at the Body Works, and it cost money. Once announced as part of the evening's entertainment, it could not be retracted without threat of riots. This evening, the groom's party hadn't showed. Either they were dead drunk in a bar in Tijuana or the groom's bride had gotten wind and forbidden the event. Whatever; they needed a groom. Our waitress had come up to me and asked me to take his place. I looked embarrassed to be here, a nice guy, she said, and that's what worked best with the Groom Show.

"Think of it as material!" cried the Samurai. "Write a story about American decadence from the first person! Win a Pulitzer! Have great big firm fake tits ground in your face!"

I agreed. I was a lonely man, really. I had spent my life trying to straddle sex and love, one a dock and the other a ship drifting away into the deep limitless blue, most often plunging into the cold, sharp water of disappointment. The few times I'd tethered the boat to the dock the rope had frayed after a year, and . . .

"Metaphor ho!" Samurai shouted. The rest of the audience was silent. I had, I realized with horror, been talking aloud. I was a bit beyond tipsy. Very, very, very—

"He's getting married!" the DJ brayed. "Signing on to work the boiler room in the old *Love Boat!* But before he does, let's have a few stokers come along to straddle his dock! Introducing: the Bridesmaids!"

Out they came. An endless series of women, all tall, all bronzed, hair tousled, feet nestled in high heels, matchbook-sized swatches of spangled fabric shining in what would have been their lap, had they sat down. And of course, one did. She pressed her breasts in my face, and my hands flew as though bidden by Norse berserkers to her buttocks. Her breasts were as hard as soccer balls, regulation size. She gave my cheek a chaste lick and stood up, waved her bottom before my goggling eyes, and strode away.

"One down!" shouted the DJ. "Eleven to go! One for each day of freedom old Simpo has left!"

"Remind me to come here three months before my next wedding," I said. Scattered resentful laughter from the audience. The next woman appeared from behind, sat in my lap, upped the ante a chip, nuzzling my ear with the rote professionalism of a surgeon probing the guts of a body on the slab. The next one, a whip-thin beauty who looked as if she got her bust from a tire-inflation pump at a gas station, put a little extra hip into my groin. I found myself warming to the idea and returned the gesture. She got up doubly quick, gave me the mesmerizing metronome of her bottom waving in waltz time, and danced away to loud applause. This was, all told, a nightmare: drunk, sitting up on stage before a roomful of strangers, arguing halfheartedly with an insistent erection.

They came and went. Riotous applause followed whenever the dancers were out of my sight. If they were doing something at my expense, I didn't see it, for as one left, another came. They had to be doing something. I feared that if I turned around, there would be a line of gorgeous women wearing rubber masks of my fiancée, all being ravaged by members of the wedding party. Then I remembered I didn't have a fiancée. A sudden surge of anger and bitterness spouted up my throat, and I wanted to stand and denounce everyone in the room.

"Anastasia!" proclaimed the DJ. "Here she is, gentlemen, the reason you've come tonight! Did you really think we'd keep her from you? Aaaaa-naaaa-staaaaaa-sha!"

"Goddamn you," said Anastasia, settling into my lap. She was naked, glistening with some sort of oil. Her skin shone in the lights, felt slick to the touch. She wore a wedding veil.

Beneath which, I knew, she was bald.

"What are you doing here?" she hissed. "I told you to stay away!"

"Cute," I said. "Dad's a communist, so your stage name is a Romanov monarch. Getting back at Dad anyway possible, I'd guess."

She stood up and slapped me. An inchoate roar of appreciation rose from the audience. Mel strode toward the curtains.

"Now you know why I brought you here?" roared a voice from the audience. "Get it now?"

Mel threw open the curtains, and I lurched after her. "Whoa!" said the DJ. "Not included in the package!" The audience whistled, and threw catcalls; I fumbled with the curtains, found where they parted, and proceeded after her. From the corner of my eye, I saw large, tuxedoed bouncers leap to the stage in a single, graceful bound. Mel was only steps ahead, clacking along in her high heels *(as though she made her living on high heels)* and threw open the door of her dressing room. I was just about to enter when I was grabbed from behind and thrown to the floor. My jaw cracked on the floor, and constellations danced before my eyes for a second. A knee dove into the base of my spine.

"Don't hurt him," she said in a tired voice. She whipped off her wedding veil, ran a hand across her skull, and bent down. "Jonathan, I don't know why you're here, but you have to go. I sent you the passwords in that picture. That's all I can do.

"I agree completely," I said to the floor. "Please make them let me up." The knee dug deeper into my spine. I was going to end up paralyzed, drooling, incontinent. I had to fulfill a book contract and would be forced to tap it out one letter at time with my teeth. "I'll go away. I'll let the police and the FBI have you. They're looking for a Mohawked man with a white stripe on his head, and I found a picture of you going all cozy with someone who fits the description. Samurai can back me up."

"You're not making sense," she said. I wished I had another piece of evidence to unload on her, but that was all I had. I'd thrown the whole damn jigsaw in her face.

The bouncers let me up and started to pull me away.

"Good-bye, Jonathan," she said.

"Hey, Mel," said a voice in the dressing room. "I had to do the G-strings on parade tonight, so I borrowed your razor. Sorry. Here. Catch."

I borrowed your razor?

Sturdy hands clamped to my shoulders like the talons of possessive birds bore me out of the bar, through the door, past a line of men in suits whose eyes grew wide at my egress. "I'm being thrown out because I complained the liquor was watered down!" I shouted. We were now outside. "Don't go in there!" I shouted. "Water and caramel color, that's what they call whiskey!" This earned me a vigorous introduction to the pavement. I felt sick; the wheat juice, of course. I staggered down the street. This was a part of the city where there was bound to be an alley nearby where I could complete my disgrace. I veered into a dark slot, felt rough brick, sought the angle where wall meets earth, and let the evening come up.

"She can grow hair after all," I said to myself. "She has hair."

"Of course," said a voice behind me. "Whatever made you think she couldn't?" Samurai stood in the alley, shaking his head. "You free of her now?" I nodded. He put his hands on his hips and laughed. Color him green, and he would have belonged in Blue Earth. "Good," he said. "Now, sober up. Now we plan strange and violent things."

"What I can't figure out," I said, "is why everyone's told so many lies when it would be easy to prove them wrong." I was riding in Samurai's Bel-Air. The cool air and purging of wheat juice had done me good, and I felt somewhat hale again. "They lied about stupid stuff. Why tell me she's bald because of a disease, for God's sake? Hardly any shame in being bald for legitimate reasons, like a twisted, self-abasing concept of beauty. And how do I know you're not out to shiv me as well?"

"You've had your quota of liars. Your card has ten punches and you now qualify for one free truth-seeking muchacho *not* unlike myself. I am embarked on a program of good works, you see." He suddenly looked very solemn, like a grade-school textbook illustration of Civic Duty. "When I realized I had spent years in sin and villainy, okay, I realized two things: I either survived by the dint of good people, in which case I owe the world, or I survived by being a very bad person myself, in which case same conclusion. I figure my karma card is pretty well maxed out, have to start earning capital again." He punched the car through an red light. "Besides, I'm curious."

"What made you come to me?"

"You're involved in the matter of my predecessor scraped off the pavement. Gets a man's attention. Now, here's the schedule. You feeling better? Roll your eyes back in your skull twice if yes. Okay, great. We got to go the Boomerang, find this Ludwig you told me about, then I'll steer him outside and beat the unholy shit from him until he talks."

"What happened to the karma business?"

"I got a lifetime more to work on it. Many lifetimes. Plus, it's bullshit, so I'm covered all around."

I leaned back and closed my eyes. "Take me home. I just want to sit and think. I'm not even going to check the computer for additional slayings, that's how bushed I am."

Samurai drove me home in silence—well, not exactly. No words. But an unending stream of whistled TV theme shows, finger poppings, knuckles drummed on the wheel, rhythms tapped on the dashboard. When we pulled up, I asked the question I'd been saving all night.

"Why did you take me to see Melodya?"

"Figured you'd want to know."

"Who cares that she's a stripper? I'd be a stripper, too, if I had her body."

"You *did* have her body, didn't you? Oh, well. Just wanted you to know where it spent its free time. Because it wasn't always alone. I met Mel at that club, but that's also where I met another dizzbag I wish I'd never clapped eyes upon, and that would be this guy who hung on the stage every night stuffing dollar bills in her fishnets till the bouncers used him to shine the pavement. I'm going to trust you with this little connection, even if it's not the sort of thing I want generally known, at least until we figure this out and you write your book and I am shown to be the hero."

"Josh Carlton hung around Mel?" I asked.

Samurai nodded gravely.

There was a pause. "So?"

"You figure it out! You're the one taking score and keeping notes and writing pieces! Just don't make me out to be an idiot when you write the book," said Samurai. "I read a true crime book a couple of weeks ago, and I think I was one of the minor characters. I didn't come off too well."

"You sure it was you?"

"The author misspelled the words on a tattoo. But they change these things to protect the innocent."

It was past one o'clock when I got back to the manor. I looked at the tape: TALK OF TOWN REEL 7. I hit play and saw Peter Byrne's mournful mug staring sadly into the camera. *"Tim, Tim, Tim,"* he said. I noted that this tape was time-coded, little numerals flickering in the bottom. 22:54:12. Following Byrne was the appearance of someone I'd never seen before, a man with a fade haircut elegantly humiliating the entire concept of Mohawks; the numbers read 15:24:20—a different tape, apparently. I rewound back to red-wigged Mel and the skins. 22:01:01.

I rewound and went frame by frame over Peter Byrne's segment. In the background of the shot, behind Byrne's mug, there was one frame of interest. A sliver of Mel and the four skins turning the corner, walking away.

All these folks just happened to pour out of the building at the same time.

I hit rewind again for another look and lit a cigarette. Pushed play. I'd overshot the segment and found myself observing the tail end of the *Talk of the*

Town show I'd done, the show the guy had dubbed for me at UCCAC. There I was, pale and sweating under the lights, trying to talk about food poisoning while a man in a chef's hat yelled at me. Good old P.D., the consummate pro. There he is shaking his fist. See him grabbing his crotch. Here is now the escalating abuse. The shoving match. I found myself laughing as I watched myself fight the man in the chef's cap. If I hadn't known the animosity was real, I'd have thought it was fake. I looked quite ready to slug him there, but then our feet tangle and he falls backward, turns around—and he pitches into the camera: ouch. The little piece of chipped tooth pings against the lens. Off flies the chef's hat. I'm in the background, on my back, looking up, at the time unable to see the Mohawk beneath his chef's hat. With a white stripe.

P.D. jammed the hat back on his head and draws his finger across his throat. Cut.

Another episode of TALK OF THE TOWN with P.D. Spaunaugle follows, the screen said. *Local party fixture Martha Lamfure explains why coats belong on the bed.*

Then the theme song.

> *He's marvelous, he's wonderful*
> *He's none of those things at all*
> *He's obvious! Pathetic!*
> *He's ab-so-lutely predictable*
> *Malignant and confusing*
> *Strives to be bemusing*
> *Indicative of an unstable*
> *Miiiiiiind*
> *It's Talk of the Town! Talk of the Town!*
> *Strips your smile and adds a frown!*
> *It's the P.D. Spaunaugle shoooooow!*

I paused the tape, hands shaking. The picture froze on P.D. Spaunaugle snarling, middle finger tapping his chipped tooth, angry, in pain, out of character, hat doffed.

P.D. glared out at me from my TV: foreign and feral.

"You're the one," I whispered. I got out Bob's card from my wallet, hoping there was more than a UCCAC number listed. There was a second number with a North Minneapolis exchange, far from uptown. I dialed it.

Bob answered on the tenth ring with a mild *"Hello?"*

"Jonathan Simpson. Listen, I need to get in touch with P.D. Spaunaugle now. You wouldn't happen to have his number?"

"I have his last number, he's been gone for a long time."

"How long?"

"Jeez, nearly a year. Why?"

"I need to get in touch with him, do an interview." My fist has some questions for his teeth.

"Good luck. He's been off on a project. No one's seen him or missed him, to be frank."

"What project?"

"I don't know." He yawned. "He got a grant to do something on violence in the media."

"A grant." *It's a talk show as performance art,* Spaunaugle had said that night. Driving around the country shooting people to spell out a meaningless phrase, was that also performance art? Did the pope pretend to walk against the wind in the woods? "Who gave him the grant?"

"I think the NEA. I saw the check." He sighed. "You could have lived five years on it. Not to say he didn't deserve it. Guy's weird, but he's a visionary."

"He's shot eighteen people."

"For real? Not an effect or anything?"

"For real."

Bob fell silent for some time.

"I should take him off my résumé as a reference," he finally said.

Mr. Obvious

1

"ALL I CAN SAY IN MY DEFENSE IS THAT I DO NOT NOW have, nor have I ever had, X-ray vision."

The judge seemed to accept that. My next-door neighbor merely snorted. She was seated at the next table, wrapped up in a plaid shawl with so much livid red that it looked like the tartan for a clan that suffered from congenital hemophilia and needed something to cover the stains. Her lawyer, the same hideously embarrassed man who'd been shoveling me subpoenas for the last year, tried not to look at anyone. When he spoke, he seemed to be addressing his legal pad. Perhaps there he had drawn a picture of a sympathetic judge.

"The point, your honor," he said, "is not whether the defendant has X-ray vision. I think we can assume, absent sufficient medical evidence to the, ah, contrary, that he does not."

"The Devil he doesn't! Ma drapes!"

"Mr. Simpson has, through a calculated program of harassment, preyed on this woman's age and led her to believe he has powers capable of causing her harm." He smiled at his legal pad. Maybe his picture of the judge had winked or blown him a kiss. "No one is suggesting that the defendant actually has, ah, X-ray eyes."

"Really?" asked the judge.

"Yes, your honor. It would be, ah, absurd to, ah, maintain in a court of ah, law that—"

"That on November 30, at four-o-three A.M.," the judge read in a droll voice, "Jonathan Anthony Simpson did cause the drapes of the home of Mrs. Edna MacPhereson to ignite, and that he employed a lethal beam of X-rays emanating from his eyes to do so."

"Eminatin'! Ma drapes!" Mrs. MacPhereson cawed.

"That is what the complaint says, your honor, but if I may suggest that the plaintiff's deposition does not reflect the, ah, main thrust of the case. It is our contention that what the plaintiff is describing, in an admittedly fanciful way, is that the defendant has harassed Mrs. MacPhereson to the point where she becomes nervous, fearful, and drops her cigarette, thereby, ah, setting various parts of her house on fire."

"Fearful of his eyes, y'mean."

"Mr. Simpson," said the lawyer. He turned to another page on his legal pad, where perhaps he had my picture drawn, looking up in fear and submission. "Where is your house located in relation to Mrs. MacPhereson."

"It's right next door."

"Would you say your windows look out onto her windows?"

"I would. They're windows. They look out where you point them."

"Do you ever look through your windows at her windows?"

"It's not beyond the realm of the possible."

"I see. And did you stand looking out your windows on . . . on November 12 of last year?"

"November 12? No."

"Why are you so sure?"

"I was in a coma."

"A coma," the lawyer said, utterly flummoxed but trying to make it sound suggestive, as though people were known to wake from comas with great and mysterious powers. "A, ah, coma."

"Judge?" I said. "I'd like to say something." He nodded. "Every month I have to come down and here and go through this. Every month. I've copies of two years' worth of subpoenas here—take a look. One piece of nonsense after the other. Before the X-ray eyes it was a vapor machine I had built in my cellar. One month I was accused of growing to a height of fifty feet just to frighten her while she pulled weeds. It's true, as they've pointed out, that I did not appear to contest three accusations of using X-ray vision, which is why we're here today. My only defense was medically certified unconsciousness, but I think it's a pretty good one. Now it should be obvious that what we have here is a law firm more than happy to bleed large amounts of money from this woman by cheerfully representing her in nonsense suits—"

"I resent that," said the lawyer.

"I take it back. You're not cheerful. The fact that you draw this duty is proof how far down on the partner ladder you are. I wouldn't be cheerful either."

"Gentlemen." The judge had no gavel. It was, small-claims court. He tapped his knuckles on the bench. "Mrs. MacPhereson, I find your claim specious and without merit. Mr. Simpson, I see from your statement that you have judgments outstanding on your nonappearance in previous cases, but I cannot act on your petition to have that judgment dismissed. Go downstairs to the main desk and they will tell you where to go. Next case."

I was tempted to turn to Mrs. MacPhereson, make the devil's horns with my fingers in front of my face and waggle them at her, but I resisted. She'd get new advice from her lawyer, and next month I would be accused of something plausible, like plotting to breed sea monkeys and train them to swim up her pipes and gnaw on her withered fundament as she sat in her bathtub.

The day's legal work concluded, it was time to work. I was still a food reviewer, after all. I had decided to write about Café Plaid, a place that had mailed me a press release a few days earlier.

The restaurant was in the same spot occupied by Café White last month. And Café Red before that. Before that, it was the Green Café. I had a dark revelation that Café Plaid was not a new restaurant at all, but the same bad café that had occupied this space in various incarnations for a hundred years.

Back when the warehouse district served an actual purpose—that is, housing manufactured goods ready to build a nation instead of galleries full of sloppy impasto paintings and sculptures that looked like a welder's feverish dream—Café Plaid had been a sturdy workingman's hash shop. A long counter, scarred with cigarette burns, slight indentations from a half-century of elbows flanking each stool like the spoor of weary ghosts. Two booths with high backs for conferring with bookies and aggravated wives. A grill where everything was fried. When I first came to Minneapolis in my college days, I'd come here once for breakfast. FRIED TOAST said a sign in the window. House specialty. Tasted of ham and eggs and bacon and beef and whatever else had laid down its life on that grill. It was, I recalled, delicious.

I went in, and a merry gnome waved me to a seat at the window, where, a minute later, a waitress with carrot-hued hair and sharp, accusatory eyes flew past and hurled a menu at me. I looked over the menu with no great anticipation, expecting the same mix of rabbit food and timorous quasi-Cajun chicken. And it was all there. But there was a new addition: FAMOUS FOR FRIED TOAST, the menu said at the top in jaunty '50s-style lettering.

"I'll have the fried toast," I told the waitress when she finally reappeared. She drew back in faint distaste and said they didn't have any.

"It's on the menu," I said helpfully.

"Yeah, but we don't have it. We found this great old, like, neon thing in the storeroom, and it said Famous for Fried Toast. They're going to put it up in the window this weekend."

"But you won't have any." She shook her head no.

"We got a mock lamb today on a bed of spring-fed sprouts." Image of a mannequin lamb bouncing on a leafy mattress, springs singing. No. "And the Cajun lutefisk is pretty good."

"This menu looks a lot like the one they had at Café White."

"Same menu except for the toast thing. Same everything except for the paint around the door. See, the owner just changes the name every couple of months and sends out press releases and gets reviewed. It's cheaper than advertising, you know? And no one catches on, so." Shrug.

Mm-hmm. "Well, your secret's safe with me," I said with a smile.

I ordered the Plaidburger, thank you, good-bye. I considered taking notes on the decor, but I had it all in my jottings from previous visits. There were no other patrons save one burly man at the counter, hairy arms, hairy neck, slurping coffee and gazing around with mild hatred. The sort you find affixed to any lunch counter, their bottoms embossed with a permanent circle from the stool. Left over from the FRIED TOAST days, most likely. They'd renovate the café around him.

The food was a horror show. My Plaidburger was just that—strips of whitish cheese, limp green peppers, exhausted strips of red peppers, and some lurid yellow extrusion, the general effect looking like a melted pile of crayons. The sort of pattern found on Reagan's jackets. Pouring ketchup over it made it look like a murder scene at a Miami Beach shuffleboard center.

I did not want to spend the rest of my life writing about the ways people tried to gussy up circular masses of ground-up ruminant. The very sight of the dish set my innards muttering in discontent, and I realized I needed to pay a visit to the bathroom. When I returned, my meal would not just be inedible, but cold.

I slid a glance toward the kitchen as I passed, just to see if Jackson Pollack was in the kitchen, drizzling cheese on burgers to demonstrate his new theory of Action Cooking. The cook was the sort of guy you find in hash houses run by postmodernists. He wore a tall, white chef's hat, no doubt meant as an ironic commentary on the elitist standards of cuisine. He had a dull, woebegone face, a weak chin, a loser's posture.

It was Peter Byrne, the Christmas escapee from the house of his benefactor, the wielder of the electric carving knife, the man who spilled blood at the holiday table and gave us that wonderful headline, BLOOD ON THE TURKEY.

Our eyes met. Byrne shuffled the worn and dog-eared deck of cards that comprised his memory, and i.d.'ed me. He stripped off his apron and hairnet and bolted.

I looked around for a door to the kitchen and didn't see one. "The kitchen!" I shouted, wheeling around to address the waitress. "Door! To the kitchen!"

"Sir, I can take it off your bill if he didn't—"

"The fucking door to the kitchen! Where is it?"

"You can't go back there," she said, flustered, for she now saw the hairnet and apron thrown over the ledge, the apron resting on a sandwich, the hairnet sinking in a bowl of soup.

"I have to! Where?"

"I mean you can't, there's no door—"

"What the hell do you do? Shove the cook in and weld the door shut? Brick it over?"

"There's no door between the kitchen and the café," she said. "There never was. Something about the liquor law or something. I don't know."

I went behind the counter and mounted the ledge. "Call the police," I shouted, and I vaulted into the kitchen. My foot went on the sizzling grill, and the sole of my tennis shoe immediately melted and adhered to the hot metal. I pulled it off, leaving cheesy strings of plastic, put the other foot on a nearby sandwich preparation table, stepping on a tomato with a sickening *plurgh!* and stepped down to the floor. Saw the door. Ran for it. One foot sticking to the floor.

"Walkout!" I heard the waitress shout. "Walkout!" I turned half by instinct, half in anger at being accused of walking out on my check. The large hairy man who'd been sitting at the counter was now squeezing through the ledge over the grill.

I ran down a hall reeking of mouse droppings, over brooms knocked down to impede my path, through a door, into an alley behind the warehouse. I sprinted to the street and looked up and down. Empty sidewalks.

I ran back down the alley, passing the café's back door just in time for the big hairy man to emerge, spot me, plot a trajectory, and launch himself at me. We went down in a clatter of trash bins, considerately provided by the city to add an expected note to alley brawls.

"Yer gonna come back in there and yer gonna pay," said the hairy man.

"Of course, I am," I panted. "I was just chasing the chef. I would have come back."

"You gotta problem with the food, take it to the management."

"Fine, and I will. Let me up!" I shouted, seething. Byrne was long gone. "I'll tell all to the stupid management, just let me the hell *up.*"

"I'm the management."

Stupid, hairy bastard. "The Plaidburger was cooked by an escaped criminal." I spit.

"We've had that complaint."

"Can you get off me now?"

"Yeah." He stood and hauled me to my feet by my shirt. "Want to tell me why I got melted sneaker on my grill? Huh?"

"Your chef is wanted for attempted murder of a friend of mine."

The hairy, burly man looked up and down the alley in shock, then regarded me with alarm. "What are you, the police?"

"Worse," I spat. "I'm a food critic."

A police car roared up the alley, lights spinning, as if to enforce my opinions of his cuisine.

"Some people like the plaid effect," he said, watching the policeman get out of his car.

"Tell it to the judge."

2

"GOOD WORK," DETECTIVE BISHOP SAID FACETIOUSLY. HE lit a cigar. It smelled of tobacco grown in fields well irrigated by goats with weak bladders. "We had seven months of observation, of careful police work. Stealth, not the usual brutality you guys in the press always love to hang around our necks."

"Yeah, restaurant reviewers," I said, "scourge of the police." I rubbed my head where it had hit a trash can, wrinkled my nose at myself. Something noxious from one of those cans had leaked on to my shirt, and I was competing with Bishop's cigar. Whoever peeled paint first was the winner.

"Stakeouts, plainclothed officers pretending to be regulars, a recruit fresh from the academy as a waitress, all keeping watch, taking notes . . ."

"Rub it in," I said. "I like to see a man enjoy himself."

". . . all in hopes that one day Peter Byrne would give the whole game away and contact Mr. Spaunaugle."

"Who *I* just found out about a few days ago," I said bitterly. "Thanks for keeping me up to speed, for warning me off."

"Oh, did we forget to alert the corps of restaurant reviewers that we knew who was behind all this? Let me see who's in charge of giving details of ongoing investigations to food critics. A black mark will go in their fuckin' file, I promise."

"Cut it out," I snapped. "If you've known anything, it hasn't been for more than a few days. If you'd known Spaunaugle was behind this, you'd have hauled Melodya, Ludwig, me, and whoever else had a bad haircut into your office and struck them across the kidneys with rubber hoses and phone books."

"Ever think we'd talked to your friends and they didn't tell you? Ever consider that maybe we decided it wasn't in the best interests of the Minneapolis Police Department to haul you in? We went through this the last time, Simpson. You tend to get in the way. If you want to come around after everything has a nice red ribbon around it and the perp of the week is off at Stillwater getting the wood put to him by the steroid fairies, great. Then we talk. Then I get *posilutely* expansive." Bishop stood, fat hands on the desk, eyes wide and white. "Until then, you are like something laying in the road. I'll swerve if I have the time, but otherwise I'll just run right over you."

"All I did was show up to review a restaurant!" I shouted. "There wasn't any yellow POLICE LINE— DO NOT REVIEW tape in front of the door, so I figured it was safe to drop by and have a burger! If you'd have told me—"

"It always comes back to that, doesn't it. If I'd told you. Well, lad, no one is in the telling business anymore. From now on, we ask, you talk. And I have some people in the next room who would like to talk to you."

"Who."

"Remember how I told you how much I hated to work with feds?" I nodded. "Time you see why."

Special Agent Gretchen Parks was a hard woman with a face of plaster and lacquer. If by chance a tear would have leaked from one of her marble eyes, superstitious peasants would flock to the site and proclaim it a message from the Virgin.

I believe the message was, in Agent Parks's case: My bra is too damn tight.

She was joined a minute later by another agent. He riffled through his briefcase with the desperation of a man who believes his keys must be here, they *have* to be here. Nothing impressive about him, though I was happy when he entered the room. After one look at Parks, I was certain I was in for the dreaded bad cop/no cop routine.

The Blessed Special Virgin looked across the table, gave what someone trained in such matters had informed her was a smile, and switched on a tape recorder.

"This is simply for our records," she said.

"Thank God it's only the FBI I'm talking to and not some organization that has any use for *records.*"

She frowned. That one came naturally. "It isn't going to be any easier if you're hostile."

"Sorry. I'm upset." I was, in fact, terrified. Her partner at last slammed his briefcase shut, sighed, and noticed me as if for the first time. He stuck out a hand and announced "Special Agent Will Try."

"More serious sounding than Willie Try, I suppose." It had slipped out.

"It's my name," he said, his face clouding over. "Will Try, T-r-i-e-g-h. Look, we'd like this to be friendly. We just have a few questions to ask. We can do it here, or if you want to be difficult, we can do it downtown."

"We are downtown," I said.

"He means downtown Chicago," Agent Parks said. Wonderful. Bad cop/bad cop. Their interrogation technique was probably consisted of taking turns beating me and waiting for me to form an emotional bond to the one who didn't lead with their class ring.

I had nothing to fear. I was innocent. "I'm not under suspicion of anything, am I?" I said.

They just looked at me with an expression common to the items sold in a fishmarket.

"I mean, I didn't do anything. I just know some of the people involved, that's all. I even tipped off the police to the disc drive with the pictures." Spoken like a true sniveling, guilty-as-all-hell stoolie, trying to reroute retribution onto someone else's head. "And now I can tell you who is doing all this shooting. I found out yesterday. Late at night, too late to call."

"We're open twenty-four hours," said Agent Triegh.

"We know who's doing this," said Agent Parks. "We knew his identity several months ago, and those pictures you gave the detective merely confirmed it. If you're wondering why we haven't interviewed you or any of your friends, it's because we didn't want to let Mr. Obvious know we were aware of his involvement."

"Mr. Obvious?"

"That is his legal name. It was originally Paul Douglas Spaunaugle III. Petitioned the court to change it to . . ." She looked at her notes. "Bix Voidoid Obvious. That was last year, before he left the state. We've been aware of Mr. Obvious since 1988, when he was arrested for performing a dance called . . ." Back to the notes. "Called Kill the President with Long Hot Phallic Pokers. He had mailed a rather elaborate death threat to the president and specified that he would be symbolically illustrating his threat on a certain date in front of the federal building. As the letter itself constituted a federal offense, we were on hand to apprehend him. Unfortunately—"

"He pled the First," Agent Triegh growled.

"He claimed it was a work of art," Parks corrected. "He had proposed a senior thesis for his theater major that involved getting arrested while performing his dance. It was all spelled out in the thesis and approved by his instructor. A judge subsequently found that he was indeed performing a work of art and thus entitled to do what he did."

"A Minnesota judge," Triegh added, his tone suggesting that a Chicago judge would have held him upside down in a bucket of slaughterhouse-floor scrapings.

"A year ago it came to our attention that Mr. Obvious had received a grant from the National Endowment of the Arts to explore violence in the media. He proposed a multimedia exhibition that—" Parks thumbed through her notepad, scowling. " 'That illuminated the dichotomy between the media's simultaneous condemnation and exploitation of violence.' His words."

"Armed and extremely funded," I said, laughing.

"Now," said Agent Parks, "Melodya Tochter. You slept with her."

"I did," I chuckled.

"As did Obvious."

"He did," I said, fighting snickers. Wait a minute. "He did?"

"They were lovers from May 1987 until his disappearance. They met at the university where he was pursuing graduate work in studio arts. Lived together off and on, various residences in Dinkytown, including this one." She showed me a picture. I felt my scrotum constrict. It was the Bijou, as we called it, one of two ramshackle boarding houses.

"You were in residence in a building adjacent to this place for approximately eleven months in 1982, were you not?" I said I was. "Did you have any contact with Mr. Obvious at that time?"

"I don't remember. There were a lot of people in the houses. They came and went. You know college rooming houses." I looked at their faces. They didn't know college rooming houses. "Did he live upstairs or downstairs?" I asked. Instant flummox. They consulted their notes and found no mention of which floor he had occupied. "Because there was a great difference between the two. Downstairs was for the loud, dissolute art majors, and upstairs was for the quiet, dissolute English majors. Our contact with each other consisted of throwing rocks at their walls when the stereo played too loud or shouting out the window on weekends for their party guests not to pee on our cars."

"I see. And do you think Mr. Obvious held you any lasting antipathy for this?"

"No one's going to shoot me because I'd complained about their loud music in a previous decade. Anyway, I'm telling you, I don't recall a thing about him."

"All right," said Agent Parks. "Look at this picture, please." It was a photo from the *Daily,* the campus paper where I'd worked for five years. I was leaning over a typewriter, snarling at someone dressed up as a skeleton.

"Do you recall this incident?"

"Sure. Our paper had neglected to sufficiently applaud the Sandinista government and was briefly occupied by the Committee in Solidarity with Illiterate Coffee-Pickers or whatever they called themselves. Don't tell me that's Mr. Obvious dressed up as the skeleton."

"Correct. Did you recognize him?"

"He's dressed up as a skeleton, for heaven's sake. His mother wouldn't have recognized him. The makeup's so thick his osteopath wouldn't have recognized him. I'm telling you, I didn't know him."

"Show him the videotape."

"You needn't. That's when I recognized him. Or at least figured out who he was."

"Not that tape. The other one." Triegh walked over to a VCR in the corner of the room and pushed a button. The TV screen showed a freeze-frame Spaunaugle with a woman wearing a flattop hairstyle. "Recognize her?"

This was the day of revelations. The woman was Daphne Johnson, one of the *Metropole*'s innumerable temporary receptionists. She'd put in a stint back while the food terrorists were at work. I remembered her only because we went out once. She had mauled me in the shower, then dragged me to a slam-dancing club. She was a go-go capitalist with a huge trust fund who did stints in the working world as a lark, a way of getting out in the world, seeing people, and screwing up their phone messages for sport.

She was standing with Spaunaugle in front of Marvel Manor, my house.

"Daphne Johnson," said Parks, "was Obvious's lover from January 1984 to approximately April 1987. She met him in graduate school, where she was majoring in performance art."

"Don't tell me she had a grant to mislead food critics into thinking they found them attractive."

"No," said Parks. "A thesis paper. Her final work was to be a temporary receptionist for a year."

"But she *was* a receptionist."

"As I understand it, the point of the work was that she was not really a receptionist, but merely behaved as one. A fine point if you ask me, but she received an A. And before you wonder whether the FBI investigates everyone with a major in theater, I will tell you that she came to our attention in connection with the food-terrorist episodes of a few years back. The police did not believe she led you to the club where you were abducted, but we thought otherwise. We have never been able to establish a link between her and the Alimentary Instruction League. The file is still open, though, mostly because of her Obvious connection."

"Why are they in front of my house?"

"They are on the way to visit you in the hospital, which is I believe next to your residence at 2880 Park. Obvious did not go in but waited in the lobby."

"This was shortly after the threat on the president," said Triegh. "We were watching him. Pure coincidence she showed up. She's also gone underground, so we can't very well ask her. In fact everyone seems to have hit the woodwork. All your skinheads, Melodya included."

"All we have is you," said Parks.

There was a long silence. I was suddenly aware that I had soaked my shirt and was about an inch from likewise despoiling my underwear. Suddenly that maternal entreaty to wear clean underwear lest the authorities be appalled when they pull it off you struck me as uninformed: It is most often the authorities who make you soil your drawers and hence cannot be too surprised when they encounter the results.

"What do you think of me?" I said. Or croaked, really. "I mean, this is all just happenstance and coincidence. You can't think I had anything to do with this."

"We don't," said Triegh. "We just want your opinion."

"Well, I . . . I wish I knew what to say."

"What you want to say is that you'll call us the moment you know anything, see anything, or come across anyone connected with this."

"I came across one of them today, and no one seems particularly happy with me." The special agents said nothing. For some reason it was a very curious nothing. "Anyway, you're the one with the telephoto lens and bursting data banks. You ought to do better than me."

"We can't be everywhere," said Parks with regret. "We rely on the input of good citizens."

"It's a big country," said Triegh. "According to the FCC there are one hundred thirty-seven radio stations he could hit for the next letter."

I looked down at the picture of Josh Carton, good dead citizen. THESE ARE THE SMILING LIARS! Eight to go.

What's your favorite punctuation mark? said that guy at KTOK, a long, long time ago. What was he talking about?

"Nine to go," I said slowly. The agents looked at me expectantly. "Nine, not eight," I said. I looked up smiling, a happy dog who loved his new trick. I tapped the exclamation point on the photo.

"He's going to shoot someone at a station with an exclamation point in its name."

"But there aren't any," said Triegh.

"But there *are*. A station in Washington, D.C., petitioned the FCC for the change. Josh told me about it." This caused them to sit up. "That would be a nice flourish, wouldn't it?"

"Carlton knew about it?"

"That's what I said. And how come he hasn't entered this little colloquy too much?"

"Because he's irrelevant," said Parks. "Thank you for your help."

And that's when I knew what was in Josh's letter.

3

THE REMAINING VICTIMS WERE SHOT ON SCHEDULE.

How Spaunaugle-Obvious, as I liked to call him— say it aloud, it's pleasant—managed to find five people willing to present themselves as targets, I don't know. I can understand the first person not taking precautions—he had knocked off for a while. But when he hit the second two weeks later, on a Friday— regular as payday—you'd think people would have been careful.

Wouldn't you? But that would suggest they knew there was something to guard themselves against. Although the papers whooped and hollered about the return of the Media Massacre, they didn't give many helpful details, such as the name of the gentleman responsible or the fact that there was a pattern to what he was doing. They didn't even release a picture.

Henk knew what was going on, though. I read his accounts of the five incidents and noticed that he wasn't mentioning which letters were targeted anymore. His thumbsucker where-the-story-stands roundups hadn't tied the letters together either. But I was certain he knew, just like the FBI knew. And he was hiding it.

That realization stoked all the cold stoves where I store my sense of journalistic obligations, and I decided I would tell the world what the authorities were hiding from them. I called Fikes and told him I wanted to do another story, and he practically came through the phone for my throat. My last piece—How I Had Destroyed a Carefully Maintained FBI Operation, by Jonathan Simpson, the *Metropole*—had been long on entertainment value but none too good for the paper's reputation as a purveyor of credible journalism. And needless to say the Plaid Café yanked its ads (although the previous week someone had handed me a flier for Shades of Gray, a new nightspot in that same locale). A few other restaurants, hearing only that the food critic for the *Metropole* had leaped over the grill and chased the cook, called to ask if I was insane in addition to being incompetent. Fikes did not want another piece that would Rip the Top Off the

Whole Story. He wanted a nice straight eat-here-you'll-love-it review he could wave in front of the investors.

He would come around, but I had to write the piece first. I made a pot of coffee, went up to my study, turned on the Mac, lit a cigarette, and thought of how to start.

But then I had the same insight that had struck Henk and the FBI: *Don't let him know.*

Don't tell him you know what he's spelling, because you might not know where he's going to hit next but you do *know where he's going to hit last!*

!

And that's where everyone would wait for him: at WDC! You couldn't tell where Spaun-Ob would be before then, unless you posted agents at every station that had the relevant remaining letters. But the decision to wait until he showed in D.C. was probably wise, although certainly costly to a few of Obvious's victims.

Bob Frank, host of a morning show for WLOT, an all-news station in Maine, was struck in the shoulder by a bullet as he entered the station. Herb Barker, afternoon newsreader at a radio station in North Carolina, took a bullet in the upper right thigh just before another bullet took the middle L out of WLLL's sign. (Really, they should have known he'd hit that one.) Mr. Barker also survived.

Hank Beauman, your Fiddling Friend on the FM dial, as Henk wrote, was hit in the shoulder as he stood outside the station having a cigarette. This was in California, where, like Minnesota, it is the height of incivility to smoke around other people. Given the number of radio personalities who had been popped while standing out back beating a butt, it gave you an insight into the denial mechanism of smokers.

Harvey Baxter was killed in northern Minnesota. Henk was able to get there before the police tape came down and write a front-page close-up. Witnesses say Baxter was standing outside talking to the man who was weeding the flowerbed around the station and that as he crouched down to examine something—a rose, a bug, the design on the elastic of the gardener's underwear—he flew back in a tumbler's kip and sprawled on the lawn. Spaun-Ob was probably aiming for something nonlethal, and the man moved at the wrong time, after which Spaun-Ob put a slug through the window on which the station's letters were painted, a slug that buried itself in a filing cabinet of billable accounts and stopped at a file for the local mortuary.

The winner of the last bullet was not a media person at all, but a gaffer for a small television station in Minot, North Dakota, a college student named Jeff Anderson—a name so common half the state probably looked up in alarm when they heard the news. He was wounded in the groin while walking to his car. I can imagine the barber-shop conversation. "Don't know what a gaffer does, but I do know what he *won't* be doing."

Each on a Friday, two weeks apart. No sign of Spaunaugle-Obvious.

I knew where to look for him, and I planned to be there when he showed up. He owed me for three unconscious months. The question was how to bill him for it.

I had been at the New French Bar for three scotches. That's a long time. They pour with a heavy hand. Somehow, I was not yet cheerful. Indeed, the prospect of cheer was receding at a stately pace. I could probably catch it if someone gave me a push.

Happy hour had been spent at Thanks a Lot, an old bar in a building slated to close for demolition the next day. The rest of the buildings on the lot were boarded and marked for destruction, making the Thanks a Lot sign particularly bitter. I had coffee there with an old friend from college who worked downtown, but he had to go home and tend to his kid. I went across the street to Peter's Grill, where in college I had spent hours at the counter writing in my journals. I considered walking to Dinkytown, right by the campus, but the idea of ending up sitting alone in a booth at the Valli watching the fresh-faced and firm-fleshed stride around slinging burgers, looking at me with the same mild pity I'd given solitary people in their thirties when I'd worked there—ah, it was too much. I decided to go to the French, see who I met, and ignore them.

I'd met no one. The people I knew who would show would roll in at midnight when their plays or showings were done. In the meantime I would hold down this table. Midnight was only four hours away.

I sipped scotch and read a novel I'd bought on the way over. It was something of Henk's. I hadn't known he'd written a novel, but there it was in the dreaded Regional section: *Pothole Fever.* The story of one man's travels around Minnesota on a bike, written five years before when he wasn't just a bad writer but a bad writer at the height of his talents. I was reading the chapter where the hero, a boisterous young man named Honk, has climbed up to the top of the Jolly Green Giant statue and is standing there hands on hips, when someone tapped on my shoulder.

"I'm saving the seat for someone," I said, not looking up.

"Me, I hope," she said, and that got my attention. It was Tara.

"I can't stay," she said, sitting down. She took out a pack of cigarettes, waved for the waiter, and ordered a margarita.

"I'm over at the restaurant? And I was heading off to the ladies' spiffy? and saw you sitting here. I haven't seen you for such a long time, and wanted to see what was up?" She looked tired. Perky as ever but falsely so, as if jerked about by wires. "You don't return my calls."

"I didn't know you were making them."

"I call and call and call, and all I get is a whistle, like I'm calling a fax machine?"

Damn: the computer. I had kept my phone line hooked up to the computer, and anyone who called must have gotten the modem. No wonder my answering machine was full of clicks.

"Nothing's up," I said. "Haven't been shot or run over lately. Brain's doing fine. And you?"

"Fine, fine, fine." She lit a cigarette and shook the match like a thermometer, with a little more vigor than necessary, and placed it carefully in the ashtray. "Fine."

"What have you been calling about? Don't tell me you're doing a piece on all the shootings."

"What shootings?" she said. "You mean *those* shootings? Well, maybe." The wires tugged, and she gave a quick smile. "You can probably guess."

"How's Henk?"

"Henk?"

"Your husband. The guy I was cuckolding for half a year."

"He's fine, just great, great." The waiter brought her drink with regret. Ordering a margarita at this bar was like yelling out a request for the *Star Wars* theme at an orchestra concert. I merely touched my glass to indicate another. "Can I get a pen?" she asked the waiter.

"Thanks! Anyway, Henk just got an offer on the next book. The violence one?"

"Right. He's still pretending he's writing a book about the effects of crime on survivors?" I scowled. "Any huge million-dollar offers for that one?"

"Only one. Actually, a half million." Another quick smile. "It's turned out to be something quite different of course, what with all those shootings. The radio ones?" She stubbed her cigarette out and lit another. "There's so *much* he knows. Things he doesn't write about. I hardly see him anymore. He's on the road all the time running after the Mohawk man." She flicked me a look to see if I reacted. I didn't. "He drives everywhere—silly old Henk, afraid to fly." The waiter returned with a drink for me and a pen for Tara. There was a television journalist for you: no pen. She thanked him and fumbled in her purse, produced a business card, and scrawled something on the back. Then she took a sip of my drink and made a face. "Yuk. I don't know how you can *drink* that. Well, nice talking! See you." She stood, tossed her hair back and smiled. It brought back the days when I slept with women who had hair. I watched her go, heard her meet someone at the door with an insincere squeal of delight, then pass out of sight down the hall. To the spiffy.

I looked at what she'd written on the card.

Wash DC next Fri—pls be there—We're taking the train—I am afraid!

I used it as a bookmark for *Pothole Fever*.

I was two blocks up the street before my leg started to hurt, and I realized I'd left my cane at Thanks a Lot, where this evening of heedless joy had begun. Perhaps I could find it in the rubble tomorrow.

I would go to Washington, D.C., to get my head

blown off or, if not, take notes for another bad book to be joylessly slapped together and earn me another bleak month on the pimp 'n' shill circuit. All this would be tolerable if I didn't feel so goddamn *alone*.

You see, I finally realized I would be facing the man who'd shot me. While I fully trusted there to be agents of the government who would shoot him good and properly, the thought of being present still scared the hell out of me. I did not want to do it by myself. I did not want to do it alone.

I do believe I'm going off to die. Who wants to keep me company?

Then I looked over at the bus shelter, saw the big ad for the big man with the big tart draped bigly around his big shoulders, and started to laugh, laugh the stupid laugh of the drunken.

Who, indeed.

4

YOUR SEATMATE ON A TRAIN IS USUALLY ONE SORT OF nightmare or the other—a gasping asthmatic; a baby who behaves as if his diaper is full of nettles; a Rabelaisian mound that will eat, sweat, eat, snore, sweat, and take up half your seat. But none of that troubled me this time.

"This is *happening*," Samurai said.

It was too early for this much radiant humanity. "Wherever you look, things are happening."

"I don't know about that." Samurai struggled to fit his huge body into the contours of the seat, clearly designed for people who fell within certain genetic parameters, that is, not given to pointlessly overdeveloped buttock muscles. "This *place* isn't happening.

Few things are happening, really. But the general idea of what we're doing is *happening*."

Eight hours to Chicago, an eight-hour layover, then sleeper cars to Washington, D.C., via the Capitol Limited, all courtesy the *Metropole*.

The conductor came by and glowered at our tickets, punching them with rancor as though they were something obscene he'd ban if he had the authority. The train gave a violent shudder. There was the squeal of giant scissors drawn against a fresh whetstone, and we lurched forward.

"Explain to me again what we're doing," Samurai said. I told him.

"Good thing I brought guns," he said when I'd finished. "Do you know how *cranked* you sounded when you called me up for this job? Like the hounds of hell were peeing on your leg. Almost made me feel frightened—*technically* impossible. Anyway, I'm not going halfway across the country to bodyguard my little buddy without some serious munitions."

"Are they registered?"

"Sure." He frowned. "Well, to *someone* they are."

After eight hours Chicago lumbered toward us, the Sears Tower leading the mob. Fabulous skyscrapers capped with spumes of light surrounded it like bodyguards hired for their fashion sense. The dim lights of the rail yard played on the tracks, glinted on the sides of boxcars waiting, dumb, dozing beasts yoked with rust and chains.

A conductor with a fat welt on his forehead ushered us off with no particular joy. Samurai and I strode down a harshly lit platform to the waiting room. Upstairs we found a cavernous waiting room in such disrepair you didn't know if they were fixing it up or had just unearthed it. Scaffolding hugged one wall. A tired American flag was unfurled beneath one arch in case there was any doubt which nation we were in. Standing above the entrance were two statues symbolizing—and I'm guessing here, God forbid there should be a plaque around to help the metaphorically disabled—Night and Day. Night was a woman drawing a cloak over her face, Day was looking with classical dispassion into the distance.

"Look," I said, pointing to the statue. "See the one hiding her face? That symbolizes the Chicagoans' attitude toward organized crime: I didn't see nothing."

"Fascinating," he said with no conviction. "What about the other one looking out into the distance like she's trying to see if there are any cabs coming?"

"That represents the ability to overlook the petty reality of civic corruption," I said. Samurai nodded, enlightened. He breathed deeply, flexed. "You know, this feels familiar, running around the country with guns. Maybe I was a cop."

"Or a drug dealer."

"Oh, I know I was a drug dealer. But maybe I switched sides. I saw a movie about that once. On TV. Wasn't very good. Had that guy who's now on that game show based on—what is that game of pool, except it's British?

"Snookers."

"Snookers." He stared contemplatively at Night.

We spent a gray hour in the waiting room, seated across from a man who chain-smoked and ground out the butts on the floor, then arranged them with his foot into a semicircle, like a boundary that would keep germs and bums out. We could have spent the time in the first-class lounge, but if Tara and Henk were on this train, that's where they'd be. No man with a half-million-dollar book deal takes coach on a cross-country train trip. If they were on it. The idea that Tara had been sent by Henk to put me on this train was a notion that had been gnawing at me since we left. Perhaps he was going to keep me from showing up and catching Spaunaugle myself. Maybe he planned to derail the train. Maybe he'd tie ropes around Tara and put her on the tracks.

At eight o'clock they announced the Capitol Limited was boarding sleeping car passengers. We plodded back to the platform, passed the waiting hordes of coach passengers with little guilt—aristocrats en route to the palace. We were met by a short, doughy attendant who held up a clipboard and demanded our names. Simpson, I said, and I snuck a look at his manifest: *H. Gruesse. T. Sarnoff. Room H, Car 3901.*

"Pull up a toilet and sit down," said Samurai, gesturing to the shiny steel commode in the corner of the room. There was hardly any room for the two of us. Samurai occupied about 80 percent of the room, provided he didn't flex anything. He could have done the Marx Brothers' stateroom scene as a one-man show. "You want some poisonous nitrite-filled wine?" I shook my head. "Artificially made cheese?" He held out a foil triangle with a picture of an inordinately happy mouse. I took it. It was as spongy as a baby's arm.

"Dinner's in an hour," I said, handing him back his cheese. "Why fill up on bad food when there's so much bad food ahead?"

"I'm hungry." He scowled at grim Chicago, crawling along outside the window. Check-cashing storefronts, exhausted houses leaning into one another, tattered billboards of happy people holding long unlit cigarettes. "Where is the bed in this place? I thought beds came with this deal."

"It's in the wall," I said. "Everything folds out of the wall." I leaned behind me, pulled a tiny latch, and conjured a sink out of the wall. I depressed the spouts. The cold-water spout spat out a greeting. The hot-water tap sighed. "You get the bed down by pulling that big lever. The one marked BED. It's understandably confusing," I added. "Look, we have to figure out what to do about Henk. He's in the car behind us, and we're bound to see him coming or going."

"Who the hell cares? Let him know. If he has a problem, I can throw him off the train."

"You can't do that. You'd kill him."

"Not if I taught him how to land right. See, you have to keep your knees loose. Like this."

"No throwing Henk off the train. I don't want his book more exciting than mine, okay? He'll know where we're going and why. He may want to talk. Maybe not. Just be prepared."

"I'll take the gun to dinner."

"Well, wear something where it won't be noticeable." Samurai looked at me quizzically. "Don't you own any clothes that aren't designed to show off your arterial system?"

"Oh. So it's *formal,"* Samurai said. "I'll get out my sweatpants. What does this Henk look like again? So I know."

"Tall guy, thin, red hair, expression of someone with flaming piles." There was a knock on the door. "Ah. That'll be the porter for dinner reservations." I pulled the door back.

"Hello," said Henk. I stared, agog. Henk grinned. "Hey. When you guys going to eat?"

"It was pointless to hide," said Henk, leaning back in his chair with the relaxed look of a man among friends. Or vanquished enemies. Tara was in her room, he'd said, complaining of a headache. Something ached, anyway. The train was rattling and banging at high speed now, wheels screaming beneath the floor. I hoped Tara didn't really have a headache, or she'd been needing an aspirin the size of a tractor tire.

"We were going to run into each other eventually—if not here on the train, then in Washington," said Henk. "Crime makes strange bedfellows." He twirled beard hairs into a point.

I looked down at my steak. Sometimes meat is rather up front about being dead flesh carved from a dead animal. This was one of those times. "So what takes you to D.C.?"

"Oh, please, Jonathan. You don't have to dance." He continued to twirl his beard hairs. "I'm on this train for the same reason you are. The bad guy enters his final act, and we, scribes of true crime, have to be there to record it."

"I'm doing a piece on museums. A travel piece."

"With a bodyguard?" Henk pointed a fork at Samurai, who was staring with great malevolence at his Vegetarian Harvest Medley.

"It's a dangerous city." I took a bite of the meat. It tasted like burnt kapok. "People murdered every day. Fifteen killed on line to see Titians just the other day. Gang warfare. Tell the wrong person you prefer baroque to mannerism, and they'll just as soon shoot you as argue."

"Killing people for artistic reasons." Henk smiled. "What an unusual idea."

"Listen, Henk," I barked, a little too loudly. "I own this story. I got shot, not you." Henk rolled his eyes. "Plus, I have your sister as a source, and you probably don't, and that's going to look just great when our books come out. Right? So eat your meat and get out of here. I'm not telling you anything."

"Give me a break," Henk growled. "Tell *you* anything? I was a police reporter for ten years. I have more sources in the cop shop than you have leaks in that tinshit roof at your big, fancy house. What are you, a food critic? And I'm supposed to be worried about what you can dig up? You didn't even read that letter from Spaunaugle. I know, because I've read your pieces, and if your letter said what mine did, you'd bark it all over the first graph. But you don't have anything. You don't know anything. I don't know why you think you're going to get anything out of this trip at all." He took a sip of his coffee and winced: too hot.

"Why should you care?" I asked.

"Whatever I say, I can prove. Whatever you'll write is guesswork or stuff you've stolen from my articles. Anyway, friend, after this trip, whatever you have to say won't count for shit." Henk looked down at his coffee cup, then gave me a cold and empty look. "You really don't have any idea what's going to happen out there, do you?" he said. "You don't. Well, you can always write interesting color features on the trial, if there's a trial, which I doubt."

"Ever parachute?" said Samurai. Henk looked puzzled, shook his head. Samurai continued. "Well, the thing is to keep your knees bent. Don't fight the ground. Fall into it, like it was the softest bed in the world."

"He always this irrelevant?" said Henk.

"Actually, he's being uncharacteristically pertinent," I said, kicking one of Samurai's titanium shins under the table. "He's referring to how you should behave if he throws you off the train."

"Hey!" said Samurai. "Don't spoil it for him."

Henk blanched. "Why do that?"

"I don't know. Why warn me off? Nothing you say makes sense here. The only thing I know that you don't is the contents of the skinhead's computer disk, which I gave to the police, who you say tell you everything. So I don't even have that. So I know nothing you don't. If I write a book, who cares? You have the big contract. You have the dutiful audience and the good day job and the promotional apparatus. You'll do well, and if my book comes out at the same time, it'll probably get lost. I don't care. But I think you'll read every word. I think you'll look for that one little bit of writing or scene setting that you know in your bitter little heart is better than anything you could do, and you'll realize that your wife just didn't sleep with another man, but a better writer. And that will drive you nuts."

"Whoa!" said Samurai. "I don't know what you're talking about, but I am *frankly impressed*. I think you hit a nerve. Did he hit a nerve?" he asked Henk.

"Think what you want," said Henk. He stood up and tossed some money on the table. "See you at the studio," he said and he left.

"He's really a poor use of skin," Samurai commented after Henk had stamped off. "Is he going to bug us the whole trip?"

"Probably."

"Not if I can help it. He's going off the train tonight."

"Samurai, you can't throw a man off the train."

"I gave him the instructions." Samurai drank off an entire glass of water. "Do you want him off?"

"Of course I do," I snapped. "Tomorrow's the Friday Spaunaugle-Obvious finishes his stupid little thesis and sends it off to whatever bindery a performance artist-slash-serial killer uses. If Henk goes off the train tonight, he'll never make it. He won't fly, and it's too far to drive. But you can't throw him off. If you somehow manage not to dash his brains against the crossing gate, he'll identify you and we'll both get thrown in jail."

Samurai sighed. "I wish this kind of stuff wasn't so

familiar. Thrashing drunks. Using guns. Throwing people off trains. I don't know if I should be guilty or proud, you know? It *taxes* a man."

"Doesn't mean you were bad," I said, scowling into my coffee. "Sometimes the interests of society require that a jackass gets thrown off a train."

"Yeah, but bad people fly or drive around in fast cars. Not likely I threw a *bad* guy off a train. Probably some innocent family man. A guy in a witness protection program, maybe. All that work by the government, and I screw it up. And for what?" he added, not depressed but philosophical.

"Maybe you did it in Europe, where everyone takes trains, including the bad guys."

He brightened. "Sure. Hell, my passport has stamps from all these countries I can't remember visiting. Maybe I was CIA." Then he frowned again. "Or KGB."

"I'm going back to the bar car." I put down a tip, waved a farewell at my half-eaten steak. "Don't throw him off. Please." He nodded and tore into his eggplant. It didn't stand a chance.

I'd been down in the smoking lounge for an hour or so and, as is the custom with trains, fallen into easy conversation with fellow smokers. The bar car is a traditionally charmless place. The air is always blue with smoke, the floor littered with crushed snacks, the bartenders generally surly, and the selection of food limited to ghastly pizza squares; dry, oversugared pastries; and sad, damp sandwiches that tasted of chemicals. In other words, a neighborhood tavern towed across the country. Except, of course, the phone numbers written on the walls have area codes.

I was seated at the back, right below a machine that ate the smoke electronically, uttering an occasional vindictive *pzzt!* as it did so. I had my back to my destination, and the world unraveled in a long, fluid monologue. Within minutes I was joined by others with cups of brackish Amtrak coffee and amber drinks, shaking cigarettes from their pack, ready to stare out the window and act like old friends. We got destinations out of the way first—that always comes before names—and settled in to marking the miles with talk.

I was talking with the usual assortment of snaggle-toothed ex-felons and fat, brassy travel agents on vacation when Tara slid into the seat across from me.

"I can't stay long," she said.

"That's becoming your signature," I said. "Tara, you don't look well." Her shoulders slumped a bit. "And I say that not as an ex, but as a friend."

"I'm not sure we're friends," she said. "I think we're just two people who used to go to bed with each other."

Now she's a stickler for details. "Why did you tell me to come on this train? You should have been a little more forthcoming at the French. I knew all about the D.C. thing. Have for weeks. I like the train, but—"

"Henk's going to kill Spaunaugle. He's got a gun."

"Well, you suggested as much," I said, cross. "What am I supposed to do about it? You're the TV reporter —if you're going to be in the studio tomorrow, tell your crew to have a camera on him. That ought to cut down on any vigilante impulses."

"There isn't any camera crew," she hissed. "He wouldn't let me bring one. Do you understand the position I'm in?"

"If your husband kills the guy, he may get in big trouble. If he doesn't, you lose a couple million. Granted, it's a puzzler."

"It's not that!" she said. She leaned across the table, eyes wide and hot, suddenly the old, mad, lovely Tara I'd first met. "It's not like that at all. He—"

She must have thought I had suddenly decided to leap across the table and kiss her, for there I was, flying out of my seat.

But I was not alone.

Everyone aboard the Capital Limited was suddenly pitched from their seat as though blown through a bazooka.

A keening screech wailed from the wheels below us, and the floor froze, jerked away like a rug. I heard a dozen anvils of varying weight thud to the floor above me, heard the miniature bottles in the bar leap from their place and shatter with the sound of some anarchic carillon. I saw those sitting down and facing forward pitch into the table, and those facing backward bark out in shock as the table suckerpunched them in the stomach. It was a busy time, and I was en route to the floor, so I may have missed some details.

My head bounced once, just once. That was enough. Then I skidded on my back down the aisle. Somehow I'd turned myself around as I fell, probably grabbing for handholds. I found myself caroming off the inert pile of people and coming to rest against the bulkhead at the end of the car. Half a second later Tara flew my way, limbs flailing. Here was an eternity of screeching and howling and grinding as we slowed, slowed more, shuddered, stopped.

I looked south and saw Tara, dazed and momentarily unplugged, staring at my groin with stupefaction. The floor was littered with people and cups and cards and ashtrays and a hundred tiny liquor bottles, as though giants had invaded a Lilliputian drinking shop and been valiantly repulsed. There were groans and curses.

There had been few casualties from the emergency stop. The worst was a man who'd been hit by Samurai. The sudden stop impelled Samurai forward, his ster-

234

num striking the man in the forehead and instantly convincing his conscious mind to go hide somewhere. The man had been taken off at Toledo, his ring fingers twitching. Just his ring fingers. It was like scraping bad meat off a cold griddle. They put the stretcher under him, scooped him up. His head stuck to the carpet.

I stood in the front of the sleeper car, watching the scene, disoriented, flummoxed by the noise and confusion. Henk was screaming at Samurai, Tara was sniffling in the corner, two porters were shouting for us to return to our rooms while they helped the injured off.

"It's his fault!" Henk screamed, jabbing a finger at Samurai. "He was trying to throw me off the train!"

"Please," said Samurai.

"That's why I hit the emergency brake!" Henk shouted. "It was the only way I could—"

"*You* hit the brake?" one of the porters said, standing on the platform. "Man, you're in a whole new type of trouble." His walkie-talkie crackled a few words, and he muttered something in return. I looked out the door at Toledo, wasn't impressed.

"He was trying to kill me!"

"Henk," I said. "Let's all calm down. Come on. Let's go have a drink."

"I will not drink with this maniac!"

"Henk!" Tara sobbed. "Please! Let's just go to bed!"

"Excellent idea," said Samurai, giving a theatrical yawn.

"Oh, *you* want my wife too? You and Simpson? Little needledick Simp here wants to have my wife again and then you take seconds while I lay broken along the track bed? Was that the idea?"

"For Christ's sake, Henk, shut up!" I said. "You have to shoot a man tomorrow. Husband your strength."

It was either the admission that I knew what he was

up to or my use of the word *husband.* Henk swung at me. I blocked the punch with a forearm, and he staggered off balance, put a foot into the three-step stairwell, and toppled off the train, arms flailing.

His head cracked hard on the Toledo platform, and his eyes rolled up and closed.

The porter who'd told Henk he was in trouble for pulling the brake looked down at the motionless form, ran his tongue along the inside of his cheek. "Justice is done," he said.

5

PENNSYLVANIA ROLLED PAST. GREEN HILLS AND BROWN towns, empty mills like the ferrous skin of some long-departed beast. I was having breakfast alone in the dining car. The pancakes tasted like something originally placed in the pharaoh's tomb so that he might have breakfast on the Other Side. I poured syrup on the stack. It vanished into the pancakes like rain into thirsty soil. The sausage was a hard, dark rod that looked like something a dog had labored to extrude, legs shaking, its voice a high, pained whine. I pushed it away and turned my attention back to the window, watched the train slide through the clotted land of the eastern seaboard. More gutted factories, faded names, and ruined windows. Toxic rivers glinted with chemicals. The occasional overbuilt downtown, chastened by high vacancy rates, hiding now behind a curtain of gray smoke. Two hours of this, alternating with pastoral and unaffordable suburban developments, and then we were in the District of Columbia.

Samurai spurned the red cap, carrying both our luggage as well as that of an old lady with three hat boxes and a steamer trunk on a leash. The heat hit us like an anvil shot from a cannon. Samurai staggered and dropped every bag he carried. We recovered and joined a line of bureaucrats in suits, ties knotted right against their throats like voluntary nooses, all of them sweating Niagaras and looking as though they might pass out en masse like pin-striped dominoes. The cab stand attendant put them into cabs with the professional detachment of someone shoving pizzas into ovens.

Our cabbie spoke not a word, staring sullenly at the road while the radio played a sermon excoriating the Jewish conspiracy and the white devil. *The Protocols of the Elders of Oslo,* I thought. We passed through a blasted neighborhood that looked to have doubled as a proving ground for shoulder-fired rockets, then graduated to a street where there were actually buildings on every lot. Our hotel was a graceless concrete crescent perched on a hill. From the look our cab driver gave me when we pulled up, it was the hotel preferred by nine out of ten white devils. His contribution to helping us with the luggage consisted of popping the trunk and driving away before we had taken it all out of the back. Samurai had to chase after him and bang on the roof to get him to stop. I had, of course, overtipped.

We checked in, a pasty desk clerk enveloping us in usual clouds of insincere deference throughout the procedure. There was time to drop the bags and check the beds for tensile strength, then we had to get to the radio station. We were late as it was.

WDC! was located south from the hotel by Dupont Circle, close enough to walk. I was still unsure about what I was going to do here. I'd called the station's general manager before leaving Minneapolis and said I was doing an article on talk radio around the nation and wanted to sit in on a few shows. I had sent a copy of *Dead Bread* before calling so they knew I wasn't some wretched hack but a real, published hack.

"Oh, no," I said. "No, no, no."

Dupont Circle was a park filled with Mohawked bicycle messengers and dank, slumbering bums. There was a fountain in the middle of the circle, graceful art nouveau maidens with laudanum-numbed smiles. A banner went round the fountain.

WDC! TALKS! said the banner. LIVE TODAY, LIVE TONIGHT! YOUR TOWN, YOUR STATION!

Sitting behind a table by the fountain was a old man in a brown suit, talking earnestly into a microphone. Speakers were set up so the messengers and bums could hear his words.

". . . so if you haven't come down, well, what can I say but come down. We'll be here all day and, ah, all night. Broadcasting live from Dupont Circle, laid out by L'Enfant and named after Dupont. Hey, I made a rhyme. Anyway, management seems to insist that this is what WDC! is all about: getting among the people of this great city, and not hiding in some comfortable air-conditioned room and pretending we know what's going on. No, we're out here sweating like idiots who don't know any better. I'm, ah, Mark D. Kravips, and I'll be back after this message."

"Let me handle this," I said.

"Go ahead." Samurai snarled. "I'd just *mightily* berate him for being unhappening."

I walked over to the table. Mark D. Kravips looked up and pulled his headphones off one ear, regarding me with a wan smile.

"Hello," he said. "You want a beer magnet, I suppose. Over there in the box." He pointed to a box full of vinyl squares that said WDC! and New Columbia Beer!

"No, I'm here for the madman with a Mohawk."

He gestured to the bicycle messengers. "Take your pick."

"No, I'm not kidding. Didn't your producer tell you there'd be a guy around today, writing a book on—"

"Oh, that. I wondered if you were showing up. They had you down for the four o'clock hour. But here you are." He was a tired man who had worked better stations. "Mind coming on a little early? I'm not pulling any calls out here."

"I'm not here to be your guest, for Chrissakes! You'd better unplug and take some cover or—"

"I'm confused. You're the crime writer? Isn't this—"

"Thirty seconds, Mark," called a young man at the adjacent table.

"Have a seat."

Fine. We'd do this on the air then. I sat down and took the headphones. DJ Samurai, sensing air time in a major market, promptly trotted over and took the spare headphones. I indicated that he was with me. Mark D. Kravips appeared utterly confused but soldiered on with a shrug of his shoulders.

"This is, ah, Mark D. Kravips, and we're back on WDC! with—" He looked down at his notes. "With Dr. Naomi Mangere. No, I'm sorry, she's next hour. But you won't want to miss it and hear all about her new book *Your Prostate Is a Time Bomb.* With us now is a man who writes true crime books for a living. Let's welcome Henk Gruesse."

"No, I said. "Jonathan Simpson. Henk Gruesse is in the hospital. It's important I—"

"And *this* is Samurai Stevens, KTOK St. Paul/ Minneapolis, 1510 on your AM hemisphere," Samurai barked. "Mark D. Kravips. What kind of radio name is that?"

"It's my own," said Kravips, calm as Christ. "It's

Polish. And you, Mr. Samurai, must be a wacky, unpredictable morning jock. Would you like a beer magnet?"

Samurai was inflating en route to some sort of furious oration. I held up a hand to keep him from unloading.

"Everybody—shut—the—hell—up," I said. I leaned into the mike. "I'd like everyone to leave this park immediately. I believe a Mohawked man intends to do violence to Mr. Kravips here and anyone who happens to be nearby. This man has killed or injured dozens of people already, and if his pattern holds, Mr. Kravips here can expect to be shot before the network news. Am I clear?"

No one moved. I looked to my left and saw bored bike messengers, a few glaring at me for my blatant display of Mohawkism. Someone on the edge of the park was clapping, slowly, sarcastically.

"I'm absolutely serious!" I shouted. "And I cannot understand why no one is willing to lend a fraction of an ear to what I am talking about! *Hasn't anybody warned you?"* Another round of clapping, the same lone pair of hands stropping my embarrassment. A car honked on the street. I heard a bus groan to my right. Everything appeared normal except me.

"Excuse me." Kravips stared down at his notes. "I have here that you're going to talk about your new book, and it's about someone who shoots media people. Who was this person or will that spoil the ending?"

"He's, ah, a mentally unbalanced artist," I said slowly. "He is spelling out his thesis statement one letter at a time by shooting people employed by the station whose call letters have a letter he wants. Think of it as a game show. Except instead of buying a vowel, he shoots it out of your hand. No one's told you?

Didn't that idiot Gruesse at least *warn* you?" Clap, clap. Closer now. Kravips scribbled something on a notepad.

"My little buddy is telling the truth," said Samurai gravely. "This man shot the guy whose time slot I now occupy. It's drive time, three to six, and currently I'm the highest rated in the market. I *am* the drive time, so let me tell you, Mr. Kravips, that your style—"

I was staring at what Kravips at scrawled on the notepad:

WE KNOW!
FBI IS HERE!
CALM DOWN! YOU'RE GOING TO RUIN IT!

"Oh," I said. "Well. Oh."

"You tell 'em, Simpson!" I looked up. There was, undoubtably, the source of the clapping, limping with a bandaged head, needing only someone tootling on a fife to complete the revolutionary tableau. Henk. How in the hell did he drag his sorry corpus here? "You're the great true crime writer," he shouted. "Surely you can spare some secrets for us amateurs. Rank amateurs," he added, cliché instincts still firing.

"My competition," I said weakly.

"Hey! How was Toledo?" Samurai shouted.

"Let's swap trade secrets," said Henk, hobbling up to the microphone. His eyes were red and not entirely focused. "Let's talk about Mr. Simpson's uncanny ability to find women involved with the bad guys and then sleep with them. Let's talk about one—hey, make it two—two plots just dropping in his lap like manna from heaven! And I mean in his lap!"

"Would you like a beer magnet?" said Kravips. "Someone has to take a beer magnet."

Henk took the box of beer magnets and flung it in

the air. Magnets went everywhere. "This little—this little—this little—" Then he stabbed a finger at Samurai. "This big—this—"

"Christ and Kali and harefuckingkrishna," Samurai said quietly, staring past Henk. "It was her after all."

Henk wheeled around, scrabbling at his waist, and now he had a pistol in his hand.

Rounding the fountain, staring at the ground: Melodya.

Sweat covered her head, which was now covered with a fashionable bristle of black stubble, tough shoots from brackish topsoil. "Melodya!" I cried.

Henk's hands began to shake convulsively. She looked up, and her face was drawn—eyes ringed, cheeks hollow. She saw us and gave a sob. Her eyes went unbelievingly from Henk to me to Samurai and back through the circuit again, her eyes darting between our faces like someone etching a cat's cradle. She kept walking toward us on leaden feet, no light in her eyes. She carried a black suitcase.

She stopped about ten feet from the table and stared, shaking her head. Henk to me to Samurai to me to Henk. Tears rose in her eyes, and she backed away, shaking her head. I was frozen by the sight of her and would have sat there like the art nouveau statues, dreamy and uncaring. She slept with me, she's not going to harm me, there's nothing in that briefca —Ouch: Samurai had elbowed me hard in the ribs to wake me up, and as I snapped back, I saw a natty black man in a bow tie bolt toward Mel. A bum sprinted across the lawn toward her as well, and most of the bike messengers were on their feet and running—not away, but toward us. Henk was hobbling toward her. She backed away quickly, her eyes now frantically darting between us, the suitcase, some point beyond the fountain. She started to run as Henk and the natty man converged on her. She dropped the suitcase and cried out one long shriek of fear and despair. Then Samurai knocked me to the ground.

BAOM!

Hard in the ears and deep in the guts.

God slamming his fist on a great oaken chest.

A slap on the something that was between me and the sound.

Splinters.

Spattering of something heavy and cool my cheek.

Ringing, ringing, ringing.

Silence.

Then noise: moaning, cries, honking horns. I looked up and saw blue sky and the same old furious sun, white indifferent clouds. I struggled up, heard someone shout "Hey!" and discovered I was laying on top of Mark D. Kravips. Samurai had already bolted to his feet, and he kicked away the table that had been knocked over and shielded us from the the blast.

Melodya, I thought.

No Melodya. A hole in the concrete, tree branches splintered, leaves still drifting down. A few bikes blown into the grass, a dozen people squatting or bending over, hands over their ears, wailing high ululations of distress, one man in spandex with a bike spoke sticking from his leg. There were three or four or five sprawled on the ground, unmoving. Hideous bloody things were strewn around the ground as well, smoking. I turned to the fountain on legs of meringue, noted that one of the maidens had had her nose blown off, and vomited into the water.

"I can't hear," the Samurai bellowed. "I can't hear!"

And there was so much to hear. Car alarms were going off for blocks around, and sirens were wailing in the distance. People cried and sobbed and whimpered. The last few beer magnets fluttered to the ground. Some made a gentle plosh as they landed in the water. A few had landed on cars and stuck to their hoods. One, I observed, had adhered to the sign announcing: This Is Your Park. Please Clean Up After Yourself.

6

BACK TO THE HOSPITAL WITH ANOTHER HEAD WOUND, EX-cept that this time I was conscious. Certainly a move in the right direction.

I sat in the waiting room, watching the ambulances unload the victims. The first few that had gone in wore sheets all the way over their head. A hospital seemed to be a rather inappropriate place to bring them. I thought of a story I'd read about the discovery in New York City of several old skulls in a cardboard box, sitting on a street corner. The story said they'd been taken away by ambulance. What's the rush? Same idea here.

They had taken in Samurai. He still couldn't hear anything in either ear, and his body appeared to have deflated. There was a gash in one shoulder where a beer magnet had sliced through it, like those straws picked up by hurricanes and driven half a foot into a phone pole. Maybe he was leaking.

I was in shock but not incapacitated. Mild shock. As though forced at gunpoint to take Valium—calming but somehow unnerving at the same time. I was not certain what had happened, other than Spaunaugle's bomb had gone off—bomb! appropriate for an expla-nation point, really—and that Mel and possibly Henk had been atomized in the explosion. The ambulances had been quick in arriving. They get a lot of practice in D.C., I understand. Two paramedics had found me sitting on the edge of the fountain, sobbing without cease.

I came to my senses in the waiting room, staring at a copy of *Time*. Our Changing Economic Outlook, said the cover. Probably a special waiting room edition, good no matter how long it sits there. I picked it up and started reading, but none of the words would stay still. The magazine slid from my hands, and I leaned back and closed my eyes.

Bang and the gurney smashed through the doors to the ER, heading out to the ambulances for another load. Hard to tell how many had been in. I'd seen a bum standing in shock with all his clothes blown off. Maybe he'd been the one wearing five parkas. Strong explosion. Maybe the FBI would adopt this as a new rating scale. "We estimate the suitcase carried enough explosion to blow five, perhaps six, parkas off a bum standing fifty feet away. Of course, compared to the bomb dropped on Hiroshima, which had enough power to blow 22,390,873 parkas off a bum standing fifty feet from ground zero, it's puny."

I spent the next hour veering between reliving the explosion and observing the chaos in the waiting room, feeling as though I was stuck in a motel with a TV that only had two fuzzy channels. After a while a nice nurse came and took me away and sat me down on a bed surrounded by clean white curtains that rippled slightly with some unfelt breeze. It would have seemed like heaven except for the large enema bag hanging on the wall. "Depends on your idea of heaven, of course," I said to the nurse.

"Of course it does," she said with a smile. "How do you feel?"

"Malleated," I said. The word made perfect sense. Past tense of malleable. But that wasn't a verb. "It ought to be a verb," I sniffed. "Really, it should."

"Oh, my." She eased me down on my back. She

slapped a blood pressure cuff on my arm, that great Velcro engagement ring that announces you and mortality are an item. She registered my vitals, then talked with another doctor who had materialized in the corner of the room. The doctor spoke in that odd tongue of the physician, solid ancient Latin colliding with vaporous trade names of various wonder drugs. Then the nurse helped me up and settled me in a wheelchair. She said something, but she might as well had been talking to her aquarium for all I understood. An orderly wheeled me away, down to a pharmacopoeia, where I was given drugs. The rest of the day was a vast blank canvas. I didn't even sign my name to it.

Henk was down the hall in the ward for people who had suffered two concussions in as many days. He also had a fractured leg and, from what one of the policemen had told me, the blast slapshot one of Henk's kneecaps through a plate-glass window on the other side of the street and knocked two teeth from the mouth of a bank teller. Henk would walk eventually, but for the next several months he'd lose a footrace with a continental plate. The word from the nurse was that he was not only as unlikable as ever but thoroughly depressed, which expressed itself through arch sniffles and black sulks.

"And how are we today!" I cried as I limped into his room. He was worse than reported. Both arms were swaddled in casts from bicep to fingertips. He looked like someone in a horror movie slowly, inexorably turning into the Michelin Man.

"Go away, Simpson." Henk turned his head toward the window.

"Why? We're practically roommates, what with me just two doors down. Almost like a dorm, eh?"

"Wouldn't know." Sullen glare.

"Anyway, I could hear you weeping from my room

and thought I'd come over and give you some comfort. How's the leg?" I sat down on his bed and slapped his cast. "Take it from me, they're doing miracles with physical therapy nowadays. They'll straighten that busted one almost to the point where you couldn't tell it was broken. The chance of you coming out of this with no more than a nickname like Old Wishbone or Festus are damn near even."

"Would you go away?" Henk shouted. "Chrissakes, I saw my sister blow up yesterday! Do you know what that's like?"

"Nope. All my sisters are intact."

"Jesus, you're sick."

"No, vindictive." I smiled. "Tell me about that gun you pulled back at the circle. You were already to shoot until you saw it was Melodya. Were you really going to bring down Spaunaugle yourself?" His eyes twitched slightly. "I mean, I've had troubles with the ends of my pieces, too, but that is going a little too far."

"Get out. Just—"

"I can see where you thought it could work. Brilliant writer has suspicions, just suspicions, mind you, goes heeled to where the bad guy might show up, and in a fit of civic zeal shoots him before he pops anyone else. Or in this case blows up the park. There'd be trouble, but what a two-fisted sort of fellow you'd seem when it was all over. Right?"

"I don't know what you're talking about."

"Your wife does. She told me as much. Why isn't she here weeping by your side? Could she be any more disgusted with you at this juncture in the marriage?"

Henk just stared out the window. I sat down on the bed and patted his leg cast. "Henk, what a stupid idea. I mean, I can tell from reading your stuff that you have a poor imagination, but this poor—I stand in awe. If you thought you could get yourself out of this by killing Spaunaugle, you must have been extraordinarily desperate. Why not just go to the police?"

"I didn't know. Nothing was for certain."

"No, Henk, I mean at the beginning. When Spaunaugle shot the second person. That's when you should have gone in."

"And told them what?" he sniffed. "It wasn't until the fifth that I picked up on what was going on. With the letters and the spelling and all."

"No, Henk, you knew what was going on from the start." I drummed my fingers on the cast. "This was all your idea, after all."

Henk looked at me as though I had just suggested dipping his privates in a bucket of snapping turtles. Then he closed his eyes and looked away. Murmured: "Go away. Get out and stop bothering me."

"Only after you confess. I need to get the confession part. I'd rather have it from you than have to hear it in court. Those benches are hard." I patted the bed. "And this is rather comfortable. So let's have it then."

"Okay. I did it. I shot them all. Now go away."

"Wrong. C'mon. I'm not Catholic, but I know you can't get absolution for 'fessing up to the wrong sins. Give me the beginning. Where did you all cook it up—the Boomerang, around the kitchen table?"

Henk now had the look of a man about to make his first skydive.

"Tell me, Henk, you've got to tell someone." Nothing. "Then I'll tell them for you." I stood up. "Hasten the wheels of justice." Clichés were evidently a communicable disease. "It'll be their timetable, not yours."

"What could you tell them?"

"Who got letters from Josh before he died? You and me. No one else. Mine was probably some sort of confession, and yours was probably one long blast of hate and recrimination. It had to blame you somehow. That's why you never wrote about it. So probably you and Josh Carlton and P.D. Spaunaugle were all in on this. Right? Melodya wasn't, but she figured it out and went to stop her boyfriend and God knows what happened there, what sort of pressure he put on her, but you're prone as a result, Josh is dead, and Spaunaugle is still somewhere in this great land putting together his next grant proposal."

Hard for a man in bed to sag, but he did just that. I'd hit it after all.

I continued. "So give me the details. Or I'll make up awful stuff for *my* book and you'll be even more reviled. This is your last shot at spin control, Henk. After this it's hot lights and rubber hoses."

He stared out the window again. Spoke in a dead flat voice. "Spaunaugle's fault. All of it. Josh and I came up with this idea one night after a bottle of two of something. He—"

"How did you know Josh?"

"Met him when I bailed out Melodya one night after a fight. He followed her from work to a bar. Got into a scrap with her friends. They were all arrested. He called up to apologize later. Had some drinks. He was an okay guy. We got along. His life wasn't going well. Neither was mine. Needed publicity."

I tried to think of a time in my life when depression could be tied to inadequate publicity; couldn't.

Henk droned on. ". . . had this idea. He had read this book about a talk show host who got shot. Made me read it. One of the worst true crime books I've ever read," he added, a dark smile in his eyes. "He had been listening to me complain about not being able to write. Being in a slump. Thought it would be great to get shot at. Not shot. Shot at. Would make people listen to his show. I'd write about it."

"You can't get a whole book out of someone who is shot at without effect, Henk."

"No, but I'd resurrect the other shooting of that talk show host. I'd write about violence in America, how the unhinged fasten upon the famous. Not just a crime book. A serious book. So we talked to Spaun—"

"How'd you know him?"

"Came around to the house with Melodya. Weird guy. Never knew what he'd agree to. Brought him in carefully. Sounded him out. Hypotheticals. He loved the idea. Proposed it before we even got around to spelling it out."

"Because he had something else in mind."

"The grant. The artistic statement. But he wanted to get rid of Carlton."

"Why?"

"Couldn't stand him. Carlton loved my sister. Lit up everytime she came around. Found out what she did for a living and hung around the bars. Never introduced himself, stayed in shadow. Before the shooting he got drunk and declared his feelings. Mel laughed, told her boyfriend. When it came time to shoot Carlton at the radio station, Spaunaugle wasn't in a mood to miss. But I never thought he'd . . . ohh."

"Then he disappeared? And you got stuck watching your wife crusade for this poor guy Spaunaugle picked to make his alibi."

"He was so *obvious* about it. Was supposed to be a small thing, unsolvable, forgotten after six months." Tears surged from Henk's eyes. "But he couldn't stop. He vanished and kept doing it. Kept *doing* it."

"He must have called Josh when he rolled back into town, and that's what made him jump. Guilt, fear, who knows? Did Josh call you?" I asked.

Henk nodded. "Carlton was horrified. Had to stay drunk, couldn't live with himself, what we'd done. Fear of police and fear of Spaunaugle."

"So you came out here to shoot Spaunaugle so he couldn't get caught and implicate you. Get it over

with and take your chances. Tell the story your way."
Henk nodded, eyes shut, tears still streaming out.

"Let me do that," he said. "Let me tell them my way. All I have left on my side."

"Maybe you'll bunk with that Peter Byrne fellow."

He nodded. I reached into the pocket of my robe and pulled out a pen. Knelt and began to write on Henk's cast.

"What are you doing?"

"Signing your cast." *I am the scowling liar!* I wrote.

"What does that mean? What? I told you! Don't!"

"You're still lying. Peter Byrne wasn't even there."

"He was! He shot the pictures!"

"Spaunaugle shot me, right? You were across the road taking pictures." I wrote *Ask me about my complicity.*

"I wasn't! I wasn't!" *Nurse: Call the police and tell them I am part of the crime.*

"Of course you were. Old Spaun brought you to be assured you wouldn't turn on him. I saw the pictures you took, Henk. They zoomed in on me. He asked you get a close-up of the station call letters, didn't he? But you were too thrilled that your wife's fancyman was not only present but down for the count."

Henk stared wide-eyed at what I'd written, plastered hands waving like crab's claws. He was in full manic rage now, weeping with panic and fear. "Erase it!" he cried. "Erase it, you goddamn son of a motherfu—"

"Sorry. I'll go get some Wite-Out or something. First you tell me where I can find Mr. Spaunaugle."

"Erase it! Jesus fucking Christ erase it!"

"Where is he?"

"Take it off! Take it off!"

"Where is he, Henk?"

Henk glared at me, hair stuck to his forehead with sweat, and spat out four words.

"Go home. Find out."

A fine and noble man would have squared his shoulders and left with winged feet, off to meet and confound evil. As it was, I had enough of Henk and what he'd loosed on my life. I pulled him out of his bed by his fractured leg until he hit the floor, broken leg first, broken arms next. I'd have kicked him, but he was howling loudly enough as it was.

I'll bet he was hoarse for a week.

I checked out of the hospital and left D.C. the next day, leaving Samurai in the hospital. That wasn't easy.

I have to go back, I wrote on a note pad. He nodded, jerked a thumb toward the door, then grinned. Waved.

How are your ears? I wrote. He took the pad and pencil.

"Busted clean through!" he shouted. "I'm stone deaf! Blast didn't knock any memories loose. Bad deal all around but, hey, I will survive and prosper!"

The station doesn't know, do they? I wrote.

"Sure they do! I sent them a fax this morning! Told them that firing me would bring a discrimination suit down on their heads like a horseshoe! I'll learn sign language and have someone interpret the callers for me! I'll survive! Hey, they get the bad guy? No one's told me anything!"

I shook my head no.

"Then get my jacket! Take what's in the pocket. No, the inside one!"

I found it and shook my head no.

"Don't be stupid!" he hollered. And you know, he had a point.

I took the gun and put it in my waistband. It being cheap hospital elastic, the gun slid out, fell down my pant leg, and stuck in the cinch around my ankles, barrel pointed up. I tried to point my leg away from myself, wincing, expecting my testicles to be hit any second with the force of a roll of nickels hurled from the Empire State Building.

"Take a course on safety!" Samurai said. "Remedial level!"

I retrieved the gun. Samurai pointed to the safety and showed me how to turn it off. Then he smiled and stuck out his hand. I shook it and mouthed good-bye. He grinned and did the same. "Good luck!" he yelled as I left. "Aim true and shoot them for me!"

We weren't exactly being discreet here. Thank you, I mouthed.

"What? Come over here!" I did. "Shout it! Maybe I can hear you if you shout it!"

And so it came to pass that the nurse on duty, wondering what the fuss was all about, entered a room in the GWU hospital and found a man holding a gun shouting thank you into the ear of a big, grinning god. I was hustled out, explaining it was only a water pistol, we were friends, all the while jamming the gun back into my waistband. Of course, it fell down my leg again. I had about half a second to remember whether the lesson on the safety catch had concluded with returning it to the proper position.

It's easier to check yourself out of a hospital than you imagine. You just leave. If you're wearing civilian clothes, aren't bleeding from every available aperture, and keep the wobble out of your gait, nurses pay you little heed. At least at this hospital. At the close of afternoon visiting hours the following day, I suited up and walked out, leaving behind a sheet of paper with my insurance number and home address. I took a cab to the airport and bought a ticket for the first flight home, paying a usurious rate that suggested I would be transferring in Zimbabwe.

The flight left at eight. I spent an hour fortifying myself with whiskey at a little bar full of nervous fliers, hanging on to the railing of the bar like a magic talisman that would ward away evil spirits of gravity. When I boarded I was slightly drunk myself and so experienced only 96 percent of the bright, screaming panic I feel upon flying. The plane flung itself off the runway and I thought, distractedly, that someday I would not only have an orgasm this powerful, but one that would bank right and keep climbing. I fell asleep.

We landed in a clear evening, the sun going down like a hot coin into a vending machine that would, after some mechanical deliberation, produce the next day. I could smell trees and grass as soon as I got off the plane: Ahh, Minnesota. Even the diesel fumes smelled fresher. I walked outside into crisp, sharp air, threw my bags in the back, and told the driver to take me to the Boomerang Bar. After, that is, I'd stopped in the bathroom and transferred something from my bag to my jacket.

Whether up or down meant the safety was on, I couldn't remember.

The bar was empty. I sat at the bar for an hour waiting for anything shaved to come in and saw nothing. No Ludwig. No Philip or Stig. No one who might have known Melodya, who might want to talk about her, put her back together, if only for the span of the conversation.

"Slow night," I said to the bartender. The stage was dark. Only half the booths were filled, and these by people with standard, ideologically neutral coiffures.

"Big skin shindig tonight," he said. He glanced at my head, as if to suggest that since it was stubbled, I should have known about the bash. He left before I could get any details and spent his time talking to a woman at the bar whose head looked like a freeze-frame of a peacock pitching a fit. I finished my drink, held up my glass.

"Is this a spontaneous thing, this party?" I said. "I've been out of town until a few hours ago. Philip or Ludwig didn't say a thing about it."

Magic words. The bartender reached under the cash register and produced a flier.

It had a picture of some snarling snaggle-toothed cretin spitting useless derision at all concerned and words in big crude letters.

CALLING ALL SKINS!
CALLING ALL SKINS!
SKINFEST IMMINENT! BEER AND BEER PROVIDED!
TRASH A HOUSE ON AN NEA GRANT! ALL DESTRUCTION CERTIFIED IDEOLOGI-CALLY CORRECT!

There was an address listed: my address.

7

A BLOCK AWAY I HEARD IT: MUSIC WITH THE RAPID THUD-ding bass of an elephant's heart in cardiac fibrillation, vocals from someone getting their plaque removed with a nail. Hoots and shouts and the sound of things breaking. As the cab drew close to Marvel Manor, I saw something straight from a Night on Bald Mountain: the light from the manor pouring through the red glass windows, illuminating a lawnful of skins, most in black shirts and black jeans and black boots, throwing their limbs around and twitching in skinny abandon, shouting and hooting.

All wore Spiderman masks.

They had the entire lawn to dance on but had compacted themselves into one small corner, moshing in the roses, banging heads and hips, shrieking and hooting. Someone threw a bottle through the library window, and a shaft of yellow light stabbed out. I got out of the cab in front of the house and strode up the walk, kicking bottles out of the way. One skin veered drunkenly in front of me, grinning at me with a mouthful of busted teeth, face glistening with drink. He turned and threw a bottle at the house and yelled to the sky, raging at the elements, then turned around for approval just in time for me to punch him square in the face and watch with pleasure as he dropped to the walk like a gutshot deer. I took off his mask and put it on: When sacking Rome, do as the Huns.

The door was open. Brand-new hell awaited: The woodwork in the wall was scarred with deep angry grooves, the floor puddled with liberal servings of beer and vomit and chunks of smashed furniture. At the doorway to the main hall I saw my computer monitor, the glass kicked in, a vase of flowers stuck in the smoking hole. The glass crunched under my feet. Another skin staggered into sight, eyes unfocused, wearing a shirt that had Mickey Mouse with a Mohawk and a sneer, holding what I recognized as the leg of a dining room chair. I kicked him neatly in the shin, and he went down howling. More skins rounded to the corner to hear the source of the shout, stupid grins on their faces. They saw me—me with hair, although not much—and they stared in momentary confusion. I pulled my gun from my waistband to make things clear, and they drew back. Whoa, nonskin aggression, whoa. I entered the hall, arms out, gripping the pistol, looking, looking for him, whatever he looked like, looking for that chipped tooth and white-stripe-Mohawked arranger of skinhead perdition. The hall was destroyed. The dining room table chopped to toothpicks, books from the library tossed and sundered, covers scattered and pages soaking in pools of beer. One of the drapes had been pulled down and tied to the balustrade. A skin languidly swung back and forth from a giant knot made at the drape's bottom, spraying nothing! Nothing! Just black blasts of paint on the marble walls! I heard a crash and looked to my left. Another had taken his example and climbed up the remaining drape and was now hanging halfway up the wall like a telephone lineman. He had put one foot through the window and was now skinnying up the wall. I shouldered my way through the crowd until I reached the drape. He was maneuvering himself to kick in the face of the angel in the stained-glass window. I had never liked her, but family's family. I reached out and had my hand knocked away by the angry, glowering skin who anchored the drape for his friend.

"You can't do that," I shouted.

"Fuck off," he said.

"You can't do this!"

"The fuck I can't," he shouted and produced a knife. Well, if you insist. Obviously he did not see my gun. I brought it to his attention by pointing at his chest. He backed away and I lowered the gun, but it was a twitchy thing and I was nervous, and the gun went off. A fine pink mist sprayed from the side of his knee, and he collapsed like a cheap card table.

"Jesus!" he screamed. "Jesus, Jesus!" I stared at him then looked wildly around the room. No one had heard the shot above the din of the music. What did I have to do to get these people's attention? First things first. I grabbed the drape and yanked it as hard as I could. The skin on the wall shouted and lost his grip and came down flailing, hands scrabbling at anything and making a momentary acquaintance with the edges of the window he'd just kicked out. He landed hard on the floor and made a few spasmodic kicks. One if his blows struck another skin in the leg, who turned around and booted him for great measure.

Back through the crowd. I looked in the direction of the kitchen. Another solid mass of black and fleshy skulls winked in dim light, bobbing and surging around to a song different than the roar in the main hall.

I looked to the balcony and saw six television sets mounted on the gray metal tables. Big TVs. Each showed a series of pictures in rapid succession. The images too grainy to be made out from down here. The first TV showed a blur of pictures, then the second kicked in, all the way down the line. The sixth TV was black. I stood hypnotized for a second until I made it out: The first TV kicked off with the shot of the letter T getting blown from the KTOK studio, Josh Carlton's arm flying up, me knocked into the air. The second image was of the letter H being splattered by a tomato. E S E followed. The second TV kicked in: A R E. And so forth.

T H E S E
A R E
T H E
S M I L I N G
L I A R S

No exclamation point.

T H E S E
A R E
T H E
S M I L I N G
L I A R S

And the sixth TV stayed dark.

I shoved and kicked my way to the staircase, took the steps three at a time, bumping into one descending skin and sending him scudding drunkenly on his tailbone down the rest of the stairs, *Ow! Ow! Ow!*

all the way. The phone on the landing table—unaccountably undestroyed—was off the hook. No dial tone. Great. I went down the hall, room by room. I kicked in the door of the first bathroom and found a skin face down in the toilet, firehosing out the evening's entertainment. Another sat on the tub, smoking a cigarette. She looked at my gun, at me, and said, "Wait your turn." Next was Grue's room, door open slightly: two skins copulating on the bed, spotted shanks heaving in the light thrown from the hall. "Hey," one of them said, "wait your turn." Next room: a dozen skins with a boom box playing something that sounded like a lawn mower dragged through a chicken coop. I walked in and turned the boom box off. Someone stood up and shouted something at me and demanded that I turn it on, so I turned it on, stepped back a pace, and shot it. It flew off the table and smacked into the wall. I was beginning to see the point of guns. They got things done.

No one moved. I suddenly had no idea what to do, so I picked up the shattered boom box, set it on the table, and shot it again. This cleared my mind. "Now then. Before anyone else volunteers for some ventilation not in the original blueprints, you want to tell me where I might find the host for this evening's revelries?" Their mouths were still slack in dead shock: typical gutless poseurs. Violence? Aggression? Ah, let me show you. I jammed the barrel of the gun against one inordinately tattooed skinhead. "Spaunaugle. Where?"

"I think—I think—I think he—I think he's—don't shoot man—I think he's at the end of the hall I think—please don't—"

"Thank you." Out of the room, down to the end of the hall, my room, of course. There was my big heavy door with its big, thick lock. I kicked it in frustration until I recalled that it was my door and my lock, and I had a key. Nice how some things just work out. I unlocked the door and as was my new habit, kicked it in, and took a deep breath. I pushed my Spiderman mask up on my head.

P.D. Spaunaugle lay on my bed, smoking a big cigar and grinning like a ward boss on election night. A ward boss with a Mohawk. He was a sickly, skinny-looking man, pale as eggs, his grin unaccountably charming. His eyes were two hundred-watt bulbs in sixty-watt sockets, bright and hot and ready to burn the joint up.

He lifted a glass in my honor and blew out a ring of smoke, then broke it with a flick of his finger.

"Quite a party," he said in a flat nasal voice. "Man, I hope you're covered."

I swung the gun up and pointed it at him. It occurred to me I had never checked to see how many bullets it had. Perhaps shooting that boom box twice had been gratuitous.

"Oh, put that away. We're all friends here." The gun shook in my hands, and I lowered it. It would probably go off, and I'd miss, or I'd hit him, and then where would we be? Just where Henk had intended to stand. In trouble, but a hero. I brought the gun back up.

Spaunaugle laughed. "How can we be at odds when we've plowed the same furrow? Banged the same gong? Good old Mel. Kinda makes us brothers." He blew another ring. "Don't worry, she told all, and at first, yes, I was hurt. But I've gotten on with my life, and she's gotten on with hers, sort of. No point having hard feelings."

"Get off my bed." I steadied my hand. "You can either get shot now for the pure sport of it or wait for the police."

"There'll be no police," he said slowly.

"I know this neighborhood. Old, rich folks with bad hearts who haven't had a party since FDR died.

Skinheads thrashing on the lawn will not go over well. They'll call—"

"They'll call Manhattan. I ran a little hack on the phone lines to reroute 911 calls. It's not too hard. Kinda depresses you to see how easy it is. I mean, what if I were a terrorist? Okay, don't answer that. Anyhow, someone from this area calls the police, they'll get 911 all right. They'll just get it in New York City. And what's this street we're on—Park Avenue, right? By the time they get it straightened out, I'll be gone." He smiled a wide and merry grin. "Now put that gun away. You don't want me to lose command of my nervous system and let my hand fall from this button." He waved what appeared to be a remote control. "I let this go, and your house is, well, deconstructed. Along with all those hapless fucks downstairs."

"What's the point of this, Spaunaugle? What's the *matter* with you?" I lowered the gun. My arms were suddenly weak, shaking. "I'm standing in my own bedroom pointing a pistol at you, and I haven't the faintest idea why. All I know is that we did some cable show a few years ago."

"Exactly! And you broke my tooth! And I swore eternal revenge!" He leaned back and laughed. "No, I take it back. This is for all those parties you held at that house by the university. The ones you never invited me to. Don't think it didn't wound a sensitive soul to the pith of the quick." He put a hand over his heart. "Actually, no. This is for that article of mine on El Salvador you never published." He scowled. "That was a cause I believed in, and you crushed! smashed! my work!" The scowl slid from his face. The lopsided grin returned, and he shrugged. "We do go back, don't we? That's what really delights me about this. All these connections, and none of them mean anything." He looked at his cigar. "There's *no* reason for any of this, friend. None. It's just something to do for a living. I enjoy putting something in motion, see where it turns out. You put a nail under someone's tire—you never know if it blew on the freeway or if it went flat overnight and made someone late for work and got them fired. You take a Polaroid of a naked woman and mail it to a man whose name you take from the phone book. Does his wife divorce him? Does he go half mad wondering where it came from? You write AIDS on a dollar bill and wonder how many people will handle it before someone refuses it in change or finds it in his wallet and throws it away. My art is putting things in motion. That's all." He puffed out another perfect smoke ring.

"Tonight has been unexpectedly rich. I rarely get to view the consequences. Usually I just sit down and imagine them, and that's my opening night at the gallery. Low overhead, and I save on the wine and cheese. But this. One night I was sitting around with Melodya's dear brother, minor amigo of mine as well, and he was complaining of the dearth of good crimes nowadays. A dispiriting drought of serial crimes in Minneapolis, it seems. Poor Mr. Gruesse. 'All the good psychopaths are taken,' he moans. And I simply said, 'Why not create one?'" Another smoke ring. "His eyes took the idea and ate it whole, and that's when it all began. We came up with the idea of some maniac shooting media people. Not killing them, mind you, just winging them. The spelling out of the phrase was my idea, but it was Josh Carlton who came up with the actual words. You know, I'd like to nominate that man for the Most Wooden Signal to a Coconspirator, that being me. Josh flipped his Zippo like it was the torch on the Statue of the Liberty.

"See, he wanted to be first. He and Henk, they did like that publicity."

"How did Carlton get in on this?"

"He came to me through old Loose-Lips Ludwig. They'd met at that shitty old Boomerang Bar, got into a fight. Carlton was there and hitting on Melodya all the livelong night. He'd seen her down at her place of employment and had been following her for months. Followed her right to Boom and no doubt blended in *real* good. From what I heard, some foreign skin made untoward advances toward my Mel, and Mr. Carlton valiantly defended her. Ludwig liked that. He was equally nuts over her, and I imagine he and Carlton sat about for weeks mooning about her."

"Where is Ludwig tonight? *You kill him like you killed Melodya?*"

Smoke ring. "I set her in motion. She agreed to carry that parcel and walk away. No one was supposed to get hurt there, I'd like to say. When you write this up, mention that fact."

"You killed your lover, for Chrissakes, and you sit there—"

"I am in repose. Not sitting. Didn't mean that to happen to Melodya, really didn't." His jaw clenched slightly, and for a second his eyes went glassy. P.D. Spaunaugle went elsewhere for a moment, then surfaced with that same cockeyed smile. Dearth of psychopaths, indeed. Henk, you idiot: Here was the pick of the litter. His eyes weren't sparking as before. They belonged to someone else, someone far away and hip deep in madness. His voice was hollow. "Anyway, this is all to your immense benefit, if you survive."

"My benefit. Oh, absolutely. I've already lost a few grams of brain matter. Wasted half the year—"

"Don't say wasted, please. A person only uses 10 percent of their brain anyway. And with Henk probably about to take the fall, someone has to immortalize this. I am counting on you to do so. See, while I was on the road, flitting from town to town, I read that book you wrote. *Dead Bread*. That account of your life with the Marxist nutritionists? Good piece of work. I knew some of those fellows, and you got them right. You're a better writer than Henk, I think. I'd much prefer that you describe my consequences. It has turned out much better than you could expect. That tape I got running with the montage of the call letters spelling out old Josh's immortal quote? It's the best thing I've ever done. And I got a camcorder running in a car outside to catch the end of it, too. Now I splice that in with tape from Henk's trial, which will be on *Court TV,* I'm sure, and I add a copy of whatever TV movie they make, and I have one hell of an addition to my portfolio. You want to know the best part? When it gets out that I did this all on a grant, you can say good-bye to the NEA. No more community theater. No more dance troupes or Morris dancers. You want to talk about setting things in motion? I start by suggesting to the right guy that he should make up a serial killer, and by the time it's over, I've managed to guarantee that *Our Town* will probably never get put on again. You can clap if you like. I am *damn* impressed with myself." He gestured at the world with his cigar. "I know this isn't totally all that hot for you. I've put you in a difficult spot." He chuckled. "Your last book ended here at this house, right? Big ol' violent shootout and all that? Well, here we are again. I leave it to you to explain to your editor how these things keep happening to wind up in your home.

"I only ask that you have some say when they cast that TV movie. Someone handsome with that sort of batshit shine in the eye women find attractive." He sat up. "Listen, where's the back door here? According to your book, there are secret passages everywhere in this damned place. It really is time for me to go."

"They'll find you."

"No, they won't. I have plenty of money and a great knack for living on the old margins of the maps. And there is nothing they can prove. They can't prove I was anywhere in this country. I have visited the data banks of the credit firms and given myself credit card charges in a hundred different cities, each a sturdy alibi."

"There are the videos. The pictures of the shootings."

"Yes, there are. Did you see the TVs outside? Adds a certain note to the festivities, don't you think? People are happier when there are TVs present. It blesses things. Like having a bishop in the corner tapping his toe to the music. Anyway, there'll no proof of anything by evening's end. The only tape will be my copy. What we have just said is hearsay according to the rules of evidence. And who's still standing to testify against me?"

"Peter Byrne."

He laughed. "If he remembers his address, let alone that I lived next to him, I'd be shocked."

"Ludwig."

"He knows nothing. I think he came to doubt my general worth, but he never really trusted me.

"Henk."

"Of course!" He smacked his head with his palm. "My fatal error! Not killing my coconspirator!" He grinned. "Ahhh, let him talk. He'll incriminate himself as much as he likes. They still won't find me. Trust me. I hope you've learned that much. You ought to trust me to do what I say."

I looked at his hand and saw that his finger was off the button of the remote. I swung the gun up and grabbed it with both hands and pulled the gun's trigger.

Nothing happened but a loud and damning *click*. P.D. had rolled back in horror at the sight of me bringing my gun on him, looked at his hand, flaccid on the remote, and then stared frantically back at me.

Then his face softened and he grinned the same smile that had greeted me when I had entered the room.

"Whoa! Must be out of range. Well, you're obviously out of bullets, so I don't feel obliged to keep your company any more. If you'll excuse me."

P.D. stood, bowed, threw his cigar in my fireplace, and left the room.

I followed and beheld chaos. The destruction below was proceeding at a riotous pace. Half the people had drifted outside, and I could see great dark masses heaving and flailing innumerable limbs to the music on the lawn. There were perhaps fifty people downstairs now, all smashing whatever items remained intact: Aunt Marvel's china, Grue's favorite cups. Furniture had been tossed over the balcony, shredded to sticks and twigs. Goldfish crackers were strewn everywhere.

"One simple flier," P.D. murmured. He stood at the end of the row of televisions, hands on hips, marveling. "Four cents a copy."

Jump him? Knock him over? What to do? He stood there hands on hips, remote control in one hand, fresh cigar in another. He turned to smile at me as I approached, waggled the remote.

I backed down the stairs, watching him. I passed the windows that had shown scenes of the Marvel clan history, from their fortune-building days in the lumber trade. There had been a picture of Uncle Marvel in a black suit standing in the forest, typical rapacious despoiler of land dressed up in the uniform of legitimate avarice. It was now an empty frame, shards on the stairs winking in the light. The vest of Uncle Marvel's suit had landed on one of the steps. I bent to pick it up: sharp glass was a weapon, too.

"I am sick and fuckin' tired of the same shit on the tube, man. Like change the fuckin' channel!" The yelling skin stood next to P.D., unsteady as the Tin

Woodman, his face a meaningless boil of boredom too long on the burner. P.D. looked at him with his distinctive distaste and small smile. They seemed to never leave his face, even when the skin coldcocked him and took the remote.

"Letters! All we fuckin' get, fuckin' letters!"

T H E S E said the first TV.

A R E said the second.

T H E

S M I L I N G

L I A R S

"Let's check out some tube," said the skin, and he pressed a button on the remote.

The sixth TV fluttered to life.

! appeared on the screen. WDC! redux, I figured. I turned and threw myself out the window through the ghost of Uncle Marvel.

The ground hurled itself upward and struck me strong in the chest. No wind. Sucking a vacuum. Standing, staggering off, brisk concrete under my feet, something smacking my forehead. Waving my arms for everyone to follow. *Light.*

The sound of the world tearing its skin from its body, howling with the effort, freeing some hot, blind soul that fried my eyes dry as it passed, took my flesh as a souvenir. Then the rain of stones, like hammer-blows on a coffin lid. I sat up, banged my head on the lid, wondered for a second why it stunk of oil. I'd made it next door, rolled under a car. Then I rolled over into hot roiling air. I stood and saw a livid red world of flames and shrieks and howls, seen through two tiny holes from the hot plastic on my face. Too hot! I turned, saw stairs. Should I climb them, take them all the way to heaven? Or purgatory, maybe. N a bad place to be. Good hearts with interestin Something behind me erupted in orange found a door—locked, glass broken. I re unlocked it and staggered in, casting a glow in a dark hall. Something was on fire here.

I was on fire here, wherever *here* was.

Drop and roll, drop and roll.

I grabbed a blanket hanging on the wall. How convenient. I ripped it down.

I didn't see the bright tartan pile of bones in the corner of the room who had by God seen every nightmare she'd ever had bolt from the grave tonight. Including her next-door neighbor, his true hideous face now revealed, coming into her house with his servant Fire, burning her drapes, finishing his loathsome work. Screams of the damned outside, hell bursting through on the edge of her very *prrrrrop*erty line. But she had been warned, and she had been ready.

Through the small eyes of my mask, I saw Mrs. MacPhereson raise the shotgun.

Melanie, Terry, and Hank

AND THE VALIANT FOOD REVIEWER THREW HIMSELF INTO the window, right into the chest of the awestruck Uncle Marvel, bits of colored glass flying everywhere.

"That's not how it happened," I said. "That window was already broken yet."

*Sssssssshh*s hissed from around the room.

"Well, it's wrong. You can't throw yourself at a stained glass window from that angle and go through it." But a lot of this was wrong, as I well knew.

"Will you please shut up?" someone pleaded from the back. I sunk deeper in my chair, scowling.

I watched myself roll under a car in the driveway next door. Cut to exterior shot of a house that was only half as big and a third as ugly as Marvel Manor had been. It blew up with more light than flames.

Probably used some sort of phosphorus. They had experts who knew how to do that. Then a half-dozen people were on fire and staggered around—a far sight less than the seventy-two who'd been burned on the lawn. (Never mind the thirty-four inside the house who'd been blown to constituent atoms.) Their heads were on fire. Silly, considering they were hairless. But they were obviously stuntmen in bulky suits anyway, looking like people do when they catch fire in the movies, as if they have immediately donned a flaming parka and been commanded to do an impression of the Mummy. Cut to a shot of me being blown out from under the car, staggering to the porch of the house next door as the car went up in flames. It was a TV movie cliché, the old exploding car, but it was probably the sole accurate thing I'd seen all night. Close-up of my face, slack and wide-eyed with horror, flames reflected in my glasses. That was wrong, too. I hadn't worn horn-rims for years. Brassy discord, fade to black.

It was not a bad job, considering I had really ended up screaming in an old lady's living room, I think I came off quite well. Mrs. MacPhereson had missed with her first shot, of course, blind as she was. The recoil from the ancient gun had shattered her collarbone and pitched her backward, and she lay on the floor cursing me for a full forty minutes before the police found her. I'm glad they left that out. They also didn't note that she sued me for that incident, winning this time. She used the money to put up a seven-foot-tall electric fence around her house.

Next: a soap commercial. Everyone relaxed. There were coughs, laughs. Murmured thanks as Trygve, my butler, came by with a tray of cookies.

"Is that it?" someone asked.

"No," replied someone I'd never met. "Still seven

minutes to go. We have the wrap-up and the happy conclusion."

"I'm confused," said another strange voice. "So everyone was part of the plot? The Mohawk guy, the writer guy, the brother guy, the girlfriend, the radio guy? Like, I'm sure."

"I was not in on the plot!" Samurai bellowed. He was so good at lipreading nowadays. He could browbeat people halfway across the room who were whispering in privacy.

"What about the other radio guy, Josh?"

"Mohawk, writer, radio guy," I said. "Founding members. Bald girlfriend, reluctant later addition. All clear?"

"What *about* the girlfriend?" said the same voice.

"Guilty of terminal pheromone intoxication," said Terry. "That Spaunaugle was a hunk."

"Only in the TV movie," I said. "In actuality, he had the physique of a bicycle spoke."

Another commercial, then back to *Night of the Mohawk: A Special Movie Presentation.* I was now being loaded onto a gurney. Flashing lights of emergency vehicles flashed out of focus in the background. Firefighters ran around with hoses. Dim flickerings of a fire off screen. Someone playing Detective Bishop stood over me, grinning with affection. God knows why, considering the number of burned and maimed and the fact that every window in the hospital next door was blown out. (The coma ward took the worst hit. One guy woke up from the noise, and several others suffered singed hair. My insurance company is currently paying for reconstructive facial surgery for people who have six months to live.) But in these movies everyone standing and not in handcuffs has to end with rough admiration. Tara fell to her knees at my gurney.

Terry laughed out loud at that. "Like I really did that," she said.

"You're a composite character, Ter," I said. "They combined you with the female TV reporter. Terry plus Sarah equals Tara. I warned you."

"You're not the only one," said Melanie. "And least you got out alive."

Actually, when the police had arrived, I was standing in the street, dazed, my pants thoroughly soiled by a wildcat strike of the sphincter, half my hair burned off, muttering about bad man, bad house, bad man, bad house. That's what Bishop told me I was saying. After he took the cuffs off.

Closing moments of the movie. Wide shot of the manor in flames; close up of a pane of glass, the angel giving Uncle Marvel the ax. Odd: That was the window I'd supposedly destroyed by jumping through it. No matter; the symbolism was nice, the Muse of Destruction and all that.

"I'll bet the glass starts bubbling and boiling," I said.

The glass boiled and cracked, consuming Uncle Marvel, the ax, the angel.

"Citizen Kane," I sighed. "Last shot in the movie. If two people in America catch the reference, the director will be happy."

"I caught it," said someone.

Credits. Jonathan A. Simpson played by a soap opera star who had left his popular role two years before and clearly had intended to land choicer roles than this. He was handsome, though. Various other obscure nonentities for the other players. Cheers were raised when the words Sam "Samurai" Stevens . . . Himself scrolled past.

It all ended with a thanks to the people of Toronto and the jerky animated logo of the underfunded production company responsible. Then a disclaimer said that this teleplay was based on real events but was, in fact, fiction. Then bright stirring music: the news teaser, with the anchor revealing we'd have a word with the local man whose story formed the basis for tonight's movie right after an update on the political fury sweeping Ghana. First things first, I supposed. I had no desire to see my interview. Terry had shown me the story the day before. My bald spot glared under the lights.

I got up, slipped outside by the back door, and went around the house to the porch.

This was the new house, the good place. When the insurance money from the house came through, I bought a house on the west side of Lake of the Isles. This was where I'd always wanted to live: the middle of the city, the lights of downtown visible from my room upstairs, the sound of the lake lapping at the shore drifting in the window in the summertime. I could hear the old mysterious birds and wildcats screeching in eternal disputation on the islands. I liked being that close. I liked having the placid moat of the lake between us, too.

Samurai came out looking for me after a while, and for a moment, I resented him. There was no sitting in the dark and talking with this man. He carried a small pocket flashlight so he could train it on a person's lips and make out their speech.

But he simply sat down on the porch steps and looked out at the lake. He'd come off as a bit of a buffoon in the movie. Too bad, really, as he'd invited half the people in the living room to come see the broadcast. None of them knew him too well and were probably pleased at the depiction. I nudged him in the ribs, held out my hand, and made the motion of someone clicking a flashlight on. He fished in his pocket and produced a keychain flashlight. I held it to my face, smiled, handed it back to him. He nodded and sighed with satisfaction, then gave me a pat on the back that nearly knocked me from the steps. Then he got up, stabbed his hair with his hands, flexed before the mirror of the moon, and went inside.

Terry came out a while later.

"I didn't think it was all that bad," I said. "Considering."

"I came off as such an *idiot*. I should have known, given the book, but really."

"Well, you can't show all the nuances of a person when they're a bit player. You got boiled down and recombined like everyone else. Think of poor Melanie. She got turned into a stripper and blown up. Comparatively, you came off pretty good. Besides, if you'd told anyone about your suspicions, you'd have had a bigger role. Don't blame me."

"But he was my husband." She pounded the deck in frustration. "I couldn't turn him in. Not just because he got weird. I should have known after Iowa, you know." She shook her head. "He says he suspects the next one is going to be in Iowa City, but the only guy who gets dead is this other reporter. He was never the same after that guy died."

We fell silent. Hank's trial was two months past. His book was due out in the spring.

"No one thought they could turn anyone in," I said. "I'm beginning to see the advantages of being a free man with few friends and fewer family."

"Keep writing books," she said. "That's exactly what you'll be. Listen, I'm going to help clean up, okay? Thanks for the party and all." She stood. "Hey," I heard her say to someone as she went inside. I heard heels click on the porch. I turned as Mel put out a hand to muss my hair.

"There you are," Melanie said. She sat down. I noticed her hair was growing out well. She wore an inch of black fur now. "Well, it wasn't bad, but it was

bad enough. In an enjoyable TV kind of way, though."
She smiled. "My brother came off as stupid as I
hoped. Dear, stupid Hank. God, I'm glad I warned my
folks ahead of time, or they're going to think I'm a
stripper. Or dead."

"I think they would have heard by now."

"Samurai came off well," she said. She lit a cigarette. "Considering it was his little showgirl girlfriend
who was also sleeping with—what did you call him?"

"Spaunaugle."

"Right. Where did you get that stupid name anyway? What was it really? I forget."

"Harold Johnson."

"Tell me again what happened. I need a refresher
course after all that nonsense."

"Well, most of it was true. Put it this way: The
movie was true to the book, and the book had some
strategic lies." I smiled. "It says on the title page that
this is based on real events, which it was, except you
got combined with the stripper, and Terry got mashed
together with a TV reporter I had been dating. When I
wrote the thing, I decided to piss Hank off even more
by tweaking his name and making it look like I'd slept
with his wife. But everything else was mostly the
same. Your brother and John Corton—I changed his
name to Carlton because it's your brand of cigarettes,
incidentally—conspired with Harold Johnson to
shoot a bunch of media people for publicity and
material, for art. I couldn't make up something that
twisted. Corton committed suicide as I described,
although I made up that bit about the video harness to
emphasize his paranoia. I think I'd leave that out now
if I rewrote it. Anyway, the only really big change was
the ending."

"What do you mean? The house blew up. I saw it on
the news."

"True. But there weren't fifty people trashing the

place. There were maybe five pathetic guys around a keg in the back. I found Johnson and we had the big discussion, pretty much as it was in the book, although he was really drunk at the time. Eventually I just left to go get the cops. He comes screaming after me down the stairs telling me he's going to blow up my house, and I say fine. I don't like the place anyway. I was just leaving the front door when the place went up. I have no idea what happened—if he tripped or hit the button by mistake or what. The blast blew me out the door and something set my coat on fire, and I ended up staggering next door. End of story."

"Why did you change all the details then? Why not tell it the way it was?"

Something growled out on the island. Something else growled in response. We sat close for a while, feeling the breeze rise from the lake, swirl around us like a shadow looking for someone new to belong to.

"I don't know the way it was." I said. "My best recollection of all that time is still a guess. I can't write a book and call it true when I have no real idea of what Hank and John and Harry Johnson and Anya the Russian Stripper and all the rest of them were thinking. Whatever I wrote was going to be a lie. So I decided to lie and be honest about it. Anything but give that son of a bitch Johnson posthumous glory. This way, no one knows his name. Or yours, for that matter."

"They'll know Samurai."

"He loves it. How are you two, ah, doing?"

"It's early," she said. "I want to spend the money on the house and he wants to install a gym in the basement." She smiled. "This wasn't in the movie, but I have been meaning to bring it up ever since I read the book. You know that Christmas we spent?"

I nodded.

"We didn't."

"Didn't what? Didn't do anything?"

"You fell asleep." Melanie smiled. "But believe me, I took it all as a very large compliment. Listen, I have to fetch the big guy and head home. I have to be at the office early. We have a client coming at nine." She went into the house. I heard voices and laughter as she opened the door and the hearty boom of her husband's shout. He was still top rated in drive time. He never took calls. Just shouted what he thought. A deaf guy on radio: who'd've thunk it?

I looked at the skyline of Minneapolis, a small mountain of light rising over the trees on the other side of the lake. The Mack Tower was almost finished now, and it was just as pure and beautiful as it had been on the monitors in that studio. Back then it was just fictional, but it looked pretty good. Built, it looked even better.

They changed a few things. There's a bright glass dish on top, and it's gone through a few different names I can't remember. I'll believe it when they hammer something in granite and put it over the front door for all the ages. And then I'll wait for them to knock it down and build something else.

Everything changes and usually not to your liking. You might as well remember it the way you want.

So Mel and I didn't, eh?

I knew that, I thought, looking out at the water. I thought back to the day I was sitting on the steps of this very house and decided I would write *Mr. Obvious* as fiction. Make it turn out the way I preferred. I thought about all the scenes that Mel the editor had cut: *They didn't make the story move.*

But they did, they really did.

I stood and went back in the house to the real people and picked an argument. I won.

ENJOY SOME OF THE MYSTERY POCKET BOOKS HAS TO OFFER!

SAMUEL LLEWELLYN
__BLOOD KNOT 86951-5/$4.99
__DEADEYE 67044-1/$4.99
__DEATH ROLL 67043-2/$3.95

ANN C. FALLON
__DEAD ENDS 75134-4/$4.99
__POTTER'S FIELD 75136-0/$4.99
__WHERE DEATH LIES 70624-1/$4.99

AUDREY PETERSON
__DARTHMOOR BURIAL 72970-5/$4.99
__THE NOCTURNE MURDER 66102-7/$3.50

TAYLOR MCCAFFERTY
__BED BUGS 75468-8/$4.99
__PET PEEVES 72802-4/$3.50
__RUFFLED FEATHERS 72803-2/$4.50

JUDITH VAN GIESON
__NORTH OF THE BORDER 76967-7/$4.99
__THE OTHER SIDE OF DEATH 74565-4/$4.99
__RAPTOR 73243-9/$4.99

DALLAS MURPHY
__APPARENT WIND 68554-6/$4.99
__LOVER MAN 66188-4/$4.99
__LUSH LIFE 68556-2/$4.99

POCKET
B O O K S

Simon & Schuster Mail Order
200 Old Tappan Rd., Old Tappan, N.J. 07675

Please send me the books I have checked above. I am enclosing $_____ (please add $0.75 to cover the postage and handling for each order. Please add appropriate sales tax). Send check or money order–no cash or C.O.D.'s please. Allow up to six weeks for delivery. For purchase over $10.00 you may use VISA: card number, expiration date and customer signature must be included.

Name _____

Address _____

City _____ State/Zip _____

VISA Card # _____ Exp.Date _____

Signature _____ 958

NANCY PICKARD

THE JENNY CAIN MYSTERIES

Join award-winning author Nancy Pickard as she brings an exciting mix of romance, wit, violence and sleuthing to the Jenny Cain Mysteries.

☐ **BUT I WOULDN'T WANT TO DIE THERE**
........................72331-6/$5.50
☐ **SAY NO TO MURDER** ....73431-8/$5.50
☐ **GENEROUS DEATH** ....73264-1/$5.50
☐ **MARRIAGE IS MURDER** ......73428-8/$5.50
☐ **BUM STEER** ....68042-0/$4.99
☐ **DEAD CRAZY** ....73430-X/$4.99
☐ **I.O.U.** ....68043-9/$4.99
☐ **NO BODY** ....73429-6/$4.99
☐ **CONFESSIONS** (Hardcover)
...................78261-4/$20.00

POCKET
B O O K S

Simon & Schuster Mail Order
200 Old Tappan Rd., Old Tappan, N.J. 07675
Please send me the books I have checked above. I am enclosing $_____ (please add $0.75 to cover the postage and handling for each order. Please add appropriate sales tax). Send check or money order–no cash or C.O.D.'s please. Allow up to six weeks for delivery. For purchase over $10.00 you may use VISA: card number, expiration date and customer signature must be included.

Name _____

Address _____

City _____ State/Zip _____

VISA Card # _____ Exp.Date _____

Signature _____ 828-05